# TOXIN

A peaceful demonstration on the outskirts of
Sheffield against a new landfill site turns into a
pitched battle between police and protesters, and
freelance journalist Mike McLean is convinced it
was sparked off by hired *agents provocateurs*.

The demo's organizer, Rob Fielding, claims to
have evidence that the landfill will be used for
illegal toxic waste dumping but is shot dead before
he can hand over the proof. It seems clear something dodgy is going on . . . so McLean investi-
gates the murder and his inquiries lead him to the
mysterious death of a ten-year-old boy who lived
near a fertilizer plant. Apparently his death was
caused by asthma, but why is everyone so reluc-
tant to talk about it?

Then a second man is murdered and McLean
begins to unravel the sordid threads of the mystery before, in a terrifying climax, he must put his
own life on the line to get to the solution.

# TOXIN

**Paul Adam**

HarperCollins*Publishers*

Collins Crime
An imprint of HarperCollins*Publishers*
77–85 Fulham Palace Road, London W6 8JB

First published in Great Britain
in 1995 by Collins Crime

1 3 5 7 9 10 8 6 4 2

© Paul Adam 1995

The Author asserts the moral right to be
identified as the author of this work

· A catalogue record for this book is
available from the British Library

ISBN 0 00 232548 9

Set in Meridien and Bodoni

Photoset by Rowland Phototypesetting Ltd
Bury St Edmunds, Suffolk
Printed and bound in Great Britain by
HarperCollinsManufacturing Glasgow

# 1

The police were expecting trouble that day. I could see it in the faces of the officers drawn up along the side of the lane. A tension, apprehension, maybe a glint of controlled excitement behind the eyes which turned to follow me as I walked past.

They were on edge, waiting for something to happen. One or two sitting in the open backs of the vans, their riot shields and batons propped against the wooden benches. Others standing around on the grass verge, not talking much. Just an occasional nervous exchange, a joke, laughter a little forced, a cigarette flicked away into the road. Then a sudden silence.

I'd seen it many times before. After closing time on a Saturday night in the city centre, in the streets around Hillsborough on match days. The uniforms made no difference. These were young men readying themselves for a fight.

I continued on down the hill, the road levelling out and curving round through a copse of beech trees. Branches overhung the lane here, the leaves almost grazing my head as I passed underneath. I could hear shouting up ahead, a rhythmic chanting that jarred the gentle tranquillity of the valley. I turned a corner and came suddenly on the crowd of demonstrators blocking the road.

There were perhaps eighty or ninety of them, a curious collection of disparate people. A core of young men and women in anoraks and cagoules, but on the periphery an older group, many past retirement age, a few in suits and ties or Barbour jackets and wellies. Home-made placards wafted around above their heads. 'No Tip Here', 'Stamford Out', 'Stop the Landfill'.

The police were down here too, observing from a discreet distance. A couple on horseback, but none in riot gear. It seemed a peaceful enough demonstration. Noisy, but ordered. I wondered why the police reinforcements were waiting up the hill.

I approached the demonstrators. They were packed together outside the entrance to an old quarry, their backs to the high wire fence and mesh gates that had been erected around the site. Beyond the fence, the sun glowed rust on the sheer sandstone walls at the rear of the quarry.

The chanting had started up again and I noticed for the first time the figure in the centre who appeared to be orchestrating the protest. He was small, his body so slightly built that his head seemed abnormally large in comparison. He had an unkempt beard, gold-rimmed granny glasses and a few strands of hair pasted down across a rapidly balding pate. His hands were in constant, furious motion, waving around in the air as he directed the different sections of the crowd through the rehearsed shouts and responses.

I watched him for a time, fascinated by his energy, his appearance. He looked like a renegade garden gnome on speed. Then a slim woman in jeans and a fleece jacket detached herself from the group and came towards me.

'Hello, Michael. I wondered if you'd show up.'

It took me a moment to realize who it was. 'Maria, I didn't expect to, well . . .'

She smiled wryly as my words petered out. 'Nor did I. But there's a first time for everything.'

'A demo? You?'

'For the right cause, why not?'

She pushed a strand of dark hair out of her eyes. The sunlight caught her face so she had to screw her features up into a squint to see me. She still looked pretty good.

'You know what it's all about?' she said.

'The basic facts, not much more than that.'

'Come and meet Rob Fielding. If you want any quotes, he's your man.'

She took me across to the gnome and whispered something in his ear. He glanced at me and nodded before breaking off in the middle of his conducting. We drifted away to one side as the crowd began to talk amongst themselves. Fielding held out a hand. I shook it. His grip was hard, the fingers knobbly, like rheumatic twigs.

'Maria's mentioned you,' he said.

'Really?'

'Nothing good, of course,' Maria said.

'You doing a story?'

'That's why I'm here.' I pulled out my notebook and pen. 'You've got a good turnout.'

'People feel very strongly about this tip,' Fielding said. 'Everyone's opposed to it. Residents, environmental groups, climbers and ramblers, naturalists.'

'But not the council.'

He looked at me sharply and gave a contemptuous shrug. 'No, not the council. They've turned the East End of the city into a wasteland. Now they're going to do the same to this side. It's not necessary. There's no need for a dump here. Look at it. This is one of the few areas of real natural beauty left to us. At weekends that sandstone face is crowded with climbers, families come here for picnics down by the stream, people walk their dogs through the woods. And now it's going to be desecrated by refuse.

'Have you any idea what it'll be like, how this whole area will change? It's not just the tip. People are worried about their children. The bin lorries coming through the estate up the hill, the noise, the pollution, the traffic dangers.'

He spoke rapidly, with an intense passion no newspaper quote could ever hope to convey.

'Do you live round here?' I asked.

'No. But you don't have to live somewhere to want it preserved. Why do you think we're here today? A lot of

7

these people aren't going to be directly affected by it, but they want it stopped nevertheless. We have to take a stand against people like Russell Stamford and the lackeys on the council who gave him the licence. They're morons with hardly a brain cell to rub between them. They see a hole in the ground and they immediately want to fill it with rubbish. They can't think what else to do with it. They're complete cretins, the lot of them.'

'Can I quote you on that?' I said.

Fielding grinned at me. 'Of course. That's why I'm talking to you.'

Maria said drily: 'Rob never likes anyone to be unsure of his views.'

'Not that they take the blind bit of notice of them,' Fielding added. 'That only makes me shout louder.'

'But is anyone listening?' I said.

'We wouldn't be here if we didn't think so. The landfill got the go ahead, but that doesn't mean we're going to make it easy for Stamford. We intend to block the first lorry that tries to get through those gates.'

'And if the police intervene?'

'We've made our point. This is a peaceful demonstration. Confrontation is no part of the plan. If we fail, then we'll quietly disperse and continue our campaign by other means.'

I looked up from my notebook. My shorthand could barely keep pace with his quick-fire delivery.

'Russell Stamford is an influential man. You really think you can block his plans?'

Fielding hesitated, taking his time over his reply. It was uncharacteristic. He sized me up carefully.

'You're freelance, aren't you?'

'Yes.'

'Maria says you're pig-headed, an awkward bastard.'

I flashed her a sideways look. 'Those are just my good points.'

'How are your contacts in the national press?'

'As good as anyone else's round here.'

'Willing to stick your neck out?'

'That depends,' I said. 'What did you have in mind?'

'I've got a few facts about Russell Stamford. Facts I think it's about time the public knew.'

I pursed my lips. 'I'm not interested in dirt. I don't do tabloid stuff, marital problems, drink, call girls, that kind of crap.'

Fielding looked amused. He tilted his head. I caught a glimpse of my own reflection in the lenses of his spectacles.

'Well, a rare find. A journalist with principles. Where on earth do you sell your stories?'

'It's not easy,' I said. 'Ask my bank manager.'

'Or your accountant,' Maria said. She was smiling at me gently.

'This isn't that kind of dirt,' Fielding said. 'It's information about his business affairs. You interested?'

'Try me.'

'It might cause you a lot of trouble. I mean serious trouble.'

'I hate a quiet life,' I said.

'Stick around till the end. It'll take me time to tell you.'

He patted me on the arm and moved away. I watched him go. A reporter and photographer from the *Evening News* and a second photographer from an agency in town had shown up and were taking pictures. A white transit van was just pulling in under the trees by the road. A camera crew from Yorkshire Television. I studied them thoughtfully as they unloaded their gear and began to tape the demonstration. For a small, localized protest about a relatively insignificant landfill site it was attracting a lot of press coverage.

I turned to Maria. 'Someone must be very persuasive, to get a TV crew out here.'

'Probably Rob. He's good at publicity.'

'Mmm. Have you been here long?'

'About forty minutes.'

'You notice the police in vans back up the hill?'

'No, the police arrived after we got here. Why?'

'Nothing in particular. He's quite a character, isn't he?'

'Rob? Yes.'

'You know him well?'

'His wife's an old friend. Aren't you, Cathy?'

I looked round to see a small, delicate woman coming up to join us. She had a soft, English rose beauty. Fair skin and wispy blonde hair tied back with an elastic band and topped with a white woolly bobble hat. She was wearing hiking boots, baggy leggings and a long Arran sweater pulled down over her bottom like a mini-skirt.

Holding her hand was a little girl I assumed was her daughter. About four or five years old. Pale and blonde like her mother, her cheeks pink from the wind and fresh air. On her back was a tiny rucksack shaped like a koala bear. Its arms were looped over her shoulders as if it were clinging to her.

'Aren't I what?' Cathy said.

'An old friend.'

Maria introduced us. Cathy Fielding gave me a frank look of appraisal.

'So you're Mike McLean.' She caught Maria's eye and half smiled. Maria looked away.

Cathy's gaze came back to me. She had sleepy hazel eyes and a slow, placid way of looking at you as if she'd only just woken up and was trying to remember who you were.

'Has Rob been assaulting you with his opinions then?'

'He did have the odd thing to say. I think I got it all down.'

'If you didn't, he'll happily repeat it all for you.'

She looked round and smiled affectionately at her husband. He was in the middle of giving an interview to the television crew but that didn't stop him pulling a face and waving to her. They seemed a happy couple. An odd match maybe, but happy.

'Did he organize this?' I said.

'Partly. The residents' association did their bit too.'

10

'Let me guess, they're the ones in the suits and green wellies.'

'Some of them, yes.'

'And the others?'

'Mostly members of various local environmental groups.'

'Including the lads at the back? Over there on the right. Six or seven of them.'

Cathy craned her neck to see who I was indicating. 'I don't know. I don't recognize them, but they might be friends of members. Rob wanted as many people here as possible.'

The little girl tugged impatiently on her mother's hand.

'Mummy, can we go home now? I'm bored.'

'It won't be long, Jenny. Just be patient.'

'I'm getting cold too. Why can't we go?'

'We have to wait for Daddy.'

Jenny pouted sulkily. 'Can't you tell him to hurry up? What's he doing?'

'He's talking to someone from the television station.'

The little girl perked up. 'Is he? Is he going to be on it? Is Daddy going to be on television? Can we go and watch?'

'All right.'

Jenny pulled her mother away eagerly, then held out her other hand to Maria.

'You come too, Aunty Mia. Come on. Yes.'

Jenny grasped Maria's fingers and pulled her after them. Maria looked back over her shoulder at me.

'Catch you later.'

I nodded and slipped my notebook and pen back into my jacket pocket. There seemed to be a hiatus in the activity around me. The demonstrators, their leader otherwise engaged, appeared unsure as to what they should be doing. The crowd was beginning to fragment, small groups breaking off at the edges. Some were taking out Thermos flasks and sandwiches, or scratching their legs to relieve the tedium.

I yawned. I'd covered a lot of demos, marches, picket

11

lines, protest meetings and they all had three things in common. Cold feet, boredom and a singular failure to achieve anything. Sound and fury, but no results. That was democracy for you.

I took in a bit more of my surroundings. The beech trees, their leaves just turning to gold, the stark beauty of the sandstone cliffs, the brook trickling through moist grass and rosebay willowherb at the edge of the road. I could see why Rob Fielding felt so strongly about it being turned into a refuse dump. Some things are worth fighting for.

Yet I didn't give much for his chances of winning. There'd be a few paragraphs in the papers, maybe a soundbite on television, but ultimately nothing would change. The landfill would go ahead, the press and public would soon lose interest and the world would return to the comforting embrace of the status quo. That's how things worked.

You're getting too old for this game, McLean, I thought. Too many years spent spectating, not participating. Watching cynically without involvement. Everything about journalism was vicarious. Reporting what others did, never really doing anything yourself. Sometimes it made me feel there was an aching hole in the centre of my life.

Something flashed suddenly up the hill in the trees, catching my attention. I ran my eyes over the slope, trying to see beyond the shadows. There it was again. The glint of sunlight on a mirror, or glass. Then one of the shadows changed shape and I saw the outline of a figure by a tree. A man. He was holding something up in front of his face. I couldn't make it out clearly, but I knew it was a camera.

I skirted round the back of the demonstrators. The six or seven lads I'd noticed earlier were leaning on the fence around the quarry, smoking. Something about them set them apart from the others, but I didn't give it too much thought. I was more interested in who was taking photographs from the cover of the wood.

I pushed through the undergrowth and scrambled up

the steepest part of the hill, pulling myself up on branches and tufts of shiny rabbit grass. The ground was wet and several times I slipped to my knees, caking my trousers with mud.

On the brow of the hill I turned left, attempting to come round behind the man. Maybe he'd seen me, maybe I'd made too much noise for he was no longer there. I paused and listened. I could hear the rustling of leaves, the breaking of twigs as someone retreated through the forest. I ducked under the low bough of a sycamore tree and ran towards the noise.

Thirty seconds in, I saw them. Not one, but two men, stumbling clumsily over the uneven ground. They were out of condition, both carrying too much weight. The one at the back had the additional burden of the camera and long telephoto lens. He glanced around and saw me. I registered the fleshy face, the double chin and pale gingery hair before he looked away and followed his companion through a clump of rhododendron bushes.

Car doors slammed and an engine started up. I plunged through the rhododendrons to see a bottle-green Rover slithering away down the rough forest track. The wheels spun on a patch of mud as the car took a corner too fast. For a moment it skidded sideways, grazing a thin silver birch sapling, then it was back under control and out of sight in the trees.

I stood there staring down the track long after the car had gone. I hadn't seen the first man's face, but I'd remember the second all right. I wondered who they were, who would be interested in taking covert photographs of a demonstration. They certainly weren't press. Then I heard something else. Another engine – deeper, throatier, like a lorry – in the distance with people shouting over it. I turned and sprinted back the way I'd come.

From the top of the hill I had a perfect view of the scene outside the quarry entrance. The first refuse lorry had arrived and been blocked by the demonstrators. People were milling all around it, banging on the bodywork and yelling. A few were lying down on the tarmac to block its path. There was too much confusion for me to identify anyone in particular.

The police were moving in now to clear a path for the lorry. More demonstrators lay down on the road, offering no resistance as they were dragged away. I saw Rob Fielding in the thick of it, sitting down quietly in front of the gates to the quarry. Maria was nowhere to be seen. I scanned the crowd for her and saw the group of lads in close formation at the back. As I watched, they nodded at each other and launched a barrage of stones at the police. One officer was hit and went down clutching his head. More stones came over. The crowd disintegrated into a chaotic melee. Rob Fielding leapt to his feet and pushed his way through, trying to reach the group of youths.

The police retreated under another hail of stones. But then behind them came the police vans I'd seen up the road earlier. Reinforcements tumbled out of the doors, helmeted riot police, batons and shields at the ready.

I went over the edge and slid down the hill towards them. The police charged the demonstrators, laying into them violently. In quick succession, I saw a man knocked to the ground and beaten about the body, another smashed in the face, Rob Fielding being punched by one of the stone-throwing youths and then, up the road, the two mounted policemen charging down into the throng.

I hit the road and took a second to regain my balance. The crowd was breaking up as individuals tried desperately to escape the police onslaught. The nucleus was little short of a pitched battle. I watched helplessly. It made no sense to join in and I could do nothing to stop it. A woman came towards me, blood oozing from a gash above her eye. It was Cathy Fielding. I ran out and hooked an arm around her shoulders, half guiding, half carrying her to safety.

She yelled in my ear: 'Jenny – she's gone. Find Jenny.' Then she slumped down in tears under a tree.

I went back out into the road, staring about wildly.

14

There were too many people, the chaos overwhelming. A police baton slammed into my back and I spun round, ducking instinctively, shielding my head until I was almost crouching. Through the moving curtain of legs and arms I saw her. Frozen to the spot, her hands clutched to her eyes, her mouth open in a scream no one could hear.

I elbowed a youth aside and forced my way through, lashing out at everything and everyone in my path. Jenny pulled her hands away from her face and saw me. I swept her up into my arms and there was a sudden look of terror in her eyes. I twisted round. A police horse was almost on top of us. I jumped back, spinning Jenny round to protect her with my body, and the horse's flank brushed past my sleeve.

I staggered away, Jenny held close in against my chest with one arm while I broke a path out with my other. We burst through into open space and then Cathy was there in front of us, Maria at her side. Cathy held out her arms and embraced Jenny, hugging her, weeping, mother and daughter sobbing as one. I held them both tight, feeling their bodies shaking. Not moving, not saying anything, just holding them.

In time, Cathy Fielding pulled away and lifted Jenny out of my arms. Her cheeks were wet.

'Thank you,' she said. Then she looked past me into the road. It was all over now. There were just a few demonstrators left, wandering about or standing quietly in small groups. Dazed, shocked, some with blood on their faces and clothes. A uniformed police inspector was asking them to disperse.

'Rob! Where's Rob? I can't see him. Rob!'

Maria said: 'He's OK, Cathy. He's not hurt. The police took him away in a van.'

'You sure?'

'I saw it.'

'I mean, you sure he wasn't hurt?'

'Yes. They just picked him up and tossed him into the van with half a dozen others.'

Cathy sighed. 'Thank God. What happened?'

Maria shook her head. 'I don't know.'

She was pale. I could see her hands were trembling.

'You all right?' I said.

'Yes. I got out early. Before the fighting started.'

I touched her arm. 'I think you should go home. It's all over here. You got your car?'

'I came with Cathy and Rob.'

'Do you feel up to driving?' I said to Cathy.

She nodded. 'But what about Rob? What's going to happen to him?'

'I'll go down to police headquarters and find out.'

'Would you? I ought to get Jenny back. She's badly shaken.'

The police inspector came across to us and told us curtly to move on. Maria gave him a look, but didn't argue.

We made our way slowly up the road. Jenny clung to Cathy, her face buried in her mother's shoulder. Just once she looked up and stared back at the quarry. The gates were shut, the refuse lorry safely inside. Outside on the tarmac was the debris of battle: scattered stones, a broken baton, items of torn clothing, a discarded shoe and, in the middle, a sorry heap of smashed placards.

# 2

Maria came with me to police headquarters. She sat in the passenger seat of my car boiling over with anger. At the police, at the violence, the uncontrolled brutality, the injuries, arrests she'd witnessed. Shaking with fury, saying the same things over and over.

I waited until we were driving down Fulwood Road, the city sprawled out in front of us, before I said: 'You were set up.'

She turned to look at me. 'What?'

'The whole thing. Someone arranged it.'

'The demo, you mean?'

I shook my head. 'You didn't see it, did you?' The television crew, the police reinforcements, it all made sense now.

'See what?'

'You think the police started it. Waded in to break up the crowd when you blocked the lorry.'

'That *is* what happened.'

I told her about the youths at the back, the flying stones. 'Didn't you notice?'

'That was later. After the police attacked us. It was self-defence. Jesus, did you see what they did? They clubbed everything that moved. Smashing people's heads in, trampling on women on the ground. You saw Jenny. She was nearly killed by that police horse. They were savages. And you know what? They were enjoying it. Bashing a few Greens, a few lefties. They were enjoying themselves.'

'Maybe,' I said. 'But they still didn't start it. I saw it from up on the hill.'

Maria looked at me again. I could tell she didn't believe me. It was only half an hour ago but her memory was way adrift, the sequence of events confused.

'You any idea who those lads were?' I said.

'No. But then I didn't know who anyone was. I was only there because Cathy and Rob roped me in at the last minute.'

'I'll bet no one else knows who they were either.'

'What are you saying?'

'I'm saying that someone wanted that demonstration to get out of hand. Someone wanted a confrontation with the police. Those lads weren't there by accident. Nor were the police, nor the press. I arrived after the demo had started. The police back-up was already in position. In riot gear. They were waiting for it to happen.'

'You mean they *knew* there was going to be trouble?'

I nodded. 'And someone tipped off the press. Why else was there a television crew there?'

'Because it was a newsworthy event.'

I gave her a sardonic grin. 'Don't kid yourself. A protest about a minor landfill site on the outskirts of Sheffield? A bunch of middle-aged, middle-class residents complaining that the value of their houses will plummet with a dump on the doorstep.'

'That wasn't what it was about.'

'That's how the TV guys in Leeds would see it. They don't give a toss what happens down here. Someone told them there'd be more happening. Maybe not in detail, but enough to make them think it was worthwhile turning out.'

'You were there. Did someone tip *you* off?'

'No. But this is my patch. I was always going to be there.'

Maria watched the traffic in front of us. We were down to one lane, crawling towards the city centre. The middle of the road was a building site, dozens of men in hard

18

hats leaning on shovels and killing time between tea breaks. They were laying track for the new cross-city super tram. Laying it right on top of the old tracks they'd buried in the fifties when trams were deemed obsolete. Funny how progress always gives you a sense of *déjà vu*.

'You think those lads just wanted a good brawl?' Maria said.

'Possibly.'

'Or?'

I thought it over. 'Or someone hired them to do it.'

'Why would anyone do that?'

'Well, it diverts attention from the real issue, doesn't it? Violence always does. It discredits those who take part in it. The stories on the news tonight and in tomorrow's papers will concentrate solely on police and demonstrators fighting. Not on whether the landfill should be there in the first place.

'A violent clash is always more interesting to journalists than the issue that causes the clash. A peaceful protest has right on its side. What happened today will be condemned by every rent-a-quote clown in the county. Your cause will lose a lot of friends.'

Maria was studying my face. I caught it out of the corner of my eye.

'You love conspiracy theories, don't you?'

'They're so much more interesting than facts. You don't believe me?'

'I don't know. If those yobs were *agents provocateurs*, who might have hired them?'

'I bet your friend Rob Fielding has a few ideas,' I said.

Rob Fielding wiped the beer froth off his shaggy moustache and beard with the back of his hand, fidgeting in his seat, unable to keep still. Listening to what I had to say. He didn't seem particularly surprised.

'That's pretty much what I figured,' he said. 'I'd never seen them before. They weren't from any environmental

19

group I know of, and they certainly weren't local residents.'

We were sitting in the lounge bar of the Two Chuffs near police headquarters. He'd been charged with causing an affray and released on police bail to appear before the magistrates in three days. He had a swelling bruise on his forehead, a black eye and cuts on both cheeks.

'Did the police do that to you?' Maria asked.

'Some of it. One of the lads gave me the black eye when I tried to stop them hurling stones. The coppers just added their bit on the way to the van.'

'You should sue them.'

Fielding shook his head. 'No point. It comes with the territory. You cause a disturbance, you expect to get worked over by the filth.'

'You didn't cause it.'

'You think anyone will believe me? With my record.'

I said: 'This has happened to you before?'

'Twice. Once on a demo in London, once with the hunt saboteurs.'

'Causing an affray again?'

'Behaviour likely to occasion a breach of the peace. Bound over once, a fine the second time.'

'A hardened criminal,' I said.

His mouth twitched ironically. 'Yet both times I didn't do anything. Just being there was enough to get me arrested. Same thing this morning. I was out on the side-lines when the police moved in. But they came straight for me. They knew who they were looking for.'

Maria said: 'You mean they targeted you in advance?'

'Oh yes. Whatever I did, I was always going to end up in the back of a van with two coppers sitting on my head.'

He took a sip of his beer. He was being pretty phlegmatic about his experience.

'Why you?' I asked.

'Because I'm a troublemaker. What the police would call a troublemaker, at any rate. Because I make a noise about things I think are wrong. And not just a noise. I *do*

20

something. That's what gets up their noses. They can live with people making noises, writing to the papers, lobbying their MP. They know that never achieves anything. What they hate is people who get up off their arses and actually try to change things.'

'You don't think you're being just a bit paranoid?' I said.

Fielding pulled his glasses off. His eyes were grey, heavy-lidded, the skin around them pale and delicate as if it was only rarely exposed to direct sunlight. He blinked at us short-sightedly and rubbed one eye with the tips of his fingers. He replaced his glasses and shrugged.

'They know who I am. They know what I stand for, and they don't like me. If you get involved in any kind of protest movement in this country, it pays to be paranoid. Because you can bet your life someone is out to get you.'

'And on this occasion, who was out to get you?'

Fielding pushed his empty glass across the table to me.

'Get the drinks in, and I'll tell you about Russell Stamford.'

I put two pints of bitter, and a gin and tonic for Maria, down on the table and settled into my corner seat. I knew a bit about Russell Stamford. I knew he ran a waste disposal business from an office in the city, that he owned and managed landfill sites and incinerators across the country. But that was about it. I'd never met him, never spoken to him on the phone, probably never given him a real moment's thought in my life. Waste disposal does that to you.

'He's respectable enough now all right,' Fielding said. 'Leading light in the Chamber of Commerce, on the board of a couple of obscure quangos, contributor to Tory Party funds. But about twenty-five years ago he had a different name. Derek Kent.

'He was working in a garage as a mechanic. He was good with cars, but he also had an aptitude for business. He noticed that getting rid of spent motor oil was a prob-

21

lem, and could only become more of a problem as the number of cars on the road increased. He saw it as an opportunity to set up on his own, disposing of oil for local garages. This was down south, near Slough.

'He started off doing it properly, on a regulated, legal site. But after a time he realized there was more money to be made if he cut a few corners. Took less care about how he got rid of the stuff, dumped some of it illegally where no one could trace it back to him. It's easy enough to do. Take a few drums out in the middle of the night and slip them into the nearest tip, or bury them in the woods.

'Then he expanded. He took on contracts to dispose of other materials. Paint, dye and drug by-products, canisters of hazardous chemicals. But he didn't dispose of them, which is expensive to do properly. He just dumped them. Inspectors from the local council came out to his site and found drums of toxic waste rusting and leaking in a hole in the ground. In a holding pond they found drums of hydrochloric acid mixed with barrels of cyanide. Any leakage of the two could have produced a cloud of lethal gas, hydrocyanic acid. And he was operating at the back of a housing estate, near open land where kids played.'

'So what did the council do?' I said.

'Closed him down, of course. But he was declared bankrupt so the council had to foot the bill for cleaning up the mess he'd left.'

'No prosecution?'

'He disappeared before the lawyers got round to it. Then he surfaced again in Wolverhampton under a false name. Joseph Clements. He did the same thing again. Went bust and skipped town with a long list of creditors owed money. That's when he came to South Yorkshire, changed his name to Russell Stamford and decided it was wiser, in the long term, to establish a legitimate waste disposal business.'

Fielding gulped down some of his beer and looked around the pub. It was crowded with drinkers, but no one was paying us any attention. Maria asked him how he knew so much about Stamford. Fielding said he'd been checking his background for months, travelling around, asking questions, looking up newspaper cuttings.

'Why?' I said.

'You any idea how much money there is in waste? Stamford's company has an annual turnover of nearly thirty million. And it's the most secure business around. The amount of rubbish we produce is never going to decrease. There are always going to be toxic chemicals, poisons around that need to be got rid of. Britain is the dustbin of Europe. We've got the smallest, most crowded country on the continent and we import waste for disposal here. We take in other country's crap to pollute and destroy what little remains of our countryside.'

He continued for a time in the same vein. Denouncing the madness of modern society, the profligate use of dwindling and irreplaceable resources, the way we're burying our problems in the earth for our children to sort out. He quoted statistics, reports, evidence to back up his analysis of insane environmental policies. He knew his stuff and, unlike most people, he knew what he wanted done about it.

Maria and I listened to him, not needing to say anything. He was a good talker. Obsessive, but not boring with it. He had passion, a clear integrity and an appealing, almost boyish, innocence about him. I'd met him for the first time just a few hours ago, but already I knew he was a man untainted by corruption or self-interest. It made a refreshing change.

Then, finally, Maria said: 'Rob, this is all very well, but what has it to do with Russell Stamford?'

Fielding grinned sheepishly. 'Sorry, got on my soapbox again. It has everything to do with him. He's one of the main culprits. He handles thousands of tons of waste each year. He is filling up this country with a lethal cocktail of chemicals which, sooner or later, is going to escape with

23

disastrous consequences. And he's doing a lot of it illegally.'

'I thought you said he'd turned legit?' I said.

'On the surface, yes. But underneath he's still the cowboy he was all those years ago. That quarry we were outside this morning, what do you think it's going to be used for?'

'Low-grade waste, domestic refuse. That's what the licence covers.'

'But that's not all he's going to dump there. I've been inside. Well out of sight of the road, he's been building concrete tanks lined with asphalt. You know what that means? Toxic waste storage. You fill the tanks with drums and then seal them in with more concrete. The asphalt forms a membrane to stop leachate seeping out.'

'You sure?' I said.

Fielding nodded. 'I've got photographs of them. And a dossier an inch thick on Stamford.'

'Does he know you've been checking up on him?'

'I don't know. And I don't care.'

'Can I see this dossier?'

'You bet.'

'How much of it is speculation and how much fact?'

He couldn't resist needling me a bit. 'Do journalists know the difference?'

'Libel lawyers do,' I said. 'You want a story in the nationals on this, you'd better be damn sure of your case.'

'I'm sure. Do you want to see the tanks at the quarry for yourself?'

'Yes.'

'I'll meet you there tomorrow morning. Six o'clock. Before it opens.'

'There's a twelve-foot fence all around it,' I said. 'How are we going to get in?'

'Same way I did last time.' Fielding paused, watching me. Maybe enjoying himself a little. 'We abseil in down the back wall.'

I knew there had to be a catch.

# 3

I left the car on the estate at the top of the hill and walked down to the quarry. The sun was just coming up but the damp chill of night remained, gnawing at my guts. I waited under the trees opposite the quarry entrance for Rob Fielding to arrive.

But he never showed. I gave him until half past seven, standing there freezing my balls off. Then I went to take a look at the quarry myself.

I went round the perimeter fence, peering through the mesh. It was solidly built, the top three strands barbed and angled outwards to deter intruders. I didn't fancy trying to climb it. Inside, the ground was barren and stony, coarse grass and weeds poking up through thin soil. It was big, maybe five or six acres in total. The escarpment at the rear was too sheer, too smooth to be natural, and below it the ground had been hewn away to form a deep basin.

I climbed the hillside, still following the line of the fence, and scrambled round until I was standing on top of the rear wall. I was only a couple of yards from the edge. I looked down and studied the quarry.

The landfill had already begun at one side. An earth ramp had been constructed to allow the refuse lorries down into the basin and mounds of household waste were piling up in the bottom. A bulldozer and a JCB were parked nearby. I could see no sign of any concrete tanks lined with asphalt. But that didn't mean they weren't there.

From my vantage point I could see probably less than

25

half of the quarry. The sandstone had been removed in blocks and at various points there were spurs of rock remaining, forming enclosed bays into which I couldn't see. I was quite relieved Rob Fielding hadn't turned up. The thought of abseiling down that sheer face was unnerving, even if it did lead to an exclusive. You can take dedication to duty too far.

I made my way back to the car and called Fielding's home from a telephone box on my way into town. The line was engaged. I gave it five minutes then tried again. Still engaged. I shrugged and drove to Hunter's Bar. Fielding lived in one of the streets off Sharrow Vale Road, but I stopped at a café for some breakfast first: frazzled bacon and eggs that tasted as if they'd been fried in Brylcreem. Then I went over to the house.

The first thing I noticed was the small group of people loitering outside on the pavement. A couple of greasy-looking men in overcoats and a brassy blonde in a leather jacket. I recognized all three. The blonde and the older man were local correspondents for the tabloids. The other man was Craig Mills, crime reporter on the *Evening News*. Doorstepping a man on bail for a simple public order charge. Sounded like overkill to me.

I parked up the road and walked back to join them. Craig Mills nodded at me, a cigarette wedged in the corner of his mouth. He looked cold and bored. His face was the colour and texture of congealed porridge.

'You won't get anywhere,' he said. 'We've tried. No quotes, not even a snap of the husband. Stupid bitch. If she just came out and said a few words, we could all piss off and leave her to it. All we want is the grieving widow shit.'

I stared at him. 'What?'

'They never have a clue, these people. Bit of cooperation and we'll leave her alone. I mean, do they think we enjoy it out here?'

'Did you say widow?'

26

Mills gave me a funny look. 'You winding me up, McLean?'

I double-checked the number on the front of the house in case I'd made a mistake.

'This *is* Rob Fielding's house, isn't it?'

'You think we'd be here if it wasn't? It's all right for you. You show up halfway through the morning. I've been here since half past fucking seven and I've got sod all to show for it.'

'Just tell me what's happened, Craig.'

'Eh? Look, if you think I'm going to . . .'

I took him by the lapel of his coat and shook him. 'I don't *know*, Craig. Now tell me.'

'OK, let go. Christ, what's the matter with you? He was found dead this morning.'

'Rob Fielding?'

'Who else? Listen, why are you here if you don't know?'

'Where? How?'

'Out at Castleton. He was shot through the head.'

I knew it wasn't likely, but I had to check. 'Suicide?'

Craig shook his head. 'Not according to the fuzz. 'Course they're not telling us much. Never do, the bastards.'

'What time?'

'Early this morning, they think. The body was found about half-five. Postman out on his rounds.'

I turned and went in through the gate. As I started up the steps, Craig called out: 'You're wasting your time, McLean. Believe me.'

I rang the doorbell three times in quick succession. No one came to answer. I pressed the bell and held it in. Craig Mills was grinning at me smugly. I wanted to wipe it off his face with a baseball bat. I *knew* these people. Maybe for only a day, but I'd liked Rob Fielding. I'd held his wife and daughter in my arms, for God's sake. I wanted no part of this doorstep scavenging, but I was going to speak to Cathy Fielding if I had to climb in through the letterbox.

The door swung open violently and Maria came out, her fists clenched into tight balls.

27

'I've told you parasites before. Fuck off and leave us alone.'

'Hey, it's me,' I said quickly. She looked all ready to throw a punch.

She took in who it was and her expression changed to one of utter contempt. That got to me.

'You? I thought you at least might have more decency.'

'I'm not working,' I said. 'Rob arranged to meet me at six this morning, remember? You were there.'

Maria ran a hand over her eyes. 'I'm sorry, Michael. I thought . . . those vultures have been ringing the bell for the past two hours. Come in.'

She stood back to let me pass. Outside, Craig Mills was yelling. 'Oi, what about us? Give us a break. Hey!'

Then the door slammed shut and I was alone with Maria in the hallway. She looked tired, stressed.

'How is she?' I said softly.

'Bad.'

'You want me to go?'

'I don't know, Michael. I don't know anything. She called me after she got the news. I came over straight away.'

'Jenny?'

'She doesn't know. She's out at playgroup all morning.'

'Do you know what happened?'

'Only the bare details. He was found dead in his car. Somewhere near Castleton. Winnats Pass, I think. Cathy hasn't really said. She's in a state of shock.'

'You don't look too good yourself.'

'I'm OK. It's just that . . . God, who would want to kill him? Why? I can't take it in. Part of me still doesn't believe it.'

Cathy came out into the hallway through the open kitchen door at the far end.

'Maria, is there some –' She stopped, seeing me there. 'Oh.'

'I didn't mean to intrude,' I said. 'I didn't know. I'm sorry.'

She nodded at me. The hall was dim, the shadows giving her face a gaunt, almost haunted look.

'I'd better be going.'

'No,' Cathy said. 'Come through.'

She turned and went back into the kitchen. I glanced uncertainly at Maria.

'She mean that?'

'She needs company.'

We went into the kitchen. It was a narrow room, protruding from the back of the house, a window down the side giving a view of a paved yard and whitewashed brick wall. The units were pine, the walls above them tiled in a Wedgwood pattern. It smelt of coffee and burnt toast.

Cathy Fielding was sitting at the farmhouse table, her head propped in her hands. Her face was very pale, strands of her straw-blonde hair straggling across her cheeks. Her eyes were red from weeping.

'Have some coffee,' she said.

'I'll make a new pot,' Maria said.

I sat down at the table, trying to think of something to say. But words have no real power to console, they just patch over the surface of grief. So I remained silent. Maria made the coffee, saying nothing either. Just being there, the familiar chink of crockery, the kettle boiling, seemed enough for Cathy.

She waited until we all had cups of coffee in front of us before, unprompted, she started to talk.

'He went out last night. Around nine. He took the car. He didn't say where he was going. He said he'd be back this morning. He mentioned he was meeting you at the quarry very early.' She looked at me.

'Six o'clock. I waited there for him,' I said.

'That's about the time the police came round. Maybe a little later. A postman in a delivery van had seen our car at the bottom of Winnats Pass. In the car park opposite Speedwell Cavern. The driver's door was open. Rob was lying across the front seats. Dead.'

She paused, swallowing hard. She took a quick sip of

coffee and gazed at the table, not looking up as she continued.

'The police said he'd been shot. They checked the registration number of the car and got our address. Then they came round to see me. They asked me a few questions, but they didn't tell me any more. That's all I know.'

She lifted her head. Her expression didn't change, but the tears flooded out over her cheeks. No sobbing, no sound, just tears and a bleak sorrow in her eyes that caught at my throat. Maria put her arms around her and pulled her close.

Then the doorbell rang. Persistently. Maria gave me a look over Cathy's shoulder, her mouth pulled tight.

'I'll deal with them,' I said.

I got up and went down the hall. Through the frosted glass in the front door I could see dark shapes outside on the steps. I ripped open the door, preparing to give Craig Mills and the others a mouthful. But it wasn't them.

There were four men waiting there. Two in front, two a little way below on the steps. The man at the top on the right held up a folded document and stopped, his hand halfway to his face. He was staring at me, his mouth sagging open. I recognized him the moment he recognized me. It was the man with the camera who'd been taking snaps of the landfill demonstration. He took a second to recover.

'Police,' he said. 'This is a search warrant.'

He started to come in, but I blocked his passage.

'You must have the wrong house,' I said.

He thrust the warrant under my nose. Pugnacious. 'Read the address, sonny boy.'

There was no mistake. 'You know he's dead, don't you?' I said. 'Just a few hours ago. His widow's back there in the kitchen, distraught, and you people come here to turn over her house.'

The man stuck his face closer to mine. He was shorter than me, but bigger. Fourteen or fifteen stone. Somewhere in his mid-forties. His face and features were pudgy

30

and characterless, as if a child had sculpted them out of plasticine and not bothered to finish them off.

'Who the fuck are you?' he said.

'I might ask you the same. You want to come in, you'd better show me some ID.'

'Get out of my way before I have you for obstruction.'

I stayed where I was. 'You want the search to be legal, don't you? So show me some ID.'

The other man at the top of the steps said: 'Let me handle this twat, Ray.'

I ran an eye over him. He had a face like a frog. Bulging eyeballs and a wide, prominent mouth, the lips pushed out by swollen gums. You could've played Chopin on his teeth. I turned back to the other man.

'I guess you're the organ grinder,' I said. 'Who's your monkey?'

Frogface started to come for me, but his partner put out a restraining arm and shook his head almost imperceptibly. Then he looked directly at me. His eyes were chilling. A pale, icy blue, the life washed out of them.

He pulled a wallet from his inside jacket pocket and flashed me his warrant card so quickly I had no time to read it. I caught his hand as he pulled the card away and held it still long enough to read the identification. He was a detective superintendent called Ray Coltrane. But what interested me more was the fact that he wasn't from the South Yorkshire force, he was from the Met.

He tore his hand loose and snarled at me: 'Now stand aside.'

The four men barged into the house just as Maria emerged from the kitchen. She stood in the middle of the hall, not letting them pass.

'What's going on, Michael? Who are these people?'

'Police,' I said. 'They've got a search warrant.'

'A *what*?'

Coltrane tried to get past Maria but she stood her ground. Her eyes were narrowed, burning red hot.

'Get out,' she said furiously. 'Get out of here. Jesus,

what kind of people are you? Have you no feeling at all?'

'Are you Mrs Fielding?' Coltrane said.

'No, I'm a friend. Here to look after her. And there's no way you're coming in. She's in no fit state for this. Her husband was murdered this morning.'

She looked slight, fragile, standing there in front of Coltrane. But he seemed wary, even intimidated by her. She was all charged up, only a fraction away from taking a swing at him.

I stepped between the two of them. 'We've got no choice, Maria. Come back into the kitchen.' I took her by the shoulders and turned her round. At first she resisted, but then the fight seemed to drain out of her and she let me lead her away.

'Get on with it then,' I said to Coltrane. 'Do what you came for, then get out.'

We sat in the kitchen for the next two hours, drinking endless cups of coffee and listening to the police banging around all over the house.

'What are they looking for?' Cathy Fielding said repeatedly. 'There's nothing here. We've done nothing wrong. What are they searching for?'

At one point, I stood up and headed for the door.

'You're not going, are you?' Maria said hurriedly. 'Stay if you can. I don't want us left alone here with those men.'

'I'll stay,' I said. 'I'm just going to see what they're doing.'

I went upstairs and found Coltrane and a sidekick in the small front bedroom which had been used as a study-cum-office by the look of it. There was a desk in front of the window and shelves on the walls stacked with files and books. The two coppers were removing the files and putting them into black binliners. They weren't bothering to read them first, they were simply taking everything.

'You're a long way from home,' I said to Coltrane.

He didn't reply.

'Why's the Met interested in Rob Fielding?'

Coltrane tossed a wad of papers into a binliner and said to his colleague: 'Sort out the computer.'

The other man nodded and turned his attention to the word processor on the desk. He knew what he was doing. He searched around for the start-up diskette and inserted it into the system unit. Then he followed the instructions on the screen for parking the heads in preparation for moving the system. They didn't want to lose any of the data on the word processor's hard disk.

'You've done this before, haven't you?' I said.

Coltrane said belligerently: 'Shift yourself. You're in our way.'

'Your photos been developed yet?' I asked. 'Any interesting snaps?'

He studied me carefully, his cop's eye no doubt filing away a description for future reference.

'You want us out of here, you'd better let us get on with our jobs.'

'I will. Let me see the warrant again.'

'You're not the owner of the premises.'

'But Mrs Fielding is. She asked me to check it for her.'

'Go screw yourself. I don't have to show you shit.'

I stood by the door and watched them. Not interfering, not speaking. Just crowding them a little, getting up their noses. I'm good at that.

After five minutes, Coltrane had had enough. 'Listen, arsehole, you're obstructing us in the execution of our duty.'

'I'm watching you,' I said. 'Making sure you don't nick anything. That's not unlawful. If I want to follow you around the house, taking notes of what you remove, then you can't stop me.'

Coltrane gritted his teeth, glaring at me, weighing up his options. He decided on the course of least resistance. He pulled out the search warrant and threw it at me. I read through it slowly and gave it back to him. Then I went downstairs into the kitchen.

'What're they doing?' Maria said.

'Removing files and papers from the study.'

'Can they do that?'

'Oh yes, they can do it all right.'

'But why?'

I turned to Cathy. 'That was Rob's study, I assume?' She nodded listlessly. 'And the files on the shelves, were they all Rob's?'

'Yes.'

'What's in them?'

Cathy shrugged. 'Cuttings, newsletters, magazine articles, I don't know. Most of it was to do with his environmental campaigning. He had piles of stuff on waste disposal, pollution, global warming, acid rain, public rights of way, God knows what. He spent all his spare time writing letters, organizing protests.'

'Why would the police be interested in them?'

'I don't know. I don't *know*.' She got up from the table and wandered around the kitchen, twisting the rings on her fingers anxiously. Maria caught my eye and shook her head, warning me off.

Cathy said: 'I need some fresh air.'

She opened the back door and went out into the yard. Maria got up to follow her.

'Don't ask her too many questions,' she said. 'She's not up to it.'

I nodded. Maybe now wasn't the right time. But pretty soon she'd have to answer some questions. The police would see to that. And not solely about her husband's death, but about his activities before he died. According to the warrant, they were searching for stolen documents.

The police left shortly after noon with six bags of files, the word processor and all of Rob Fielding's personal papers. Bank statements, cheque stubs, insurance details, everything.

I made us some sandwiches and we had a brief moment of respite before Jenny was dropped off from her play-group. She came into the house excited, full of chatter about the morning's activities. Cathy forced herself to respond and seem interested, but I could see it was hard work. I looked at the little girl sitting next to her mother at the kitchen table and felt a pang of pain in my heart. Before long, she would have to be told.

Then Maria signalled to me behind Cathy's back and stepped out into the yard. I went after her. She closed the door.

'Have you got much on this afternoon?' she said.

I thought fleetingly about Rob Fielding's murder. How, if I was smart and callous enough, I ought to write it up, flog the story to the nationals, the regional TV stations. Make some money out of it. But I knew I wasn't going to do it. This was too close to home. And Maria would despise me for it. That mattered to me.

'Nothing important,' I said. 'Why?'

'Cathy has to go and identify Rob's body at the mortuary. The police asked her this morning when they first came round. I said I'd drive her over when she was up to it.'

'You want me to do it instead?'

Maria shook her head. 'I think it's better if I'm with her. But would you look after Jenny for a couple of hours?'

'Me?'

'She knows who you are. You probably saved her life yesterday. She'll feel safe with you.'

'I don't know, Maria. What am I supposed to do with her?'

'You'll be fine. She'll take a nap for most of the afternoon. You won't have to do anything much except be here.'

There was no getting out of it. When Maria and Cathy had left, I went into the sitting room with Jenny to play with her toys. She was a sweet kid. Unself-conscious, at ease with me from the start, she burbled away happily on the carpet while I slouched in an armchair and pretended to listen. Then she suggested we did a jigsaw.

'You do it,' I said.

'No, you have to help. Come on. It's Postman Pat.'

I sighed. 'OK.' I got down on my knees and tipped the pieces out of the box. Then we put it together on the floor. Or rather I did. Jenny supervised, pointing out where all the bits went.

'No, not there. That goes in the middle.'

'You do it.'

'No, you.'

'What about this piece?'

'That's Jess's tail.'

'Who's Jess?'

'She's his cat. It goes there.'

We finished the jigsaw and I said: 'Right, it's time for your nap now, isn't it?'

'I'm not tired.'

That's what I'd feared. 'Oh, I think you are. Why don't you go and lie down for a short while?' Like a couple of hours.

'No, I want to play with my Lego. You can help.'

'Well, I'll just sit in the armchair and help you from there,' I said.

'No, down here. You have to be down here with me.'

She tipped a huge pile of Lego bricks out on to the carpet and pushed them towards me.

'Build me an aeroplane.'

'What?'

'An aeroplane.'

'You sure you don't want a nap?'

'Here's the wheels. You can start with them.'

I could see I was going to be battered into submission. Her will was stronger than mine. I started to stick the plastic bricks together while she looked on. This was her idea of building an aeroplane. I did all the work while she watched and gave a running commentary on my performance.

'What's that?' she asked.

'It's a wing.'

'It's too short. Make it longer. It doesn't look much like

36

an aeroplane. You're not very good at this, are you?'

I smiled feebly, wondering if there were any sleeping tablets in the house I could slip into her Ribena.

After half an hour or so she got bored with Lego. She stood up.

'Let's play something else now,' she said.

'Good idea,' I replied. 'How about the game where you go upstairs and lie down on the bed with your eyes closed while I stay down here and help myself to a stiff whisky?'

She studied me solemnly, as if she was giving this original idea a great deal of thought. She didn't like it.

'No, I want to draw.'

She took hold of my hand and led me into the kitchen where she produced paper and wax crayons from a drawer, then sat down at the table.

'You sit here next to me.'

She began to draw the outline of an animal on a sheet of paper, leaning over, concentrating, her tongue sticking out of the side of her mouth.

'What's that?' I said. 'A dog?'

'No, silly. It's a horse.'

'Oh. One of the short-legged variety, I see. A dachshund stallion.'

'No, it's a horse. I told you.'

She coloured it in, scribbling right across the outline with black crayon. When it was finished, she gave it to me.

'Will you put it up on the wall for me?'

I looked around for a space. The walls were covered in her drawings and paintings.

'There's not much room,' I said. 'Can I pin it to the noticeboard instead?'

Jenny nodded. I rearranged some of the bits of paper attached to the cork board. Memos, reminders, surgery times for the doctor, important phone numbers. And a cutting from the *Evening News*. I glanced at it. 'Asthma attack tragedy', was the headline. The intro said something about a ten-year-old Mexborough boy dying

37

suddenly, but I didn't read beyond it. I pinned Jenny's drawing to the board and stood back.

'How's that?'

'Good,' she said, looking up briefly. She was already engrossed in another drawing. I took my opportunity.

'You'll be all right for a few minutes, won't you, Jenny? I'm just going upstairs.'

I walked out before she could reply, and went up to the front bedroom. The police had virtually cleaned it out. There were a few paperback books left on the shelves, but all the files had gone. I checked the desk drawers. Some bits of stationery, envelopes, Sellotape and drawing pins. That was it. I thought about searching the rest of the house but I knew it was a waste of time. The police had been thorough. If Rob Fielding's dossier on Russell Stamford had been in the house, it would have been taken with all the rest.

I crept quietly downstairs and took the telephone off the hall table and into the sitting room. The lead was just long enough. I called Derbyshire police press office and asked what they had on Fielding's murder. Not much was the answer. Or not much they were telling the press. So I called Gordon Crieff, the South Yorkshire Constabulary's press officer. I knew him better.

'It's not our case, laddie,' he said to me. 'Outside the jurisdiction.'

'I know, Gordon. But do me a favour, will you? Phone your counterpart at Ripley and find out what the situation is. I know the bloke's widow. I'm at her house now. Anything you tell me is off the record; I won't use it. I just want to know what's going on.'

There was a weary sigh on the other end of the line. 'The things I do for ye. OK, give me your number. I'll ring ye back.'

I put down the phone and waited. Jenny's Postman Pat jigsaw puzzle was still out on the floor. My eyes kept coming back to it, and all I could think of was that a postman had found Rob Fielding's body. A postman in a van, out on his rounds like the cartoon character in the jigsaw.

And I thought of Jenny. Sitting in the kitchen drawing pictures, not knowing her father was dead. I didn't want to be around when she found out.

Gordon Crieff rang back ten minutes later. His thick Glaswegian accent sounded muffled, as if his mouth was full.

'You eating, Gordon?'

There was a pause. 'Aye. Doughnut. Just let me finish.' He swallowed, then said: 'There's not much more I can tell ye, laddie. The body was found at five-twenty-five. Postman driving past. But ye know all that already, I assume.'

'They done the postmortem yet?'

'Aye. Cause of death, bullet through the head. Dressed up in pathologist's jargon but that's what it was. One bullet, thirty-eight calibre, the pistol held to the skull. There were powder burns on the skin.'

'Time of death?'

'Between midnight and five this morning.'

'Any witnesses?'

'Not so far.'

'Is that it?'

'Just one other thing. The body had been stripped. The fellow was stark naked when he was found. No marks on the body, but someone took his clothes. Every single item.'

'Have any of them been found?'

'No.'

'How did they ID the body?'

'From his car, and his fingerprints. He's on the computer. Got a record.'

'Pretty small beer. A couple of demo arrests.'

'He's still on file. That's all I've got.'

'Thanks, Gordon. I'll buy you a drink sometime.'

'I've heard that one before,' he said, and hung up.

I lingered for a time in the armchair, pondering why anyone would take a dead man's clothes. Not just his

39

wallet and valuables, but his clothes. Underpants, socks, the lot. Not to prevent his being identified, that was for sure, or else why leave him in his car?

I was interrupted by the sound of the front door opening. I went out into the hall to meet Maria and Cathy as they came in. They were subdued, sombre. Cathy's face was paler than ever. They didn't say anything.

Jenny came out of the kitchen and ran down the hall to her mother. Cathy picked her up and hugged her as if her life depended on it. Maybe now it did.

Maria said: 'I'll make us some tea.'

I followed her into the kitchen and leaned on the sink while the kettle boiled.

'When's she going to tell her?' I said.

'Later. When they're alone.'

'You cope all right at the mortuary?'

'It was awful. Awful. I don't even want to think about it again.'

She turned away to hide her face and busied herself with teapot and cups.

'Was Jenny any trouble?' she said.

'No. I feel as if I could do with a holiday now, but she was no trouble.'

Maria tried to smile but didn't get very far. The day was weighing heavily on her.

'Thanks for doing that. It was a big help.'

'Any time.'

Cathy came in then, Jenny still in her arms. Jenny pointed to the drawing on the noticeboard and said: 'I did that one. And' – she stopped to wriggle down out of her mother's grasp – 'I did this one too.' She picked up another picture from the table and held it out to me.

'This is for you.'

'Really? Thank you.' I took the piece of paper. 'That's very good. What is it, a mouse?'

'No, it's a cow.'

'Oh, sorry.' I folded it up and put it in my jacket pocket. 'I'll stick it up on my wall when I get home.'

40

I stayed for some tea, then said I had to be going. The atmosphere was strained, conversation awkward. I needed to get away and Cathy, I suspected, needed time alone with her daughter. Maria got her coat and came with me. At the door she gave Cathy a final hug.

'I can stay, you know.'

'It's best like this, just the two of us.'

'All right. I'll pop round tomorrow.'

'Thanks. And thank you for everything. It makes such a difference having . . .' She didn't finish.

Maria nodded. 'I know.' She kissed her on the cheek. 'Give me a call if you need anything.'

We walked down the steps. As we reached the pavement, I took a deep breath.

'I could do with a drink.'

'Not just one,' Maria said.

We went to a wine bar near the City Hall. A dimly lit joint with fake marble pillars and a chipped copy of the Mannequin Pis in an ornamental pool in the centre. A few office workers were leaning on the bar sucking Happy Hour cocktails through garish plastic straws but it was quiet for the time of evening. We had a corner to ourselves and a bottle of Australian chardonnay. Right now we didn't want anything more.

Maria was talking about Cathy and Rob Fielding, getting it out of her system.

'I've known Cathy for years, long before she married Rob. We lived in a shared house together when I first started work. Doing my training after university. She was a nurse at the Hallamshire, new to the city.

'We did everything together. Shopping, exploring the Peak District, going out with men. She always had men chasing after her. They liked that soft beauty she has. You know what I mean? The looks of a young girl. Shy, innocent, very sweet. They wanted to look after her, to protect her. That's what they told her anyway. Actually, all they wanted to do was bed her.'

41

'You're such a cynic,' I said.

She smiled. 'Not really. Cynics believe what they say. I'm still trying to convince myself.'

'About men?'

'Men, everything else. Experience makes you wary, but it doesn't make you any less optimistic. You know what's happened before, but each time you hope it's going to be different. That this one will be right. It makes such fools of us.

'Cathy was like that. She'd fall for someone, devote herself to them and they'd string her along for a while and then dump her. Heartlessly, as if there'd never been anything between them at all. That hurts. It cheapens, destroys self-esteem and, God knows, women have little enough of that to start with.'

She finished her glass of wine and poured herself another. Her third. I knew she wasn't just talking about Cathy.

'Then she met Rob. He was unlike any of her previous boyfriends. Not just in looks. He didn't seem her type. She'd usually gone for the bastards. The smooth, self-centred, confident ones. You work in a hospital, you meet plenty of them. They call them doctors.

'But Rob was really quite shy. To meet him you maybe wouldn't think that. He was so noisy, argumentative, opinionated, but on a personal level he didn't have much confidence. They were really quite similar in that respect. Two shy people, needing each other. And now he's gone.'

Maria swallowed hard, then gulped down the rest of her wine. 'Let's have another bottle.'

I looked at her, concerned. 'I'm not sure that's such a good idea.'

For an instant she flared. 'Don't patronize me, Michael. Just get another bloody bottle.' She fumbled in her purse and thrust a ten-pound note across the table.

I took it reluctantly and went to the bar. While I was waiting to be served, I looked back across the room at Maria. Sitting there at the table, a complete contrast to

Cathy Fielding. Her beauty darker, somehow wilder, less controlled. Sitting there, dabbing now at her eyes with a tissue and getting slowly, deliberately drunk.

When I returned with the second bottle, she had a hold on herself. But the make-up around her eyes was smudged. I filled her glass with the last of the old bottle and topped it up with the new. We made small talk for a while, letting the emotions subside, but there was only one topic on both our minds.

'Who would have done it?' Maria said eventually. 'A gentle, harmless man like Rob. Who would have done that?'

I didn't say anything.

'It's somehow connected with his environmental campaigning, isn't it? What else could it be? It wasn't an accident. Him just happening to be in Winnats Pass and someone kills him. He was out there doing something that someone didn't like.'

'Did you ask Cathy why he went out last night?'

'Yes. She doesn't know.'

'Didn't she ask him where he was going?'

'They didn't have that kind of marriage. Having to explain, to justify everything they did.'

'Most wives would have asked.'

Maria was on her fifth glass of wine now. I wasn't even trying to keep pace with her. She said: 'And what about the police? That was no coincidence either. A few hours after Rob's killed they're taking away his papers.' Something occurred to her. 'I suppose that file he told you about yesterday – on Russell Stamford – I suppose that went too.'

I nodded.

'That's pretty convenient for Stamford, isn't it? Information that could ruin him, maybe put him in jail, has now disappeared.'

'Not disappeared. The police have it. Or we assume they do. What makes you think they're going to bury it?'

'What if Stamford put them up to it?'

43

'He doesn't have that kind of clout. Besides, I think they were after something else.'

'What?'

'I don't know.'

She narrowed her eyes. 'Do you know something you're not telling me?'

I shook my head. She leaned closer across the table. Her smoky blue-grey eyes were slightly glassy. The wine was sweet on her breath.

'Because I want to know everything about this. Everything you find out, I want you to tell me.'

'What makes you think I'll find anything out?'

'How long have I known you, Michael? You're going to snoop around, I know you are. It's in your nature. And it's also in your nature not to confide in anyone. Well, I want you to confide in me.'

She leaned back in her seat, swaying sideways unsteadily. 'Pour me another glass of wine.'

'I think you've had enough.'

'Pour it.'

I didn't argue. I'd never seen her drunk before. It made her unpredictable, aggressive, but I understood why she was doing it.

She drained half her glass. 'You know what Rob had that most people don't? He had a quality of goodness in him. Do you understand what I mean? It's an unfashionable word, makes me sound naïve, but he had it. Cathy has it too. They're good people. We need people like them, who believe in making this world a fit place to live in. But who don't want anything out of it for themselves. We need them.'

Suddenly she started to cry, her shoulders heaving. She looked at me through a film of tears.

'And Jenny, that darling little girl. How do you tell her? How do you tell a four-year-old child her daddy won't be coming home any more? That he's gone forever.'

I didn't answer. We'd talked enough. I moved to the chair next to her and put my arms around her. She tucked her head in against my chest and sobbed her heart out. I let her weep, stroking her hair, the grief pouring out in torrents.

When, in time, the tears stopped, I held on to her. Closer than I'd ever been. But she pushed herself away and said: 'Take me home.'

She slept throughout the journey to Ranmoor. A heavy, drunken sleep. I tried to rouse her when we reached her house, but she was too deeply under. I found her doorkey in her handbag, lifted her out of the car and carried her inside and upstairs to the bedroom. There was a big antique pine double bed with a blue and white striped duvet on it. I put Maria down gently on one side. She didn't stir. I looked at her for a moment before pulling the other half of the duvet over her. Then I clicked out the light and left.

When I got home, I stuck Jenny's drawing to the wall above my desk with Blu-tack. It still looked like a mouse to me.

# 4

I spent the first part of the next morning on the phone. Speaking to the Derbyshire police press officer about Rob Fielding's murder, then Gordon Crieff. Neither had anything new to tell me so I called Detective Sergeant Chris Strange at South Yorkshire police headquarters.

I tried to soften him up with some preliminary chat about his health and the weather, but he knew me too well for that.

'Cut the crap, McLean. What do you want?'

Such grace, coppers. 'You ever come across a Superintendent from the Met called Ray Coltrane?' I said.

'What is this? The Met?'

'You know him?'

'Why should I? You any idea how many superintendents there are down there?'

'He's not down there. He's up here.'

Strange took a moment to reply. When he did his voice was casual, trying not to sound interested.

'What d'you mean, up here?'

I told him about the search at Fielding's house. 'They clear that with you?'

'Me, personally?'

'You know what I'm asking, Chris. They're on your patch, they should let you know what they're doing. Shouldn't they?'

I had him hooked. He wasn't going to admit it, but no cop likes outsiders on his territory. Particularly ones from London.

'How do you know this?' he said.

'I was there. I watched them do it.'

'They say what they were after?'

'I thought you might be able to tell me that.'

'Oh yeah? Even if I knew, why should I do that?'

'Because I'm helping you out. And one good turn deserves another.'

I heard the click of a cigarette lighter on the other end of the line, then a wheeze as Strange inhaled. I pictured him there at his desk on Snig Hill, leaning back in his chair, sweating a little around the mouth, his shirt straining over his beer gut, a Woodbine between his fingers. A living advertisement for coronary seizure.

'Rob Fielding,' he said. 'Why do I know that name?'

He knew all right, but I helped him out anyway.

'He was murdered yesterday morning. Winnats Pass. Remember?'

'Ah, yes. The Ripley boys are handling that one. And you say you were at his house when this bloke Coltrane showed up?'

He was fishing. Always wanting to know more than he needed to.

'Chris,' I said, 'I'm tipping you off. Something's going on. The Met are sniffing around in your back yard and I'll bet you haven't even had a whiff of the scent.'

He gave that some thought. Neither denied nor confirmed it, but I didn't expect him to. I knew I was right.

'What's in it for you?' he said.

'Some information. I want to know who Coltrane is and what he's doing here. So do you now. When you find out, will you let me know?'

'Well, I could ask around,' Strange said noncommittally. 'But what makes you think I'll pass anything I discover on to you? For years now you've interfered in police business, pissed me about. Why should I give you any help? I hate you, McLean.'

'I know. But you hate the Met even more,' I said, and put the phone down.

47

I made myself a cup of coffee, Continental roast, then called the offices of Stamford plc in the city centre. I asked to speak to Russell Stamford. The switchboard put me through to his secretary who gave me the usual run-around.

'I'm afraid Mr Stamford is unavailable today. Would you like to speak to our PR agency? They handle all press inquiries.'

God, no. I'd yet to meet a PR agency that could tell me a single remotely useful thing about anything. Overpaid office boys in striped shirts whose only purpose was to stop reporters getting to the people who mattered.

'What does unavailable mean?' I asked. 'He's out, in a meeting, in the bog taking a piss? What does it mean?'

The secretary's voice was icily polite. 'If you'd like to state your business, sir, I'll make sure Mr Stamford gets a message.'

'I want to speak to him personally. Is he "unavailable" all day?'

'I'm afraid so.'

'Is he actually in the office? If he is, I'll come down and see him.'

'Mr Stamford is not in the office today, sir.'

'Then where is he?'

'I'm not permitted to reveal that.'

These people. Why not? Was it a state secret or something?

'Is he abroad? Or taking a day off? Are these difficult questions?'

She hung up on me. I put the receiver down, thinking, you need to work on your phone technique a bit, McLean.

I looked Stamford up in the telephone directory. There were eight R. Stamfords listed. Too many to ring, and he was probably ex-directory anyway. So I called Alan Dobie, the industrial reporter on the *News*, and traded him a couple of numbers from my contacts book in exchange for Stamford's home address and number. I was right, it was ex-directory. I dialled it. It rang for a long time before a woman answered. I could hear voices, the chink of glasses in the background.

'Mrs Stamford?' I said.

'No, Mrs Stamford is unavailable at the moment.'

It obviously ran in the family.

'Can I take a message for her?'

'Actually, it was Mr Stamford I was wanting. Is he there by any chance?'

'Yes, he is. But he isn't taking calls until after the party.'

'Party?'

'Yes, sir. Mrs Stamford's birthday party. Shall I say who called?'

'No, it's all right. I'll catch him later. By the way, what time does the party end?'

'Three o'clock.'

I checked my watch. Plenty of time to get there. It was a long time since I'd been to a party. I didn't have an invitation, of course, but why let a small technicality like that get in the way?

The house was on the outskirts of Dore village, on the western edge of the city. An expensive neighbourhood, encroaching gradually on the boundaries of the Peak District National Park. I kept the car window open as I drove through, inhaling the heady aroma of money and exclusivity, hoping some of it might rub off on me. A select area in terms of wealth and property, but if Russell Stamford lived there, maybe not so selective about its inhabitants.

I sensed I was getting near when the side of the road started to fill up with parked cars. Then I passed a gateway manned by a couple of squat men with thick necks and lounge suits and I knew I was there. I slowed down to examine them. They didn't look the types to let me in without an invite. I drove on past and left the car out of sight at the entrance to a farm track.

I had a clear view across a field of the side and part of the front of Stamford's house. It was a big red-brick place

49

with wings and outbuildings and about two acres of land. Virginia creeper smothered the gable end in dense copper foliage. A forest lap wooden fence marked the edge of the grounds, but it wasn't much of an obstacle to a determined gatecrasher. I squeezed through a gap in a hedge and walked across the field, the damp grass soaking my shoes and trouser bottoms.

When I reached the fence, I pulled myself up on one of the posts to see over. There was a shrubbery on the other side and, beyond that, a gravelled drive and turning area in front of the house which was jammed with closely parked cars. I could go over here, but then I'd still have to get through the front door and probably identify myself. I preferred to slip in unnoticed and unannounced if I could.

I followed the fence round to the back of the house and heaved myself over it into the bushes. There was a lawn like a bowling green in the centre of the garden, flanked by stone paths and, at the near side, a rustic pergola draped in roses and wisteria which shielded anyone behind it from view. I crept along close to the pergola to within a few yards of the house. Then I stopped.

A York stone terrace was all that lay between me and the French windows that gave access to the house. Inside there were people moving around holding plates of food and glasses of wine. The murmur of voices trickled out. I straightened my jacket and sauntered casually across the terrace. I tried the French windows. They were unlocked. I slid them back and stepped through into the room without attracting the slightest attention. Everyone was too deeply engrossed in talking and eating to take any notice of me.

I was in what looked like the dining room. A long, broad room running the full width of the terrace, its walls adorned with a collection of abstract modern paintings. At one end the caterers had set up their tables and were serving guests with a buffet lunch. I wandered over to check it out. It looked pretty good, but I felt I ought to reserve judgement until I'd tasted it.

I picked up a plate and allowed a young girl in a white blouse and black skirt to fill it with salmon and an assortment of salads. I'd got the first forkful to my mouth when a man's voice said quietly in my ear: 'We don't want any trouble, pal. Just put down your plate and step outside and you won't get hurt.'

I lowered my fork and turned my head to look at him. He was just behind my right shoulder. A big fellow with a haircut like a startled hedgehog and the complexion of a pebble-dashed wall. I was glad I hadn't started eating yet: his face was enough to give anyone indigestion.

'I beg your pardon?' I said innocently.

'You heard.'

I thought about trying to bluff my way out of it, but he didn't look the patient type.

'Any chance of clearing my plate first?'

He shook his head slowly. I put the plate down on the table.

'You work for Stamford?' I said. 'Tell him I want to see him.'

'Outside.'

'I mean it.'

He took my arm and gripped it hard, guiding me towards the exit. I didn't attempt to argue with him. I was concentrating too much on the pain in my arm.

On our way down the hall I said: 'I want to talk to him about someone called Derek Kent. Why don't you mention that to him, see what he says?'

He stopped dead. His grip eased off. 'You what?'

'You heard.'

He took a long while to reply. He knew what I was talking about, but he didn't know what to do. I didn't give him any assistance.

Finally, he said: 'Who?'

I rolled my eyes. 'Is that the best you can do? Just tell Stamford what I said. He'll see me.'

He looked at me doubtfully, then made a decision. He walked over to a woman in a maid's uniform who was standing by the front door looking after the guests' coats. I guessed she was the one who'd answered the telephone. He said something to her and she nodded, then hurried off. He came back to me.

'You can wait in the study.'

We went down another long hallway running at right angles to the first. At the far end of it we went through a door into a book-lined room which smelt of stale tobacco smoke. There was a heavy walnut desk under the window and a couple of high-backed leather armchairs opposite it. I wandered around, fingering the books on the shelves. They were all beautifully bound, but almost certainly never opened. They looked as if they'd been bought by the yard.

Russell Stamford came in a short time later. He was irritated, impatient.

'What is it, Vince? I've got guests.' He noticed me. 'Who's this?'

'He came in over the fence,' Vince said. 'Across the lawn and through the windows on the terrace. No invitation. I watched him from the kitchen.'

'Then throw him out. Don't bother me with it.' Stamford turned to leave.

'He mentioned Derek Kent.'

Stamford paused. I couldn't see his face fully, but his body went suddenly taut. He looked back at me. His expression gave nothing away.

'I don't believe I know anyone of that name,' he said.

I sat down in one of the leather armchairs. 'Oh, I think you do, Russ.'

He came round the back of me and lowered himself into the swivel chair behind the desk. He had the looks of a fading matinée idol. His chin and neck beginning to sag a little, the grey hairs creeping backwards from his temples. Still handsome, but the surface starting to crack despite his attempts to hold time at bay. He must have been in his mid-fifties, his body trim and elegant in a light grey suit and matching silk tie. I could see him watching his diet, working out to keep himself in shape, but he was fighting a losing battle. He was staring at me with eyes like flints.

'Who are you?' he said.

'My name's McLean. I'm a freelance journalist.'

'I find your methods rather intrusive, Mr McLean. This is a private party for my wife and a few friends. I don't take kindly to reporters gatecrashing it.'

'No, I'm sure you don't. But still, as I'm here, why don't we have a little chat about Derek Kent?'

'I told you, I don't –'

I interrupted him. 'I know what you said. But maybe I don't believe you.'

'I've never heard of this man, so I have no intention of wasting time discussing him.'

I nodded and said nothing. Stamford didn't move. I waited. I was in no hurry. The ball was in his court now.

Eventually the silence got to him. 'You're trespassing on my property. I could call the police and have you removed.'

'Trespass isn't a criminal offence,' I said. 'I doubt the police would be very interested. Besides, your mate here asked me to stay so we could talk. That makes me a guest.'

His eyes flickered towards Vince. There was no emotion in them.

I continued. 'I got the impression he knew who Derek Kent was. Perhaps he could enlighten you.'

Stamford placed the tips of his fingers on the edge of the desk and leaned back in his chair, watching me.

'Why don't you do it instead,' he said.

I gave him the bare facts that Rob Fielding had outlined in the pub. He listened attentively, his body motionless. When I'd finished, he gave a contemptuous snort and said: 'You have proof of these absurd allegations?'

I didn't answer directly. 'Are they true?'

'Absolutely not.' He tilted forwards across the desk, his manner suddenly aggressive. 'And if one word of what you've just said appears in print, I'll have no hesitation in suing for libel. I can afford the very best lawyers.'

'Then maybe you could fill me in on the early part of your career,' I said. 'So I can check it out for myself.'

'I'm not going to fill you in on anything. My career is my business and no one else's.'

'Really? You're the chairman of a publicly quoted company. I think your shareholders might disagree with that.'

'What do you want, McLean?'

'To clear up a few questions, that's all. How's the new landfill going?'

The change of tack took him by surprise. 'What? Which landfill? We have dozens all over the country.'

'You know the one I mean. A lot of people don't like it.'

He shrugged dismissively. 'A few hooligans. Rent-a-mob thugs, that's all.'

'Rented by whom?' I said.

'How should I know?' He saw my sceptical expression. 'Are you implying I might have had something to do with that disgraceful episode on Sunday morning?'

'No. Did you?'

'I won't even bother to answer that.'

'Try this one then. What are the concrete tanks inside the quarry for?'

That caught him momentarily off balance. He glanced across at Vince again. His composure was slipping.

'There are no concrete tanks. It's a domestic refuse landfill and nothing more.'

'Can I come in to see for myself?'

He evaded that one. 'Who's giving you all this nonsense? Misguided environmentalists? The Not-In-My-Back-Yard crowd on that executive estate up the hill? They're spinning lies to discredit me, can't you see that?'

'You think the protesters are misguided?'

'They're making trouble, inciting violence over a site which has been properly authorized by the council and which will be well managed by my company.'

54

'It will also destroy an area of considerable natural beauty.'

Stamford blew air through his teeth impatiently. 'Natural beauty? That quarry? It was dug out to provide building stone for the Victorians. It's an eyesore.'

'And what will your tip be?'

'You think it's going to be a hole full of rotting garbage, don't you? That's the problem with ill-informed people like you. You have no idea how these things are done. When the tip is full it will be covered with soil and allowed to settle, then landscaped. In fifteen years' time you won't know it's there. Believe me, it'll look an awful lot better than it does now.'

'And the concrete tanks? What will happen to the stuff you dump in those?'

He shook his head in exasperation. 'There are no concrete tanks. You think I'm going to dump toxic waste there illegally?'

'You might be tempted.'

'Why? I've got plenty of other sites where I'm licensed to handle hazardous waste. Why on earth would I take the risk of dumping it in that quarry? I run a sizeable business legitimately and make a reasonable profit from it. I don't need to cheat.'

He stood up and moved away from the desk. 'I have a party to get back to.' He came round close. 'I don't expect to be bothered again, you understand? Nor do I expect any of these unfounded allegations to be repeated by you or anyone else.'

He was going to say more, but the door opened and a tarty woman in a short black skirt and silvery blouse entered.

'Here you are. What are you doing, Russell? People have been asking for you.'

'Just coming, dear,' Stamford said. 'Vince, show Mr McLean out.'

I was escorted along the hall and out through the front door. Vince stayed with me all the way down the drive.

At the gateway, he turned and said to me: 'You heard what Mr Stamford said, didn't you?'

'Sure.'

'But maybe you didn't get the subtext.'

Subtext? There was more to Vince than I'd thought.

'Go on, spell it out for me,' I said.

'Just remember what might happen to you if you don't take heed of his words.'

'His lawyers, you mean?'

Vince shook his head, then hit me hard in the stomach. I doubled up in a ball, choking for breath.

'No, this,' he said softly in my ear and walked away.

On balance, I think I'd have preferred the lawyers.

# 5

I'd been home less than fifteen minutes when Cathy Fielding rang. I was slumped in an armchair, sipping hot tea and rubbing my stomach to relieve the dull ache left by Vince's fist.

'Can you come round?' she said.

'Now?'

'Any time you're free. I need to talk to you.'

She sounded calm, but there was something forced about it. A woman on the edge, trying hard to hang on.

'I'll be over right away,' I said.

I wondered about it on the drive across town. What else could I have done? Her grief was not mine, her loss was not mine. Maybe her husband's death diminished me too, but I wasn't the right person to share her bereavement. I was on the outside, a bystander. I didn't want the burden of a widow's pain on my shoulders. Yet I couldn't turn her down.

There was no sign of emotion when she opened the door. She nodded gratefully and led me down the hall to the kitchen. Jenny was sitting on a chair, her legs dangling in space. Cathy knelt down and finished tying her shoe-laces. Jenny looked up at me brightly.

'Hello, we're going to the park.'

'I hope you don't mind,' Cathy said. 'She wants to feed the ducks.'

'Fine by me,' I said.

The afternoon had a crisp, autumnal feel, the watery sunlight taking some of the bite out of the breeze. We walked to the roundabout at Hunter's Bar and crossed the road into Endcliffe Park. There were wet leaves everywhere, a russet carpet turning into a slippery pulp beneath our feet. The River Porter was high, foaming against its banks. Jenny ran on ahead of us, kicking at the piles of leaves.

'She's taking it well,' I said.

'She doesn't understand yet,' Cathy said. 'I've told her but she doesn't know what it means. She keeps asking for him. Look at her. It hasn't touched her. Not so far, anyway. It will hit her later.'

I watched the little girl on the path in front. Running now towards the playground, jumping on to a swing.

'What do I tell her?' Cathy continued. 'I'm not a religious person. I have no faith, yet I've told her he's in heaven. You have to give her some hope. Let her believe he's just gone somewhere else. She can't comprehend complete extinction.'

Her voice cracked momentarily. I looked at her. She bowed her head, pushing her hands deeper into the pockets of her duffle coat. She seemed very small. A child in adult's clothes, struggling to comprehend too.

'And you,' I said. 'Who's helping you to cope?'

'Maria's been very good. Other friends too. But what can they do? Jenny and I have to learn to live without him on our own. No one else can help.'

She lifted her head, taking a deep breath, bracing herself. Jenny was calling to her from the playground, dangling forwards by her arms in the swing, wanting someone to push her.

We went over and I stood a little to one side while Cathy played with her daughter. Pushing the swing for a time, then sitting with her on the roundabout while I watched and gave an occasional push to keep it turning.

It all seemed so normal. There were other mothers there with their children. Laughing, shouting, chasing, indulging them. Yet underneath those contented exteriors I wondered what private agonies they were suffering.

We moved on, following the banks of the river. The stepping stones near the café were partially submerged under the torrent of water. We reached the lake and Cathy took out a plastic bag containing the remains of a loaf. She handed it to Jenny who immediately started tearing off chunks of bread and throwing them into the water. The ducks converged on her from every quarter, snapping and squabbling over each morsel as it landed on the surface.

Cathy and I sat down on a park bench to watch.

'I didn't intend us to go out,' she said. 'But Jenny wanted it and, well, I suppose I welcomed the chance to distract her. To do something.'

'I don't mind.'

She was silent for a time. Then she said pensively: 'It's easy to dwell too much on it. A part of me wants to dwell on it and nothing else. I feel I owe it to him. But God, it hurts. Just the two of us in that house and Rob gone. It's more than I can bear.'

'Is there anything I can do?'

'You've come round, that's enough.' She glanced at me. She'd put on make-up today. A touch of mascara on her eyelashes, a subtle hint of colour in her cheeks. You could still tell she'd been weeping though.

She said: 'I needed a break. Something to take my mind off it. I hope you don't mind.'

'No.'

'I wanted to talk about Rob. That sounds contradictory, doesn't it? Wanting to take my mind off it, but wanting to talk about him.'

'I understand,' I said. 'There's a difference between talking about Rob and talking about his death. One you want to remember, the other you want to forget.'

'The two are really inseparable, I know that. But it helps to think about one more than the other. Do you see that?'

I nodded. 'So tell me about him.'

She started to talk. About how they met, how she loved

him, their marriage, their life together. She hardly knew me, but that made it easier for her.

'He had this incredible energy, I don't know where it came from. A passion for all sorts of things, but particularly the environment. I couldn't keep up with him. He enjoyed stirring up trouble, annoying the Establishment. Sometimes I found it hard to take. You know he'd been arrested a couple of times before last Sunday?'

'He told me in the pub, with Maria.'

'That worried me. I didn't like him going off on protests, not knowing if he was going to come back, or if he was going to get hurt. Rob didn't mind those risks. I admired him for what he did. But I found it hard to join in. I suppose it was complacency.'

'Most of us are like that,' I said.

'I know. But doesn't it make you feel guilty?'

'You were there on Sunday.'

'That was different. It was close to home and I could take Jenny. I thought it would be a pleasant morning out in the countryside.' Her mouth twisted wryly. 'Shows how much I know. Without you, Jenny would probably be in hospital now.'

I looked at the little girl throwing bread to the ducks. 'It doesn't seem to have affected her.'

'She's blotted it out of her memory, I think. At least, I hope she has. She's resilient. She takes after Rob in that respect. He could be tough, uncompromising. He never saw two sides to anything. He held his beliefs stubbornly. Everything black and white. He didn't accept there's a grey area in the middle in which most of us live.'

She looked away over the lake. The light was beginning to fade, the gloom of dusk smudging the shore on the far side.

Then suddenly she said: 'I want to know why he died.'

I waited for her to continue, but she didn't.

'Have the police told you any more?' I asked.

Cathy shook her head. 'Will you help me?'

I didn't have to think about it for long. 'Yes. Are you up to it now?'

'I think so.'

'If I ask too many questions, just say so.'

She nodded, hunching her shoulders so the collar of her coat rode up to cover her ears. It was getting cold.

'What was he doing out at Winnats on Sunday night?'

'I don't know.'

'Did you know he was going there?'

'No.'

'Didn't he tell you?'

'No.'

'And you didn't ask?'

'He told me not to. He said it was better if I didn't know.'

'Why?'

Cathy shrugged. 'He sometimes said that. He went off a few times recently and told me it was safer if I didn't know where he was going.'

'He used those words?'

'Yes.'

'And he gave no indication of what he might be doing?'

'No.'

'Had he been away overnight before?'

'Several times. Once he went somewhere for the week-end. I don't know where.'

'Surely you must have been curious.'

'Of course. What wife wouldn't be? But I thought – well, suspected really – that he was doing something . . .' She searched for the word. 'Unorthodox.'

'You mean illegal?'

She nodded. 'And that he wouldn't tell me what for my own protection.'

'Did he ever mention Winnats Pass, or Castleton, to you?'

'No. I can't think why he went there on Sunday.'

It occurred to me then that Rob hadn't necessarily gone to Winnats Pass that night. He could have been killed somewhere else and then been driven there to be dumped.

But I didn't say anything. I wanted to keep things simple for the moment.

'What about enemies,' I said. 'Did he ever indicate he thought his life might be in danger?'

'Not seriously.'

'What do you mean by that?'

'Well, he was always speculating that someone might be out to get him. Not someone specific, just someone in general. But he had no real grounds for believing it. Not that he told me, anyway.'

I was beginning to think there were probably quite a few things Rob Fielding hadn't told his wife. I started to ask another question, but Jenny trotted over to the bench and interrupted me.

'Mummy, did you bring any more bread?'

'I'm afraid that was it.'

'But the ducks are still hungry.'

'They'll be all right. They can find their own food.' Cathy glanced up at the sky. 'It's time we were going home.'

'Can I have one more go on the swings?'

'We'll see. It's getting very dark.'

We walked back down the path, almost feeling our way in places, the light was so poor. At the playground we made a brief stop for Jenny to go on the swings, then continued our way home. We didn't talk any more about Rob.

'Come in for a cup of tea,' Cathy said when we reached the house.

We drank it in the kitchen while Jenny had spaghetti hoops on toast and a glass of milk. It was only after Jenny had disappeared into the sitting room to watch children's TV that I said: 'Did Rob mention a file he had on Russell Stamford to you?'

'Yes. But it's gone. The police took it.'

'You sure of that? He didn't have some secret hiding place for it?'

'Yes, he did. He was a secretive man in many ways. But

the police found it. It wasn't very difficult. It was in a box under some towels in the airing cupboard. Not just that file, a few others too. I went up last night and checked everywhere. The police took the lot.'

She topped up her cup of tea and sipped it. 'The search and his death are connected, aren't they?'

'Oh yes,' I said. 'It's too much of a coincidence to be otherwise. Do you have any idea how?'

'Sorry. I've been thinking about it since yesterday without coming up with anything.'

'Did you ever read any of the stuff Rob kept?'

'No.'

'So you don't know what else he might've been up to?'

'Up to?'

'You know, people he might've been investigating the way he did Stamford. Or other issues he was interested in that might have made someone want him out of the way.'

'He never mentioned anything. Not that I can remember.'

'What about . . .' I stopped as the telephone started to ring in the hall.

Cathy stood up. 'Excuse me.'

What about . . . what? I thought. There were so many questions I could ask, but Cathy was not the person to give me the answers. She knew virtually nothing about her husband's activities. The problem for me now was: did anyone else know more?

She came back into the kitchen. 'It's Maria. She'd like a word.'

I went out into the hall and picked up the receiver. 'Hi.'

Maria's voice was hesitant, a little embarrassed. 'Look, about last night. I'm sorry.'

'There's nothing to be sorry about.'

'It must have been awful for you. I don't remember too much about it. I hope I didn't make a complete idiot of myself.'

'Forget it.'

'To pass out like that. God, I've never done that before in my life.'

'You had an excuse. In the circumstances, it was understandable.'

'At my age? Come on, that's what undergraduates do.'

'Maria, stop apologizing. How're you feeling, anyway?'

'Terrible. I woke up this morning with a splitting headache and it's not much better now. Thank you for putting me to bed, by the way. You didn't even remove any of my clothes. That was very gentlemanly of you.'

'Yeah, well, I was tempted,' I said. 'But I didn't think my hormones could stand it.'

She gave a low chuckle. 'What're you doing there anyway?'

'Cathy asked me over. She wanted to talk.'

'How is she?'

'Coping well, all things considered. She's a lot tougher than she looks.'

'And Jenny?'

'It hasn't sunk in. You want another word with Cathy?'

'No. I'm coming over after work.'

'OK. Listen . . .' I hesitated. Make a move if you're going to, McLean. I thought of dinner out. A restaurant some place. Then I thought of the state of my bank balance.

'Yes?' Maria said.

I hit on a compromise. 'Why don't you come round to my flat for dinner, say tomorrow night? I'll cook us something.'

'You'll *cook*?'

I didn't like her tone. 'I'll have you know I'm a dab hand in the kitchen.'

'Will I have to bring my own Alka-Seltzer?'

I ignored that. 'Anything you don't like to eat?'

'Just cabbage, turnip and gooseberries.'

'Damn,' I said. 'That rules out my cabbage, turnip and gooseberry stroganoff. Seven-thirty OK?'

'Fine. But you don't have to cook, you know.'

64

'No, I insist. I'm cooking.'

Well, we all make mistakes, don't we?

I hung up and rejoined Cathy in the kitchen. She looked up over her cup of tea. 'Everything OK?'

I nodded. 'I ought to be going.'

She came to the door with me.

'There was just one other thing,' I said. 'Do you know what Rob was wearing on Sunday night? His clothes.'

Her brow puckered. 'His clothes? Some old jeans and a jumper, I think. Nothing special. Why?'

I shook my head. I wasn't going to tell her he'd been found naked. She could do without that kind of thing right now. She was looking at me strangely, her arms folded across her breast, almost hugging herself as if for comfort. I had an inkling she didn't want to be left alone.

'Thank you for coming. It helped.'

'I could stay, if you like,' I said. 'Until Maria gets here.'

'It's all right. I'll be OK.'

'She won't be long.'

'I know. She's a dear friend. One of the most generous people I've ever met. I knew her before she was married, you know. Did she tell you that?'

'Yes.'

'Her husband was a . . . well, let's say she deserved better.' Cathy looked me directly in the eyes. 'It's time she found someone else. It's not good for her to be on her own.'

Hell, I knew that. I'd been trying to convince her of it for years.

There was a message waiting for me on my answering machine when I got home.

'You know who this is. I've got something for you. Meet me after I knock off. Six o'clock. You know where I'll be.'

I played it back a couple of times. It was Chris Strange's voice. He was being very cautious, not leaving his name, not even mentioning the place we were to meet. I wondered why.

65

I put my coat back on and went out straight away, driving into town and parking in a side street behind the *Evening News* building. I walked down towards Snig Hill, cutting across in front of police headquarters before heading past the Crown Court to Castle Market.

The Two Chuffs pub was off a dank, gloomy alleyway near the River Don. I went through the door of the saloon bar and hit a wall of cigarette smoke, beer fumes and off-duty cops. I pushed my way through and waited for Don Soper, the landlord, to get round to serving me. He looked up at me over the Ward's pump and scowled.

'What the fuck d'you want?'

'Nice to see you too, Don. You well?'

''Course I'm not fucking well. Would you be well if you had to stand here all day serving pisspots like you?'

'A pint of bitter, please. And have one yourself.'

'I'll have a half later, when I've got shut of all you wankers.'

That's what I liked about the Two Chuffs. The friendly ambience and sophisticated conversation.

'You got any sandwiches left?' I asked.

'Cheese.'

'Anything else?'

'You want a fucking à la carte menu?'

'I'll take the cheese.'

I took a sip of my beer while Don extracted a cheese sandwich from a plastic display case on the bar. It was greyish and curling at the edges. It looked in serious need of artificial resuscitation. He slapped it down in front of me.

'That it?'

I nodded and paid. Then I looked around for Chris Strange. He hadn't come in yet, but I knew he would. He came here every night when he finished work.

Then I noticed someone else at a table behind the door. A lugubrious character in a tatty tweed jacket and a frayed white shirt. I picked up my pint and sandwich and wandered over.

66

'Hello, Harry. Mind if I join you?'

Harry Raymond glanced up without interest. He shook his head and took a bite of his meat pie.

'You all right?' I said.

He nodded unconvincingly. He was dour at the best of times, but this was something different. I'd known him long enough to realize when things weren't going well for him.

'You sure?'

'Yes, I'm fine.'

There was definitely something wrong. Harry was a committed, almost pathological hypochondriac. If he said he was fine, then I knew he was lying. But I didn't push him. He'd tell me in his own good time.

'I didn't expect to see you in here,' I said. 'You working late?'

'Something like that.'

'Business OK?'

'Yes. Ticking over.'

He didn't volunteer anything else. I took a bite of my sandwich. It was so old it should have had a 'bury by' date on it. We sat there in silence for a time, Harry chewing his pie, staring down morosely.

Eventually, I said: 'Come on, tell me.'

'Tell you what?'

'I'm a friend, Harry. Get it off your chest.'

He didn't reply, so I hazarded a guess. 'What is it, something personal? You might as well tell me because you know what I'm like. I'll keep asking questions until you're ready to scream.'

Harry sighed. 'It's the wife.'

'She's not ill, is she?'

'No, worse luck. She's in rude 'ealth. Rude being the right word.'

'You fighting again?'

'We're really getting on each other's nerves.'

'That's normal in marriage.'

'Not like this. The atmosphere's terrible. That's why I'm

67

'ere. I'm stopping out as long as I can. Avoiding going 'ome.'

'What's the problem?'

'I dunno, Mike. We've got along fine for years. Well, you know, muddled through like everyone else. Now all of a sudden she's giving me stick all the time. On me back for this and that. She says I'm boring, stuck in a rut, but what does she bloody expect? I'm married to 'er, aren't I?'

'Maybe you should talk to her.'

'Talk to 'er? I can hardly get a word in edgeways she's yacking on that much. I'm keeping me 'ead well below the parapet until it all blows over.'

'You sure that's wise? My wife used to hate it when I did that. Women like to get things out in the open, discuss them. It used to really piss her off when I tried to dodge an issue.'

Harry gave me a look. 'Oh aye. And 'ow long did your marriage last?'

He had a point. 'OK, so I'm no expert.'

'I'll do this my way, Mike. You don't know 'er the way I do.'

'Well, if you need any help, you know where I am. You can always count on me.'

'Thanks, Mike. Sorry I were a bit short wi' you. You want another pint?'

'No thanks, Harry. I'm supposed to be meeting someone here. He's just walked in. I'll see you around.'

I stood up. Chris Strange had come in through the door to the lounge and was looking around at the customers. The way cops do, taking it all in. His suit was crumpled, his tie and top shirt button undone. He fingered his bushy moustache lightly, as if checking it was still there, and nodded at me. I cut diagonally across the room and joined him at the bar.

'I'll have a pint,' he said. Getting the important business out of the way first.

I put the order in and let him light up a cigarette before saying: 'I appreciate this, Chris. What've you got?'

He was going to make me wait for it. 'They doing any food tonight?'

'I can recommend the sandwiches,' I said.

'Yeah? Hey, Don, give us a sandwich 'n' all.'

'I suppose I'm paying for that too, am I?' I said.

'Well, seeing as you're offering.' He smirked at me. 'Ta.'

I didn't say anything. He hadn't tasted it yet.

'Crowded in here tonight, isn't it?' he said. Enjoying himself, stalling.

'Coltrane,' I said. 'Or are we going to make small talk all night?'

He settled himself against the bar, his elbow resting on the surface so he could lever up his pint without straining too hard.

'I asked around,' he said. 'It's funny you should be interested in Coltrane, because he's very interested in you.'

I straightened up and paid attention. 'Is he? In what way?'

'He was in the office this afternoon, asking questions. With a mate. A DI called Jack Carson. Ugly little shit.'

'What sort of questions?'

'Who are you, your personal habits, inclinations. All straightforward stuff.'

I was intrigued, wondering where he'd got my name. I hadn't told him who I was.

'And I suppose you gave him the answers,' I said.

Strange shook his head. 'Not me. He's no friend of mine. If the Met wants to know, they can find out for themselves. I'm not doing it for them.'

'Is this what they call inter-force cooperation?'

Strange grinned. 'We gave him a cup of tea, let him take a piss. What d'you want?'

'Did you ask him why they searched Rob Fielding's house?'

'Yes.'

'And?'

69

'He told me to mind my own business. Only not as politely as that.'

'Yeah, he does have a certain crude charm, doesn't he? Someone must know what he was doing there.'

'My guvnor. But he's not confiding in me.'

He took a bite of his sandwich and chewed on it. It took a lot of chewing.

'Christ, was this made today?'

'Exhumed today,' I said.

Strange pulled a face and threw the sandwich into an ashtray.

'So tell me, McLean, why should Special Branch be interested in you?'

It had the effect he'd intended. I stared at him wide-eyed. 'Coltrane and Carson are Special Branch?'

He nodded. 'The real thing. And you know something? They've taken a big dislike to you.'

'I'll get over it.'

'Don't play it too smart, McLean. Those guys are serious. So why don't you tell me what you're doing and maybe you won't get burned.'

'I'm not doing anything.'

'You're always doing something. That's why you asked me to find out who they were.'

I concentrated on finishing my pint for a moment. Strange inhaled on his cigarette and waited.

'I was at that demo on Sunday. At the quarry landfill,' I said.

'The riot, you mean.'

I let that pass. 'Coltrane and Carson were there taking photos of the demonstrators.'

'That's their job.'

'A few residents protesting about a dump is hardly subversive activity.'

Strange gave an amused snort, eyeing me cynically. 'You're not that naïve, McLean. Those guys would photograph a bus queue if someone told them it was a dangerous political gathering. They see conspirators everywhere.'

70

'Including Rob Fielding?'

'Probably. I looked him up. He had a track record of political activity.'

'Environmental activity.'

'You think that's not political? You think the Branch don't keep an eye on people like him?'

'Is he supposed to have done something?'

'I don't know,' Strange said. 'Nobody's telling me. Unless you do.'

'All I know is that he was murdered.'

'And you think there's a story in it for you.'

I didn't answer. Strange sighed and drained his glass.

'I'll give you some advice, McLean. Coltrane and Carson mean business. If I were you, from now on I'd watch my back.'

He pushed himself away from the bar and turned to go.

'Thanks, Chris.'

He shook his head. 'I'm not doing it for you. I'm doing it for me. We all know who has to clean up the shit after it's hit the fan.'

It was pitch black under the trees. I pressed myself close to the trunk of a thick beech and poked an eye out cautiously. My instincts were right. There was something different about the quarry. At first I couldn't identify what. Then something moved over by the gates. Not a figure, more a shadow, a subtle change of light, of texture in the enveloping darkness.

I ducked back into the forest and moved stealthily through the undergrowth until I was directly opposite the entrance. I lay down on my belly on the bank at the side of the road and looked out.

Just inside the gates, set back from the dirt track which led into the quarry basin, was a small, prefabricated wooden hut. It hadn't been there on Sunday, nor yesterday morning. On one side of the hut was a window covered with a roller blind. Behind the blind a light glowed dimly, flickering now and again as if someone were

71

moving in front of it. A night watchman. Someone had been busy since my last visit.

I crept across the road and tried to see under the blind and inside the hut. But from outside the gates it was impossible. Still, it made no real difference to me. It was a nuisance, another factor to take into consideration, but it wasn't going to stop me taking a look around.

I moved left along the fence, staying next to it as it turned at ninety degrees to enclose the side of the quarry. I gave myself another twenty yards before I crouched down by the wire mesh and removed the small rucksack from my back. I took out a pair of bolt cutters and a flashlight. The hut was still in view but far enough away not to trouble me. Very carefully, I snipped through the bottom strands of the fence and pulled them apart, bending them out of the way to create a hole slightly bigger than my body. Then I dropped to my stomach and slithered through. I pulled the wire back into place behind me. It wouldn't pass a close inspection but it was the best I could do. I put the bolt cutters back into the rucksack and, keeping the torch in my hand but not switched on, moved out across the quarry.

I spent little time on the outer section. What I was looking for would be further in, hidden away in the depths of the basin. I kept going, the ground dropping away in a gentle slope under my feet. The walls of the quarry started to close in around me. It became harder to see. I glanced back. The hut by the entrance was out of sight. I contemplated using my torch, but decided against it. One unguarded beam on the rock face, a brief reflection in the sky and my presence might be discovered. I pressed on in the darkness, feeling my way over the unfamiliar terrain.

Then the earth suddenly ended in a sheer drop of maybe twenty feet. I was on the edge of the basin. I lay down and probed the wall below me with the torch. It was too steep to climb down but I knew there was a man-made ramp further along. I'd seen it from the top of the hill yesterday. I switched off the torch and followed the rim until I reached the ramp. I descended into the basin and started my search.

I concentrated on the back where the sandstone face must have been close to eighty feet high. I moved along the base of it, clicking the torch on at intervals to examine the ground. There was a slight breeze gusting and I could smell the sour odour of decomposing household rubbish from the beginnings of the landfill.

The rock face became less uniform, broken up now into clefts and hidden recesses. I explored some of the larger cavities but there was no sign of any concrete tanks. I rounded a spur of sandstone and found myself in another part of the quarry. A smaller excavation hemmed in by massive overhanging slabs that partially shielded it from above. This looked more promising. I checked the whole area but it was no different from the rest of the quarry.

I sat down on a boulder and pondered my next move. I'd examined pretty much the whole of the basin. If Rob Fielding had seen and photographed special tanks for storing hazardous waste, and I had no reason to doubt him, then they were either extremely well concealed or they'd been dismantled. I ruled out the latter option at once. Concrete lined with asphalt was not easy to take apart. The tanks would have to have been demolished and that would surely have left foundations or some indication of their presence. That meant they were hidden somewhere I hadn't looked. But where?

I peered around intently, scanning the surrounding landscape for anything out of the ordinary. Anything that seemed out of place. Then I froze.

There was a light drawing nearer on the far side of the basin. Up on the rim. It had to be the night watchman with a torch. I scrambled off the boulder and ducked down behind it, curling up into a ball to reduce my size. I stayed like that for a couple of minutes before I risked taking a peek out.

The night watchman was patrolling the edge of the basin, shining his torch down across the rocky floor. I could tell from his casual manner that this was just routine. Something he had to do at intervals as part of his job. But he wasn't very thorough. He didn't even bother to come down into the basin.

The light passed over a patch of ground to my right. Passed over it and briefly illuminated a curious pattern of marks on the surface. They looked like footprints. I pulled my head back out of sight as the torch beam flitted over the boulder that hid me. Footprints? Not mine, for I hadn't walked across that area. Then something peculiar struck me. The floor of the quarry was made of rock. How could feet leave prints in rock?

I took another look. The night watchman was moving away, his flashlight dancing around his feet as he headed back towards his hut. I came out from behind the boulder and walked across to examine the marks. They were footprints all right. Not in rock, but in soft topsoil. I widened my scrutiny. There was fresh earth covering a strip approximately fifteen yards wide and thirty yards long. There was some kind of hollow in the basin that had been filled in with soil to bring the surface level with the surrounding rock.

I dug down along one edge with my hands, scooping the soil out into a mound. About twelve inches down I encountered something hard. I scraped away more soil and shone my torch into the hole. At the bottom was the top of a concrete wall, maybe eighteen inches in width and lined on one side with a layer of dark grey material that could only be asphalt.

I sat back on my heels and contemplated the hole for a time. Then I shovelled the earth back in and smoothed out the surface with the edge of my shoe. Things were getting interesting. But then that was the way I liked them.

74

# 6

The courtroom was pretty full for a remand hearing. Four or five reporters on the press bench, maybe a dozen members of the public in the seats at the back and, in the well of the court, a group of teenagers with an accompanying adult who looked like a school party on an outing to see our glorious justice system in action. They looked as bored as I felt.

For an hour we watched a sorry-looking procession of teenage boys come in to answer charges of shoplifting, criminal damage, breach of bail conditions, a whole litany of minor offences, each one adjourned for various reasons. No one convicted or sentenced, no one acquitted, just a never-ending conveyor belt of remands, reports and bureaucracy. Vending machine justice, only the machine's temporarily out of order.

Then, finally, the five demonstrators charged with affray outside the landfill site were ushered into the dock. They stood in a line, a cage of toughened glass separating them from the body of the court. The dock used to be an open, waist-high enclosure, but after a couple of villains jumped over the side and legged it for the exit they installed a barrier composed of strips of glass with gaps in between for conferring with solicitors. It looked like some kind of high security garden conservatory.

The defendants were all men, none of them the youths who'd actually started the fighting. Four were neatly dressed in suits, the fifth was unshaven and clad in a dirty T-shirt and jeans. He was the only one I recognized. I'd seen him talking to Rob Fielding at the demonstration. He looked directly across at the press seats, then turned his gaze to the magistrates on their raised bench at the head of the courtroom, his expression one of complete contempt for both sets of people.

The clerk read out their names and addresses. I wrote them down in my notebook. The man in the T-shirt was called Edward Arthur Greaves. It didn't suit him; it was too old, too pompous. I put him down as Eddie.

Their cases didn't take long. A few formalities, submissions from the CPS and defence solicitors, then the chair of the Bench, a middle-aged woman with the looks and manner of a Gulag wardress, announced that they would be sent to the Crown Court for trial. They were all remanded on bail until the committal proceedings.

I slipped out of the door and approached Eddie Greaves as he came out of the courtroom into the concourse. I told him who I was. He didn't want to know.

'Piss off. I've got nothing to say to a journalist.'

'You were a friend of Rob Fielding's, weren't you?'

'Christ, you people. You're getting nothing out of me.'

He kept walking. I stayed with him as he pushed through the swing doors and out of the building.

'You don't understand. He was going to give me a file on Russell Stamford. Information about his business activities.'

Greaves's lip curled. 'But the poor sod happened to get himself killed before you could get your front page. Is that it? My heart bleeds for you.'

I wasn't handling this very well. 'I know his wife. I know Cathy. You can check with her. I need to talk to you.'

He stopped and turned on me angrily. 'Listen, you prick. I wouldn't talk to a journalist if it was my last breath. You're scum. I saw how you reported that demo, the crap you wrote. I didn't do anything. None of us did. The pigs threw us in a van and kicked the shit out of us, that's what happened. But I don't see any of them in the dock.

And don't give me this bullshit about Cathy. I resent that. She's a friend of mine. Rob was too. And I don't sell my friends to slimeballs like you.'

He walked off. I let him go. No protestations of innocence, of integrity, would have persuaded him to talk to me. I've hardened my skin over the years but it's still a shock when someone voices such vehement loathing of my chosen profession. Nothing personal, yet everything personal. And the truth is that usually they're right.

I'd had enough of the day. Enough of my job. I drove back home to my flat and locked myself away, King Oliver on the CD player, a cup of strong coffee in my hand, flushing out the system.

Then the telephone rang. I didn't move. The answering machine clicked on and after a silence I heard Cathy Fielding's voice, hesitant, stumbling for words.

'Look, this is . . . God, I hate these things. Are you there? Um, it's Cathy. Cathy Fielding. I thought I'd . . . You know those times Rob went away? I told you. Well, I think . . . oh, I don't know. I'll call back. Or maybe you could . . .'

I lifted the receiver.

'It's me, Cathy. I'm here.'

'Oh, Michael, is that you? Am I still talking to that machine?'

I switched off the tape. 'It's me. You OK?'

'Yes.' She took a moment to gather herself. 'I don't know whether this is any use to you, but I've remembered, well not exactly remembered, more half remembered where Rob went one of those times. When he went off and wouldn't say what he was doing.'

'Where?'

'This is the problem. I can't remember the name of the place. But it's out beyond Rotherham. What's that river up there?'

'The Don?'

'No, not the Don.'

'The Dearne?'

77

'Yes, that's it. He mentioned the name too, but it's gone. I feel so stupid.'

'Wath-upon-Dearne?'

'No.'

'Mexborough?'

'That's the place. I know he went there. I know it's probably not much help, but I thought I'd let you know. Hello, are you still there?'

I came back with a start. My mind had been elsewhere. 'Sorry, Cathy. Are you in for the next hour or so?'

'Yes. Why?'

'I'm coming over.'

The newspaper cutting was still pinned to the noticeboard in the kitchen, hidden away under one of Jenny's drawings. I showed it to Cathy.

'Have you seen this before?'

She shook her head. 'I don't think so.'

'So it wasn't you who put it up here?'

'No. It must have been Rob. "Asthma attack tragedy". What is it?'

'Read it. Does it mean anything to you?'

Cathy read through the article. 'Not a thing.'

'Did Rob ever mention the case to you? Or the name of the boy who died?'

'No, I'm sure I'd remember if he had. You think this is why Rob went to Mexborough?'

'I don't know. But it's strange he put this cutting on the board.'

'Why would Rob be interested in a ten-year-old boy who died of asthma?'

I took the cutting back from her. 'Can I take this?'

'Of course.'

'It's worth a try. We don't have much else to go on.'

Cathy tugged thoughtfully at her lower lip with thumb and forefinger. She said: 'So you're not making much progress.'

'It's early days. There are the police as well, you know.

They're better equipped than I am for this kind of thing. Have they been in touch with you again?'

'No, I don't know what they're doing.'

'I was in court this morning. The five who were arrested on Sunday were up before the magistrates.' I took out my notebook and read out the names of the defendants. 'Do you recognize any of those names?'

'Only the last. Eddie Greaves.'

'That's what I figured. I saw him with Rob at the demo. I tried to speak to him after the hearing but he gave me the brushoff.'

'He would. He can't stand journalists.'

'Yes, he did give me that impression. Were he and Rob close?'

'You think Eddie might know why Rob died?'

'He might know what Rob was up to. That's a start.'

Cathy walked away across the kitchen and leaned back on one of the units by the cooker, her arms folded.

'No, I wouldn't say they were close. They knew each other, but not much more than that.'

Something in her tone made me ask: 'Do you like him?'

She made a face, then shrugged. 'Not really. He's very aggressive. There's a lot of anger in him. I don't find him easy company.'

'And Rob?'

'He saw him occasionally for a drink. He found him hard to take too. Eddie doesn't make conversation, he makes speeches. Everything you say he challenges. You know the type of person. Permanently provocative.'

'But an activist. Like Rob.'

Cathy mused on that for a while. 'They're different. Rob got angry about things but he had a fundamental optimism. He wasn't cynical. He didn't like the way things were, but he genuinely believed he could help make them better. Eddie's not like that. He's embittered. He feels the cause – the environment, politics, whatever – is hopeless but he goes on fighting for it out of sheer bloody-mindedness. He just enjoys being awkward.'

'So you don't think Rob would have confided in him?'

'I can't see it. He didn't even confide in me.'

She looked away out of the window. I could see that hurt.

'He did it for your own good, Cathy. He had your best interests at heart.'

'I know. But I'd rather he'd told me. I don't like secrets. I'm his wife. He should have told me.'

She roused herself, coming suddenly towards me. 'Still, that's all in the past. You'll let me know how you get on, won't you?'

'Yes.'

'I've been kept in the dark these past few months. I don't want it to continue.'

I drove north-east along the Don Valley, passing under the M1 viaduct at Tinsley and continuing out towards Rawmarsh and Swinton. Moving from the steel centres of Sheffield and Rotherham into the heart of the South Yorkshire coalfield. Or what's left of it.

There used to be collieries all over this area, a great swathe running from Barnsley to Doncaster. They're still marked on the Ordnance Survey map, but most of them aren't there any more. And slowly, all the rest are disappearing too, leaving hardly a trace on the landscape.

I drove down the hill through Wath-upon-Dearne, looking north over the broad river valley. A few years ago there were two collieries blocking the view. Now they're gone. The buildings, the winding gear, the stark, angular, unnatural features of a pit have been erased. Even the spoil tips are gradually blending in, their sides being colonized by grass, brambles and silver birch. The life returning to the poisoned earth faster than to the surrounding communities where virtually all the jobs have been lost.

I turned east towards Mexborough and pulled in by a row of shops to read through the newspaper cutting again. It was four months old, yellowing and limp at the edges, but the bare facts had lost none of their poignancy.

Jamie Hynes, ten years old and an asthma sufferer, had gone out playing in the woods with a friend one Saturday afternoon and collapsed in a fit of coughing. Shortly afterwards he had died. That was pretty much it. There were a few quotes from the police and the boy's family but they added nothing to the substance of the story.

There was an address for the boy, but only the street, no house number. I got out of the car and went into the first shop in the row, a newsagent's, where I borrowed a phone book and looked him up.

The newsagent gave me directions and I was there in under ten minutes. I parked outside and studied the house. It was on a small estate, a pre-war semi with the plain, characterless design of a council house. Tiny windows, a patch of lawn at the front and a low, neatly trimmed privet hedge bordering the pavement.

I walked up to the front door and rang the bell. The woman who answered looked tired and careworn. Pasty skin, shadows under the eyes, lank mousy hair. In her arms was a baby wearing a bright pink stretchsuit. It had huge blue eyes and a head as smooth and hairless as a conker.

'Mrs Hynes?'

She nodded wearily. I explained who I was. 'I don't want to reopen old wounds, but I wonder if I could talk to you briefly about Jamie?'

'Jamie?' She sounded vague, as if the name was unfamiliar to her, but no mother ever forgets a child who's died.

'I quite understand if you say no. I don't want to intrude,' I said.

'That's all over. There's nothing I can say.'

'I just want to check a few facts with you. I won't stay long.'

She hesitated, the baby wriggling in her arms. Then she motioned me in with a tilt of her head. I followed her into the front room. There were children's toys all over the

81

floor and a metal guard across the gas fire. I sat down in a faded armchair and waited for her to make herself comfortable with the baby.

'That's him,' she said, nodding at a framed photograph on the mantelpiece. 'That's Jamie. We had it took last year, for his birthday.'

I looked at the photograph. A smiling boy, hair neatly parted, a vivid red tie on a white shirt. A happy boy, posing for the camera.

'He's a handsome lad,' I said.

Mrs Hynes smiled. Some life came back into her eyes. 'He is, isn't he? He was always good-looking, even as a baby. And he always had that thick, shiny hair. He never lost it, not like this little thing here.' She was looking down at the baby.

'How old is she?' I said, guessing its sex from the colour of the stretchsuit.

'Six weeks. Emma Jane. She had a bit when she were born, but it all fell out. It's only just coming back. She looks funny, doesn't she?'

'She's pretty. Does she sleep?'

'We can't complain. She's better than the other three. Jamie were terrible, especially at night. I were up every couple of hours feeding him. But they soon grow out of it. They don't stay babies long.'

Her mouth moved wistfully, tinged perhaps with regret for what had been taken from her. Then she turned her gaze to me.

'So what did you want to ask me about Jamie?'

I chose my words carefully. 'I know this will be painful for you, but would you tell me exactly what happened the day he died?'

'It were in the papers at the time.'

'I know. But newspaper stories leave a lot unsaid. I'd rather get the facts first hand.'

Mrs Hynes took a deep breath. 'Well, he went out after dinner. It were a Saturday. Warm. It were the beginning of June, the eighth. He went off with a friend, Dean Clayton. He lives just up the road. They went to the woods down near the old railway line. On their bikes. Next thing I knew, the police was here telling me he were dead. They said he'd had a sudden asthma attack and died before they could get him to hospital. We was devastated. It just didn't seem possible. He'd been right as rain a few hours before.'

'He suffered from asthma, didn't he?'

'Yes. But not like that. He had one of them puffers, you know, an inhaler thing. For when he got chesty. But we didn't think it were anything serious. He were worse in the winter. He had the odd day off school when it were cold and damp. But this were the summer.'

'He'd never had an attack like that before?'

'No.'

'Did anyone tell you what caused it?'

'Well, at the inquest they said it were a freak attack. No one seemed to know what had caused it.'

'The inquest. Where was that held?'

'In Sheffield.'

That was unusual. We were in the district of Doncaster here.

'Why there?'

Mrs Hynes looked blank. 'I don't know. It just were. They had a doctor give evidence. He said Jamie just stopped breathing. They got to him too late to save him.'

'Can you remember the doctor's name?'

She thought briefly. 'No, sorry.'

'Did Jamie have his inhaler with him?'

'No. There were nothing wrong with him that day, you see. Why should he have had it with him? He didn't need it.' She was on the defensive. No doubt from months of blaming herself for what had happened. 'Anyway, the doctor said it were so bad the inhaler wouldn't have helped.'

'I understand,' I said gently. 'It was no one's fault.'

'He were such a lovely little boy. Good-natured, doing well at school. Everyone liked him. I miss him so much.'

Her eyes misted over and her mouth began to tremble.

The tears would be next. But then the baby on her lap started to whimper. A tiny, plaintive cry that intensified into a full-blooded yowl. She lifted the baby up and held her close on her shoulder, bouncing her up and down.

'She's hungry. I'll have to feed her,' Mrs Hynes said, her emotions suddenly submerged by more immediate, pragmatic demands.

I stood up to leave. 'Thank you for talking to me. Jamie's friend, Dean Clayton, where exactly does he live?'

'Five doors up. Number twenty-six.'

'Thanks. I'll show myself out.'

At the living room door I looked back. She was cradling the baby on a cushion across her lap and lifting her jumper to feed her. Murmuring softly to calm the baby down, absorbed completely in the bonds of motherhood. One child was gone, another had taken its place.

The Claytons' house was identical to the Hynes'. Only the paint was peeling off the window frames, a broken pane of glass was boarded up with cardboard and the grass and hedge at the front were overgrown and untidy. It had a neglected feel, a dilapidated, uncared-for aura that set it apart from the other semis in the street. Yet there was a satellite dish on the side of the house and a brand new Ford Escort in the drive.

A man in a soiled shirt and baggy shellsuit bottoms opened the door to me. He had cropped hair, a few days' growth of stubble on his chin which was almost as long as his hair, and a cigarette butt in his mouth. He smelt like a pub.

Two small boys came out into the hall behind him, punching and kicking at each other. The man turned and yelled at them.

'Nah then, I've told you before. Pack it in or I'll tan your bleedin' arses. Get back in there.'

The two boys broke apart and started arguing – 'He started it.' 'I didn't, yer liar.' 'He did.' – until the man stepped over and clipped them both round the ears.

'I said, pack it in.'

The boys retreated into the front room, muttering sulkily. Their father came back to the door.

'Yes?' he said bluntly, his manner hostile.

I told him who I was. 'I wanted to speak to Dean about Jamie Hynes.'

'He's not talking about that. We 'ad enough of it at the time.'

'It won't take long.'

'You 'ard of 'earing, pal? What did I just say?' He sucked on his cigarette and tossed the filter away into the garden.

'Just a few minutes, to check some facts.'

'You're not listening, are you?' He took a pace nearer, almost coming out on to the step. I moved back instinctively. 'Maybe I should clear your ears for you?'

'Thanks, but I quite like them the way they are.'

'Don't tempt me, pal. I 'ate bloody reporters.'

I wasn't having much luck with my job today. 'OK. You've been very helpful.'

I pulled away out of arm's reach, then turned and headed back down the drive.

'And don't fucking come back,' Clayton shouted after me as he slammed the door.

I had no intention of going back. But I wasn't going away either. I walked the fifty yards to my car and sat inside waiting, listening to the afternoon play on Radio Four.

One of the two boys came out a while later. He looked the right age to be Dean. About ten years old, heavily built, with the same skinhead haircut as his father. A thug in the making. He turned up the road and walked away from me. I gave him a head start then drove slowly after him.

At the top of the road he went into a corner shop. I parked the car and got out, waiting for him outside on the pavement. When he emerged, he was eating crisps from a bag.

'You got a minute, Dean?'

He stopped and eyed me warily. 'You're the bloke what came to our 'ouse, aren't you?'

'That's right.'

'Me dad says I'm not to talk to you.'

'I'm not going to tell him. Are you?'

He chewed on a mouthful of crisps, his lips covered with crumbs. Then he tried to walk past me. I stood in his way.

'I want to ask you about Jamie.'

'I don't know owt about that.'

'You were with him, Dean. I want you to show me where it happened.'

'I've got to get 'ome.'

'I can make it worth your while.'

I'd gauged his character well. Suddenly he was interested.

'Oh yeah? How much?'

'A quid.'

'Gissit 'ere.'

'When we get to the place, not before.'

He watched me, suspicious. He had small eyes, set deep in his face like currants pressed into bread dough. He licked the salty crumbs off his lips, thinking hard. I guessed he was reckoning up what he could get for a pound. Weighing it up against a belting from his dad if he ever found out he'd spoken to me. The money tipped the balance.

'It's in the woods.'

I followed him across the road and we walked to the edge of the council estate together. A passageway between houses led us into a small deciduous wood.

'Is this the way you came that day?' I asked.

'Yeh.'

'What were you doing?'

'Eh?'

'You know, why did you come to the woods?'

'We was just mucking about on us bikes.'

'Did Jamie seem OK to you? He wasn't coughing when you got here, showing any signs of illness?'

'No. That 'appened later.'

We were in the heart of the wood now, horse chestnut and beech trees all around us. The forest floor was almost devoid of undergrowth but covered in a thick layer of fallen leaves.

Dean stopped and turned around in a complete circle, getting his bearings.

'I think it were about 'ere,' he said uncertainly.

'You don't sound very sure.'

'I don't remember too well. It were a long time ago.'

Four months wasn't long, but I didn't say anything. Then Dean changed his mind.

'No, it were over there.' He walked across a clearing in the trees. 'About 'ere. Yes, this is it.'

'You sure?'

Dean nodded. 'Give us the quid.'

I gave him a pound coin. 'Describe to me what happened.'

'You said I just 'ad to show you where. That were the deal. Nowt else.'

I shook my head. Kids, they learn the facts of life early.

'You ever considered a career in extortion?' I said.

'You what?'

'OK, another quid. But only *after* you've told me.'

'Well, we was playing around, chasin' squirrels, throwing sticks, like. Then Jamie started coughing. Coughing right bad.'

'Just like that. Without warning?'

'Yeh. It were 'orrible. A scary noise. Like he couldn't breathe. Then he were sick and there were all this like white stuff on his mouth.'

'Foam.'

'Yeh. He were on the ground and all his legs and arms were jumping around. Like that.'

He jerked his arms about violently. 'Scared me shitless, I can tell you.'

'You're not exaggerating, are you?'

'Whassat mean?'

'Making it worse than it was.'

'Naow. I'm telling you, his arms and legs were all over the place.'

'So what did you do?'

'I ran across the road to get 'elp.'

'What road?'

Dean hesitated. 'I mean, I ran through the woods.'

'You didn't take your bike?'

'What?'

'You had your bike, didn't you?'

'Oh, yeh. I went on my bike. I forgot.'

Something about this didn't ring true.

'Where did you go?' I asked.

'To get 'elp, I told you.'

'I know. But where? A house?'

'Er, no. I found a phone. To call an ambulance.'

That was pretty resourceful for a ten-year-old. And not a particularly bright one at that.

'Where's the phone?'

He looked down shiftily, avoiding my gaze.

'Where's the phone you went to?'

'Back there, near the 'ouses.'

I waited for him to lift his head, his face all innocent.

'Dean,' I said. 'Why don't you show me where it really happened?'

There was a patch of wasteland beyond the woods. An ugly area of low undulating hummocks and pools of stagnant water. Knee-high weeds and thick grass covered most of the surface, but in places the subsoil was exposed, revealing broken bricks, plastic bags and old lumps of concrete and metal.

Dean took me towards the far side where a high wire fence marked the boundary of a factory of some sort. Inside the fence there were prefabricated cabins laid out in uniform rows like a prisoner of war camp. Then further round a more modern industrial complex with warehouses, an office block and a high chimney belching fumes.

'What's that?' I asked.

'They make fertilizer there,' Dean said. 'Stinks, dunnit?'

'And this is where Jamie collapsed?'

'The other side of that pond. By the fence.'

I examined the area perfunctorily. The pond was about twenty feet across and so dirty it was impossible to tell how deep. Slicks of oil and greenish slime glistened on the surface of the water.

'And where were you?'

'Round about 'ere. We was cobbing stones into t'pond, trying to splash each other.'

'Why did you say it had happened in the woods?'

He looked down at his shoes. He kicked at a stone half buried in the earth until it came loose and spun into the pond with a splash.

'Why?' I repeated.

Dean continued to study his feet. 'Dunno.'

'Come on, Dean. I'm not going to do anything to you. I just want to know. It won't go any further.'

'Me dad told me to.'

'Earlier this afternoon, you mean? After I'd been to your house.'

He shook his head. 'Ages ago. A few days after Jamie died. He said if anyone asked, I was to tell 'em it 'appened in the woods.'

'But you told the police the truth? That it happened here?'

''Course.'

'And the bit about the phone box. Did your dad tell you to say that too?'

'Yeh.'

'Why?'

Dean shrugged. 'He just told me to. Or I'd get clobbered.'

'So after Jamie collapsed, what did you do?'

'I ran over there to the road, to the front of the factory. There was a couple of blokes on the gate, you know, like guards. I told them.'

'And what did they do?'

'They phoned someone. Then this older bloke and a woman came out in a car and I took them to Jamie. I don't know what they did to 'im. They kept me back. Then they picked 'im up and took 'im away.'

'Where?'

'I dunno. I didn't see. They told me to get 'ome quick. I were scared. I ran back through the woods. Then the police came and asked me loads of questions.'

'Show me the exact spot Jamie was standing.'

We walked around the pond until we were on a narrow strip of land in front of the factory fence. The ground was bare earth, churned into mud in places by feet and bicycle tyres.

'It were about 'ere, I think.'

'And what you described to me, Jamie coughing, being sick, that was all true?'

'Yeh, I swear.'

'Did you try to help him?'

Dean hesitated, then he shook his head. 'I didn't know what to do. I didn't go near 'im. I just ran for 'elp.'

'Did you come here often?'

'Lots of times. All the kids round 'ere do. We play cyclo cross over the mounds on us bikes.'

'And Jamie had never had a coughing fit before?'

'No. He got out of breath sometimes. But he were always OK. That all you want to know?'

'I think so.'

'Can I 'ave that quid then?'

'Sure.'

I wandered away round the pond without handing over the money. Dean came after me.

'Does your dad work?' I asked.

'No. He stops at 'ome.'

'How long has he been unemployed?'

'Two, three years. You going to give me that quid?'

'I see you've got a new car.'

'What? Oh, yeh. A couple of months ago. You're not going to diddle me, are you?'

'Me? Perish the thought.'

'So give it me.'

'If you answer one more question. Apart from the police, have you told anyone else what happened that day?'

'Only me mum and dad.'

'Have any other reporters spoken to you?'

'Me dad wouldn't let them.'

'So I'm the first?'

Dean didn't reply immediately.

'I want the truth, or you don't get the money.'

He gave me a sour look. 'You said one more question, not 'undreds.'

I started back across the wasteland, picking my way through the nettles and brambles. Dean caught up with me.

'There were another bloke,' he said, panting slightly as he tried to keep pace with me.

'Who?'

'I dunno 'is name. He asked me the same things you 'ave. Gave me more money 'n' all. But he weren't a reporter.'

'Can you describe him?'

'Funny looking. Small, wi' a beard and little round glasses.'

So Rob Fielding *had* been out here. I took a pound coin from my pocket and tossed it to Dean.

'Don't spend it all at once.'

He scuttled away into the woods. I followed at a more leisurely pace and picked up my car, then made a detour on my way home to drive past the fertilizer factory.

I slowed down as I neared the gates. There were two uniformed security guards manning an electric barrier. A sign by the entrance read: 'CPL Agro-Chemicals.'

I drove on, thinking seriously about Jamie Hynes's death. I didn't know much about medicine, but convulsions, vomiting and foaming at the mouth didn't sound like asthma to me.

# 7

I was washing off the day's grime at the bathroom sink when an alarming thought struck me suddenly. Maria was coming for dinner. At half past seven. I found my watch hurriedly and checked the time. Six-fifty-five. Shit! Thirty-five minutes to get to the shops, buy some food and cook it. Not a chance in hell. It would take me that long just to think of a recipe.

I threw on a clean shirt and grabbed my jacket on the way out, heading at a sprint for the Chinese takeaway down the road.

Arnie Wung was leaning on the formica-topped counter leafing idly through the *Evening News*. A diminutive five-foot forty-year-old who looked all of sixteen, he was Burngreave's only Chinese Rastafarian. Away from work he wore a pink and yellow striped tea cosy to cover his dreadlocks, but on duty, as a gesture towards the hygiene regulations, he sported a large tartan chef's hat.

'What can you do me for two people?' I said.

Arnie looked up. He knew me well. I practically had a charge account there. He yawned.

'Hi, Mike. How ya doin', man?' He spoke English with a marked Jamaican lilt, one of the side effects of his religion. I'd heard it so often it no longer struck me as odd.

'I want a meal for two. And I haven't got much time.'

He pushed himself slowly away from the counter. He was so small his chin only just cleared it. Then he took an eternity to find a menu and open it in front of me.

'Come on, Arnie.'

'Hey, man, relax. What's de rush?'

I ran an eye down the list of dishes. 'What about these set dinners? They any good?'

'They any good? What kinda place you think this is? Sure they're good. You tryin' to impress someone?' He grinned at me, revealing a couple of ounces of gold fillings. 'A lady maybe. Or ain't you tellin'?'

'Which is the quickest to make?'

'They all quick.'

'You recommend one?'

'Try A2. Thassa good.'

'I'm not sure about the pancake rolls. Do me a trade for the chicken and sweetcorn soup, but keep the rest the same. That OK?'

'No problem.'

He went to the window in the back wall and rattled off instructions to the cook in Chinese. Then he came back to the counter.

' 'Bout fifteen minutes. You wan' anythin' else? A drink, prawn crackers?'

'No,' I said. 'But you can fill me in on the art of Chinese cooking.'

I was back in the flat with ten minutes to spare. The first thing I did was go into the kitchen and decant the Chinese dishes into every bowl and casserole I could find. Then I put them in the oven and turned the gas on low.

The living room was a bomb site. I collected up the mounds of old newspapers, the scattered coffee mugs and dirty plates and took them into the kitchen. There was no time to wash up so I dumped the lot on the floor in the corner and ignored them. Then I went back out and tidied up, moving the armchairs to cover the more obvious holes in the carpet and transferring a print of Monet's garden at Giverny to conceal a spreading patch of mildew on the wall above my desk. The layers of dust, nurtured lovingly over the months, were harder to hide, but I switched off the main light and lit a couple of candles on the table to make them less noticeable. The end result: a sort of Bohemian seediness rather than outright squalor. It was the best I could do.

Maria was five minutes late, which was a relief. It gave me time to spruce up the bed – well, you never know – and set the table with my last few items of clean cutlery and crockery.

She came in slowly, almost feeling her way across the living room.

'You had a power cut?' she said. 'Or is this supposed to be romantic?'

'It's cosy,' I said.

'Cosy I can cope with. Pitch black is a little trickier. Do I get issued with a white stick to find a chair?'

I switched on the lamp on the bookshelves. 'Why do you have to be so bloody practical?'

Maria smiled at me. She was wearing black trousers and a pale blue cotton shirt, the top two buttons undone. A thin gold chain glistened around her neck. I looked at her for a long moment, thinking how simple beauty was. If you had it.

'I brought some wine,' she said.

I took the bottle from her, then the leather jacket she'd removed and flung over one arm.

'Take a seat. You want a glass now?'

'Please.'

I poured two glasses in the kitchen and brought them out. Maria had settled herself in an armchair, legs crossed, and was gazing around the room.

'It looked better by candlelight,' she said.

'Thanks. You really know how to make a guy feel good. You find it all right?'

She nodded. 'It think it's my first time in Burngreave at night. It looks pretty rough.'

'Yeah, we have to take our doorsteps in at night. Even the wheelie bins are propped up on bricks.'

'You don't have to live here, do you?'

'It has character,' I said. 'And it's cheap.'

Maria watched me shrewdly. 'But I don't think that's the reason.'

'You're my accountant. You know how things are.'

'Not this bad. You move here after your divorce?'

'Yes. My wife got the house.'

'I think you enjoy it.'

'Living in a dump?'

'Not caring whether you live in a dump.'

'Why don't I switch off the lamp and we'll start again?' I said.

Maria's mouth moved. It might have been a smile. 'I'm sorry. It's just that there was a group of lads hanging around outside on the street. It made me nervous.'

'It's not that bad, Maria.'

'I've got a rape alarm in my bag, just in case.'

'You won't need that tonight. The streets round here are perfectly safe.'

She grinned at me. 'I wasn't just thinking of the streets.'

I laughed and held her eyes. She didn't look away. For one fleeting moment I thought ahead to what might happen. Then crushed the thought immediately. Sometimes dreams can hurt more than reality.

I stood up. 'You hungry?'

'Mmm.'

'It won't be long.'

'You want a hand?'

I shook my head. 'Most of it's done already. I've just got to knock up the starter.'

I went into the kitchen and carefully closed the door before removing the dish containing the chicken and sweetcorn soup from the oven. I poured the liquid into a pan and heated it up on a gas ring. Then I transferred it into two bowls and took them out to the table. Maria came over and sat down.

'I thought I could smell Chinese,' she said.

'I knew you liked it.'

'You made this yourself?'

95

'Of course. It's not hard.'

She tasted the soup. 'It's good.'

'Thanks.'

'How do you get it so clear?'

'Simple really,' I said, trying to recall exactly what Arnie Wung had told me.

Maria had paused and was looking at me expectantly. 'Yes?'

'Oh, you want to know?'

'That's why I asked.'

'It's the method of cooking,' I said confidently. 'You have to remember not to let the liquid boil. That's what makes soup cloudy. Just simmer it slowly over a low heat. Of course, it shouldn't be a starter really. In China they have the soup at the end of the meal.'

Maria nodded, satisfied. First hurdle cleared. She didn't suspect a thing. The main courses were more of a problem, but I reckoned I could brazen it out with the other information Arnie had given me.

'I'll only be a few minutes,' I said, clearing away the soup bowls. 'I've a couple of things to stir fry. You want some music on?'

'Sure.'

'Any preferences?'

'You choose.'

I put New Orleans jazz on low on the CD player and headed for the kitchen.

'Why don't I come and watch?' Maria suggested. 'I like to see an expert in action.'

I glanced at her narrowly, perhaps detecting a whiff of irony, but her face was serenely innocent.

'That's all right. It'll be quicker if I do it on my own. Have some more wine.'

I topped up her glass and left her sitting at the table while I disappeared through the door.

'Leave it open so I can talk to you,' Maria said.

'It's better closed,' I assured her. 'Keeps the smell of the frying in. You know how it is in a small flat like this.'

I shut the door before she could argue. I whipped the other Chinese dishes quickly out of the oven and tossed one of them into a frying pan with a dash of oil. Then I turned up the heat and let it sizzle for thirty seconds, banging the edge of the pan with a metal spoon for additional sound effects. I did the same with a second dish and served everything up in some Pyrex casseroles I got with petrol coupons. Not the most elegant presentation, but I didn't have anything else.

Maria pursed her lips with appreciation when I put the dishes down in the middle of the table.

'That was quick.'

I shrugged modestly. 'That's the beauty of Chinese cooking. Get the oil really hot then just throw in the ingredients. Couple of minutes and they're done. Seals in the natural flavours of the food. Crisp and tasty, that's how I like it. Help yourself.'

She spooned rice out on to her plate and added a helping of the pork dish.

'What's this?'

'Cha siew roast pork,' I said. 'A Cantonese speciality.'

She tried it. 'Mmm, that is really something, Michael. How did you make it?'

'You don't really want to know.'

'I do.'

'I'll tell you later.'

'I want to know now. I didn't realize you were such a good cook. I'm sorry I made those comments on the phone.'

There was nothing in her tone to indicate she'd rumbled me. Her face was inscrutable. Watching me, quietly interested. I pressed on recklessly.

'Well, it's the marinade that makes it so tasty. You take a good piece of fillet pork and marinate it for a couple of hours in yellow bean sauce, dark soy sauce, Hoisin sauce, sugar and dry sherry. It should be rice wine, of course, but I find that hard to get hold of.'

'And how do you cook it? This hasn't been stir fried.'

'No, it's roasted on a rack in the oven. Nothing to it.'

'For how long?'

'Thirty minutes.'

'What temperature?'

All these questions were making me uneasy. 'You want every detail, don't you?'

'I might try it myself. If it's as simple as you say. What temperature?'

'Gas mark seven,' I said smoothly. Arnie had briefed me well.

Maria smiled, but didn't say anything more for a time. We concentrated on eating. The food was good. It didn't taste or look like an average takeaway and I knew so much about how it was prepared that I'd almost convinced myself I really had made it.

'How was your trip to Mexborough?' Maria asked after a while. 'I spoke to Cathy on the phone this afternoon,' she added when she saw my inquiring glance.

'Ah. Interesting,' I said.

'Meaning?'

I swallowed a mouthful of sweet and sour chicken. 'Did Cathy tell you why I went?'

'Something about a boy dying. An asthma attack. Was that it?'

'According to the newspaper reports, yes.'

'You sound sceptical.'

I told her about my conversation with Dean Clayton, the wasteland he showed me and the symptoms he described.

She said: 'No, it doesn't sound much like asthma to me. But presumably that's what the medical diagnosis was. Maybe asthma can be more complicated than we think.'

'Maybe. Apparently, the doctor at the inquest said it was a freak attack. That's what Jamie's mother told me.'

'What was the inquest verdict?'

'I don't know.'

'You didn't cover it?'

'No. That's one of the things that worries me. Why

didn't I cover it? It was held in Sheffield. The Medico-Legal Centre's one of my regular calls. I usually know about every inquest. Yet I never went to Jamie Hynes's. I would've remembered it for certain.'

'I suppose you could've overlooked it.'

'It's something I've got to check. But none of this is clear cut. Dean Clayton was told to lie about what happened that day to anyone who asked him. His father gave him a fabricated story. Unfortunately for him, Dean's a hopeless liar. Or he's got a bad memory. Either way, his story didn't stand more than the most perfunctory scrutiny.'

'Why would his father tell him to lie?'

'I don't know. But he's got a brand new Ford Escort in his drive and hasn't worked for two years.'

Maria chased a forkful of rice around her plate. 'You think someone's paid him off?'

'Where else would he get that kind of money?'

'What if his wife works? Or maybe he was made redundant from one of the pits round there and still has a lump sum left.'

'That's possible. I hadn't considered it.' I pushed a casserole across the table. 'Have some more beef. It needs eating up.'

'You've gone to a lot of trouble tonight. How on earth did you have time if you were in Mexborough all afternoon?'

Something in her voice made me look at her sharply. But it was just a simple inquiry. My guilty conscience alone made me wonder otherwise.

'Oh, you know,' I said airily. 'Advance planning. I had everything ready before I left.'

She drank some more of her wine. 'And Rob? Was there any connection?'

'Yes. He was out there asking the same questions I did. He talked to Dean too.'

'And got the same answers?'

I nodded.

99

Maria tapped the rim of her glass with a fingernail. 'It doesn't seem very hard to get the truth out of this boy. If someone's paid his father to distort the facts – and I think that's pretty implausible – they haven't got much for their money.'

'No. But then perhaps they forgot that if the father can be bought, so can the son. Dean's greedy. Both Rob and I gave him money, put a little pressure on him and he soon came out with the real facts.'

'I don't get it,' Maria said, frowning. 'What's the point of lying months after the event when Dean originally told the police the truth? Surely all anyone who's interested has to do is ask the police what happened.'

'On the face of it, yes. But I'm not so sure. The press report of the death describes it as having taken place in the woods, not the wasteland. That was in the *Evening News* the day after Jamie died.'

'You mean even then the facts had been changed?'

'Yes. And there could only have been one source for the story. It had to have come from the police. They're even quoted in the cutting Rob had on the noticeboard in his kitchen.'

Maria stared at me. 'You're saying the police lied to the press?'

I smiled drily. 'Well, it wouldn't be the first time.'

'Why?'

'That's another thing I don't know.'

I started to clear away the dishes from the table. Maria stood up to give me a hand.

'You sit down,' I said. 'I'll make us some coffee.'

'You sure I can't help?'

'Positive. You're my guest. Make yourself comfortable.'

I took the plates into the kitchen and left them to soak in the sink. When I came back out with two mugs of coffee, Maria was over by the hi-fi examining the case of the CD I'd put on.

'Johnny Dodds, who's he?' she asked.

'New Orleans clarinettist. Early part of the century. You like it?'

'Yes.'

'He played with all the big names. Louis Armstrong, Joe Oliver, Jelly Roll Morton, Kid Ory. Died of a heart attack, I think, sometime in the forties.'

'It makes me want to dance.'

'Feel free.'

'Maybe after the coffee.'

I sat in the other armchair a short distance away from her, wishing I had a settee. A few feet can seem an awful long way sometimes.

Then Maria said: 'So why was Rob interested in this boy?'

'I haven't figured that out yet.'

'You think it has anything to do with his murder?'

'I can't see any obvious connection at the moment. Can you?'

'Not really.' She watched me, her mug poised near her lips. Her face was half in shadow, accentuating the line of her cheeks, the delicate nose, the dark curls of her hair. She turned away fractionally. The studs in her ears glinted gold in the lamplight.

'You think Russell Stamford killed Rob, don't you?' she said.

'He's on the list.'

'Why?'

'He had the motive. Assuming he knew Rob had been probing his somewhat murky past, that is. He had a lot to lose if the details were made public. And he's rich enough to pay someone to do it. It was a professional job.'

'How do you know?'

'The method.' I hesitated. 'It's not pleasant to talk about it.'

'I'm not squeamish. He was shot, wasn't he? Or is there more to it?'

'The gun was put to his head. One shot only. Clean and businesslike. Like an execution. I'd guess it was a pro.'

Maria looked down. Her eyes were screwed up in momentary pain. 'It's so easy to kill someone, isn't it? One bullet, one tiny slug of metal and it's all over. We seem such hardy creatures, yet the life in us can be snuffed out as easily as extinguishing a candle.'

I nodded. I didn't want to dwell on it. Not tonight. Maria looked back up at me. I could tell she didn't want to think about it either. In the midst of life.

'It's so short, isn't it?' she said. 'Yet we waste such a lot of it. Not asking for what we want most.'

She stood up suddenly and went towards the kitchen with her empty coffee mug. 'I'll put this in the sink.'

I reacted too slowly to stop her. By the time I reached the door she was inside, staring down at the heap of aluminium takeaway trays on the worktop. She turned.

'Nothing to it really,' she said. 'Just marinate for a couple of hours in soy sauce, sherry and a large bucket of bullshit.'

'They were left over from yesterday,' I tried lamely.

Maria burst out laughing. 'You never give up, do you? You think I didn't *know*? The number of Chinese takeaways I've had.'

'I ran out of time. I would've cooked something.'

She shook her head. Not angry. Standing there. A half smile playing at the corners of her mouth. Waiting for me.

'I didn't come for the food,' she said.

On the CD Johnny Dodds was hitting the top note of the solo in Gatemouth.

I said: 'How about that dance now?'

'Why not?' Maria said.

'I only do slow dances.'

'They're the best kind.'

I took a pace towards her. Almost close enough to feel her breath. She smiled at me.

Then the doorbell rang.

Neither of us moved. The bell rang again. I tried to shut it out of my mind.

'You'd better answer it,' Maria said.

I hesitated. Then went to the front door and pulled it open. Harry Raymond was standing outside. He had a suitcase in one hand.

'Thank God, you're in. I didn't know where else to go,' he said, struggling past me with the case.

'Harry,' I began. 'This really isn't a –'

He didn't let me get any further. 'I know it's a bother, but you said I could count on you. I'm in trouble, Mike.'

He went through into the living room. I followed him. Maria was standing over by the kitchen. I gave her an apologetic glance and introduced Harry.

'She's thrown me out, Mike. The wife,' Harry said, barely acknowledging Maria's presence. 'Told me to pack a case and get out. She'd 'ad enough of me, she said. Just like that. After twenty year. Twenty year of putting up wi' 'er. You don't mind, do you?'

'Well, this is a bit difficult, Harry.'

'Only I didn't want to go to an 'otel. I 'ate 'em. I need somewhere to stay. Just for a couple of days. I waint be no trouble.'

Maria was gathering up her jacket and handbag. 'I'd better be going.'

'No, look, you don't have to . . .' But I didn't try to stop her. The moment had passed. We both knew it.

I went with her to the door. 'I'm sorry, Maria. I don't know what else to say.'

'It's not your fault.'

'We never did get that dance.'

'There'll be other times,' she said. She kissed me lightly on the cheek and walked away down the stairs.

When I went back into the living room, Harry was removing his overcoat and sitting down in an armchair.

'Did I arrive at the wrong moment?' he said.

103

# 8

I left the flat early next morning. Harry was still asleep on cushions on the living room floor, snoring gently. I tapped his shoulder with my shoe on the way out. He rolled over and opened his eyes.

'I've left you a spare key on the table,' I said. 'Help yourself to breakfast.'

Harry peered at me sleepily. 'What time is it?'

'Half-seven.'

He sighed and threw off the layer of blankets covering him. Underneath he was wearing a yellowish string vest and old-fashioned long johns that reached down below his knees. Poking out at the bottom were a pair of fish-white calves and two bony feet with clumps of coarse hair on the toes. I averted my eyes. Some things are hard to take on an empty stomach.

'I'll see you later,' I said.

'OK. And Mike . . .'

I looked round at the door.

'. . . thanks for putting me up. I'm sorry about last night.'

'Forget it,' I said.

I grabbed a coffee and a bacon sandwich on my way into town and went to the *Evening News* offices to check the cuttings library.

There was a file on Jamie Hynes, but it contained only two articles. One was the report of his death that I'd read already. The other a follow-up piece, a shallow, intrusive story along the lines of, 'grieving mother speaks for the first time of her loss'. It was standard newspaper practice after a death. I'd written enough of them when I worked on the *News* but never reconciled myself to their tawdry exploitation of bereavement. There were no new facts in it.

I checked with the librarian to see if there might be more filed under some different heading, but she said that was all there was. Everything would be under the name of the deceased, unless there was a cross-reference on the clippings to some other file.

Puzzled, I sat thinking for a few minutes at one of the tiny desks in between the rows of grey metal filing cabinets. Only two articles. That was too few. The story was worth more than that. At the very least there should have been a report on the inquest. Maybe several if there was an adjournment. Yet there was nothing.

I put the file back where I found it and searched through the cabinets again, pulling out an envelope marked 'CPL Agro-Chemicals'.

There were perhaps thirty cuttings inside, some dating back many years. I scanned them quickly. There was no mention of Jamie Hynes's death in any of them. Too much to hope for, I suppose. It had happened on wasteland near the CPL plant and personnel from the factory had come out to offer assistance, but unless you had a particularly devious mind there was no reason to speculate that the plant and the death might be in any way connected. I'd always been proud of my devious mind.

But I was disappointed. I found nothing to fuel any suspicions, however slight or unfounded. To finish, I checked through the cross-references written in pen on the top of some of the dog-eared cuttings. 'See also: Mexborough, General', 'South Yorkshire, Industry', 'Doncaster Borough Council'. There was nothing odd about those.

Then another cross-reference caught my eye. 'See also: Animal Rights Movement.' That was more peculiar. I rummaged through the cabinets and dug out the appropriate brown envelope.

It contained even more clippings. I read through them one after the other for ten minutes before I found a couple relating to CPL Agro-Chemicals.

On the night of March 16th, some seven months earlier, a group of four animal rights' activists had broken into the factory compound and attempted to release a number of animals from a research laboratory. They'd been caught by security guards before they could free the creatures.

I was going off at a tangent here. None of this had anything to do with either Rob Fielding, or Jamie Hynes. It had happened several months before Jamie died. Then I turned to the next cutting and began to wonder.

It was a report on the trial of the four activists for burglary and criminal damage. First time offenders, they'd pleaded guilty and received the relatively lenient sentences of two hundred hours' community service each.

The name of one of the defendants stood out like a neon sign. Edward Arthur Greaves.

I left the *News* building and drove the half mile from the city centre to the Medico-Legal Centre on Watery Street. The receptionist in the foyer made me wait while she telephoned upstairs to see if the Coroner's Officer was free to see me.

'Give him ten minutes, then you can go up,' she said.

I sat on one of the padded seats, watching the clock and thinking about Rob Fielding, Jamie Hynes, Eddie Greaves and Maria. But mostly about Maria. The others were transitory diversions, preoccupations of the moment that concerned my working life but not my life. Maria was more. Our paths crossed only occasionally, never quite joining. She was a friend, a professional adviser, a distraction, yet more than that too. I thought of the opportunities missed, or never taken. Through nervousness, uncertainty, fear. Or the blundering forces of fate. Like Harry Raymond walking in at just the moment opportunity and will coincided. Sometimes one shot is all you get.

'You can go up now,' the receptionist said.

'What?' I turned to see her. 'Oh, yes.'

I cleared my head, focusing on why I was there, then went up to the first floor. Bob Davis was standing at his desk sorting through a pile of papers.

'You've got two minutes, Mike. Then I've got to be down in the morgue.'

'Visiting your relatives again?'

He didn't react. 'How can I help you?'

'The inquest on a ten-year-old boy named Jamie Hynes. Do you remember it?'

Bob stopped what he was doing and contemplated the desk top for a time. Then he said: 'I can't talk about that.'

He resumed his sorting, not looking up. It was out of character. He was usually very helpful.

'I know I didn't miss it,' I said. 'And the *News* didn't cover it either. How come?'

'I can't talk about it, Mike,' he repeated.

His head was still bowed, the ceiling light glowing on his bald pate. I could make out the ridges and bumps on the surface.

'We weren't told about it, were we?' I said. 'Why not?'

This time he looked up. 'Because it was held in camera. Relatives only.'

'In *camera*? That's pretty exceptional.'

'The only one in my experience.'

'Why?'

'I can't tell you that.'

'Come on, Bob. Off the record.'

'It's still the same answer.' He collected the papers together and slid them into a cardboard folder. 'I have to go now.'

'At least tell me what the verdict was.'

Bob shook his head. He didn't seem to like this any more than I did.

'I'm sorry, Mike. It was a closed hearing. I'm not permitted to reveal anything at all about it.'

'A quick glimpse at the file. A couple of minutes while you're out of the office. That's all I need,' I said.

'Don't push it. The matter's closed. Now, if you don't mind, I have to be downstairs.'

'The stiffs will wait,' I said. I'd positioned myself between him and the door. I wasn't going to let this one go without some gesture of opposition.

'Why were the press and public excluded? Was there something to hide?'

'Draw your own conclusions.' He stepped round me.

'I can only think of one reason for holding an inquest in camera,' I said. 'But I don't see what the death of a ten-year-old kid has to do with national security.'

'It's up to you to work that out. You're the journalist.'

'I need some help.'

Bob shook his head again. 'You're on your own on this one, Mike.'

I had a coffee and a Danish pastry in a café off Angel Street. The coffee tasted like burnt charcoal and the pastry was about as appetizing as a lump of iced chipboard, but my mind was on other things. Concentrating this time on Jamie Hynes and no one else.

I'd worked the city for twenty years, covered probably a few hundred inquests, but I'd never come across one held in camera before. No doubt the coroner had had his reasons for closing the doors, but they didn't wash with me. Not when a ten-year-old child had died in convulsions on a patch of public land. Doing nothing more hazardous than playing on his bike and throwing stones into a pond. The people had a right to know what had killed him.

I knew now it wasn't natural causes, but the truth was buried away out of reach in some inquest file. I would probably never find out exactly what had happened at the hearing. But there was one thing even the coroner couldn't conceal from public view.

I left the café and walked up the hill to High Street, then cut up Fargate and through the Peace Gardens to the Register Office behind the Town Hall extension.

The Births and Deaths inquiries desk was upstairs, partitioned off into small booths for extra privacy. One of the clerks came to the other side of the counter and I asked to see the register of deaths for the previous six months. I checked through the thick book and found Jamie Hynes in the June section. I asked for a copy of the death certificate, paid a fee of £5.50 and was told to come back in two hours.

I went to the central library and killed the time reading the papers in the reference section. The room was full of students and dossers looking for somewhere out of the cold for a kip. It was hard to tell which were which.

Shortly before three o'clock, I returned to the Register Office and picked up the copy of the death certificate. I studied it in the waiting area downstairs before I left the building.

Jamie Hynes had died of asphyxiation due to blockage of the bronchial tubes. It was possible, I suppose, that a severe asthma attack could have done that, but I wasn't convinced. Not because I knew anything about the medical aspects, but because of the circumstantial evidence. If it had been simply asthma, why hold the inquest in camera? Unless there was something else, some other complication I hadn't yet considered. The certificate was signed by a Dr Stephen Farrell. The name meant nothing to me.

I walked back across the front of the Town Hall to a telephone box on Surrey Street. A call to Directory Inquiries and I had the phone number of Jamie Hynes's mother in Mexborough. I rang her.

She sounded harassed, weary, when she answered. In the background I could hear the sound of a television and a baby yelling. I explained what I wanted.

'I told you everything I could remember about the inquest,' she said. 'Please leave me alone.'

'This won't take long,' I said. 'You must remember the medical evidence. Did they say at any point what had caused Jamie's attack?'

'I don't know. We weren't there for the whole thing.'

'What do you mean?'

'We had to leave the room at one point. We didn't hear everything that were said.'

'The coroner asked you to leave?'

'Yes. We had to wait outside.'

'Did he say why?'

'I'm not sure. We'd never been to an inquest before. We thought it were normal.'

'When I came to your house, you said you couldn't remember the name of the doctor who gave evidence. Was it Stephen Farrell?'

'I don't know. I didn't take much notice of his name. I were still really cut up over Jamie.'

The baby's cries intensified over her voice.

'You've never heard of a Dr Farrell? He's not your GP?'

'No, that's Dr O'Sullivan.'

'Was Jamie taken to hospital after his attack?'

'Yes. In Sheffield. The Hallamshire.' She murmured something inaudible away from the telephone. A soothing sound. The piercing cries only got worse. Then she came back on the line. 'Look, I have to get back to the baby. I'm sorry.'

'Thank you. That's all I wanted to ask.'

I hung up and dialled the main switchboard at the Royal Hallamshire Hospital. There was no doctor called Stephen Farrell on the staff. Then I phoned the local family practitioner committees. There was no general practitioner in any part of South Yorkshire with that name. So if he wasn't a GP or a hospital doctor, who was he?

I got home to find Harry in the kitchen tackling the enormous mound of washing up. He had a floral pinafore tied around his waist.

'Don't you ever do this?' he said grumpily.

'Only when I run out of crockery. Where did you get the pinny?'

'I brought it wi' me. You any idea 'ow unhygienic this is? Leaving plates lying around caked in congealed food.

Not even soaking in water. It's a serious 'ealth 'azard, Mike.'

'I've been doing it for years without any ill effects.'

'You're probably immune to the bacteria by now. But I'm new 'ere. I'm an easy target for all the bugs. Me and my delicate stomach. Look at this fork. See the gunge in between the prongs? Do you know how many microbes there are down there?'

'Thirty-eight?' I ventured.

'Millions. Millions of microbes waiting to poison some unsuspecting human being. Someone like me. You ought to be more careful.'

'You brought a *pinny* with you?' I said. 'Your wife throws you out after twenty years and you pack a pinny?'

Harry looked offended. 'You never know when you might need one.'

I put the kettle on and went into the bathroom to wash. There was a strong odour of disinfectant and I noticed that my shaving kit, shampoo, deodorant, all my familiar clutter, had been neatly tidied away in the wall cabinet. The place looked, and smelt, dangerously clean.

'You been messing around in here, Harry?' I called out.

He appeared in the doorway. 'I 'ad to. The muck in 'ere, you were inviting trouble. That basin were filthy.'

'Well, at least it was *my* filth,' I said. 'I knew where it'd been.'

'And I collected together all those old bits of soap you 'ad about the place. Them bits what's too small to use. You know what you can do wi' 'em? What I always do.'

'No, tell me.'

'You pack 'em all together in an old tobacco tin. Really press 'em in 'ard. Then tap 'em out and you've got a new bar of soap. Saves you a fortune.'

'One more interesting fact,' I said.

I made a pot of tea and went into the living room and called Cathy Fielding. I asked her if she'd ring Eddie Greaves for me, to explain who I was, prepare the ground.

'Ask him if I can come and see him tonight,' I said.

'I'll do my best,' Cathy replied. 'You know it's the inquest tomorrow?'

'I'll be there. Will you call me back about Eddie?'

It took her half an hour. By which time Harry had finished off the washing up and was busy cleaning the top of the cooker. 'I need a bleedin' sandblaster to get some of this off,' he commented acerbically, scrubbing away with a ball of wire wool. I drank my tea and pretended I hadn't heard.

'He wasn't very enthusiastic,' Cathy said when she called. 'But I persuaded him it was important. He'll be in all evening. You've got his address, haven't you?'

'From the remand hearing.'

'Any news? You find anything in Mexborough?'

'Nothing concrete. I want to follow up a couple of leads, but I'll let you know if anything turns up.'

I put my coat back on and stuck my head round the kitchen door.

'I'm just going out.'

Harry straightened up from the cooker. He rubbed his nose on his wrist, his hands encased in thick blue rubber gloves.

'You pack those too?' I said.

'Good job I did. State of this flat.'

'See you later.'

'You've only just got in. Aren't you 'aving summat to eat first?'

'I'll grab something later.'

Harry shook his head disapprovingly. 'It's not good for you, Mike. You should 'ave a proper meal in the evenings. Regular nutrition, that's what the body needs if it's to stay 'ealthy.'

'Harry,' I said. 'Are you planning on staying long?'

Eddie Greaves lived in a bedsit on Crookesmoor Road. A converted Victorian three-storey villa with a wooden fire escape tacked on the side and a front garden full of rubbish the binmen had neglected, or declined, to take away.

The front door of the house was open when I arrived so I just walked in. The hallway was in darkness. The lights were on a timer. I pushed in the plunger switch and made it upstairs before the power clicked off. There was a pay phone on the wall outside Eddie's door. I knocked and waited.

He took his time answering. When he did, he opened the door a few inches and looked at me belligerently. He was wearing jeans and a Class Action T-shirt with what looked like tomato soup spilt down the front.

'You going to let me in?' I asked.

He gave it some thought, then stood back for me to enter. He didn't say anything.

I looked around the bedsit. It was a big room, but so crammed with furniture and possessions that it seemed poky and oppressive. There was a single bed against one wall, a table in the bay window, a fridge, armchairs, chest of drawers and wardrobe, all scratched and ancient, stamped with the unmistakable mark of the junk shop. A bicycle was propped against the wardrobe doors and books piled on most of the available floor space. It smelt of onions, garlic and lavender air freshener.

'I won't take up too much of your time,' I said.

'Too bloody right you won't,' Eddie said.

Not a good start. I made a feeble attempt to placate him.

'I know you don't like journalists, but we're not all the same, you know.'

'Spare me the sanctimonious shit and get on with it, will you?'

He slumped down in one of the ugly armchairs and took out a packet of cigarette papers and some tobacco. He started to hand roll a cigarette. I moved a crumpled copy of *Socialist Worker* off the other armchair and sat down facing him. He hadn't shaved since I last saw him. The stubble was black with a hint of auburn. It made him look dirty.

'Tell me about the night you broke into the CPL plant near Mexborough,' I said.

113

He licked the edge of his cigarette paper and pressed it down, pinching off a few strands of tobacco protruding from one end before he put the cigarette in his mouth and lit it.

'Why're you interested in that?'

'It's complicated.'

'I'm listening.'

'I don't even know whether it has any relevance.'

He leaned forwards in his seat and tugged the cigarette from his lip. 'Listen, I'm doing this because Cathy asked me to, not because I want to. But don't think you can ask me questions without telling me what the fuck is going on. Understand? I want the full picture.'

I'd had easier interviewees. I told him about Jamie Hynes, about Rob going out to talk to Dean Clayton.

'That kid died just by the perimeter fence of the factory. Then I found out that you, a friend of Rob's, had raided the place and I wanted to know more about it, that's all.'

Eddie studied me guardedly. 'It's a chemical plant,' he said.

'I thought it made fertilizers.'

'Fertilizers, pesticides, they're all chemicals, aren't they? They're all unnatural. Basically poisons that we throw around as if they were harmless.'

'But essential to our agriculture,' I said rashly.

Eddie gave a snort of disgust. 'That's just the Establishment line I'd expect a journalist to trot out. We don't need them. The chemical companies need them because that's how they make their money, but it's a dangerous treadmill. The more we use synthetic pesticides and fertilizers the less we're able to do without them.

'We've got all these expensive sprays, systemics, God knows what, and what do they do? Pests are thriving. New, more resilient species are appearing all the time. And we've killed off their natural predators with more pesticides. We don't have a clue what we're doing. Remember Bhopal? Two thousand five hundred people dead, thousands injured. That was a pesticide ingredient

114

that leaked – methyl isocyanate. Yet the local management at the plant said it was just an acute irritant, not
lethal. They knew nothing about it.'

I nodded automatically. I didn't want to get into an
argument about pesticides.

'But you broke into the CPL factory to release animals,
didn't you?'

'They've got a whole zoo in there. Labs full of animals
for testing. I don't mean just rats and white mice. They've
got rabbits, goats, monkeys, even sheep. We saw them
through the windows.'

'I read a newspaper cutting. It said you didn't actually
manage to free any of them.'

'No, the bastards caught us before we could get into the
labs. That place is crawling with fucking security guards.'

'It's also got a pretty formidable fence all round it,' I
said. 'How did you get past that?'

Eddie smiled slyly. 'They never found that out. They
questioned us for hours at the police station but we never
told them. I'm not telling you either.'

'I'll keep it to myself.'

'No chance. You think I trust you? Dream on, pal.'

'You do a lot of raids like that?'

'No. Too risky.'

'Why CPL in particular? There must be dozens of companies that do tests on animals.'

He shrugged and took a drag on his cigarette. 'It was
Rob's idea. The rest of us had never heard of the place
until he told us about it.'

'*Rob* initiated the raid?' I was taken by surprise.

'He was the one who found the way in too. We just
followed him.'

'You mean Rob was with you?' I thought back to the
newspaper cutting. Only four names had been mentioned.
None of them Rob's.

Eddie saw where I was going. 'He was the only one
who wasn't caught.'

'How come?'

115

'I'm not sure. The whole thing was pretty confusing at the time. We all went in together. The labs are in some old wartime prefabs at one end of the site. We'd just got to them when the guards showed up out of nowhere. Rob just seemed to disappear. Or maybe he'd got separated from us earlier. I don't really know. It was a complete fiasco.'

'I didn't know Rob was into animal rights,' I said.

'He wasn't. It was his first and only raid. He was more interested in the environment than defenceless creatures.'

'And you?'

'I've always fought against vivisection. It's barbarous, unnecessary.' He blew a cloud of acrid smoke towards me. 'Cathy said you're looking into Rob's death. That right?'

I nodded. 'I'm making a few inquiries.'

'Why not leave it to the police? Isn't that their job?'

'I like to do some things myself.'

'Don't trust them?'

'Would you?'

Eddie grinned cynically. I had a point. In his book, even a journalist was preferable to a copper.

I said: 'You know of anyone who might have wanted Rob dead?'

'No.'

'Were you aware he was compiling a file of damaging information on Russell Stamford?'

'No. You think he was killed because of that?'

'I don't know what to think.'

'You can rule that one out for a start. You think someone like Stamford cares what a pygmy like Rob has on him? That's not a personal insult. We're all pygmies in this business. We might delude ourselves that we have stature, but when it comes to what counts we're almost invisible.'

'And what counts?'

'Power, of course. People like us are never going to influence the smug bastards who run this country. Who've always run it. They've spent centuries building up their vested interests, their network of friends in the right places, putting their hands in each other's pockets. You think a bunch of skint idealists like us are going to bother them? We can annoy them now and again, but nothing is ever going to change.

'A man like Stamford, rich, with influential friends wouldn't give a toss what Rob knew about him. It's like a flea on an elephant's backside. Rob could never see that. You're wasting *your* time too.'

'You don't think the press has any power either?'

Eddie pinched out the remains of his cigarette with his fingers and put the stub down carefully on an ashtray. He stood up and moved to the door.

'Do me a favour,' he said. 'What little power you have is on the side of the Establishment. If it wasn't, they'd soon take it away from you. You're lackeys, every one of you, so don't give me any shit about the power of the press. You're part of the problem, not the solution to it. Now, have you finished?'

He was holding the door open for me.

'It looks as if I have,' I said. 'Thanks for your time. If I need to check anything, maybe I could give you a call?'

'Maybe you could shove your head up your arse.'

I walked out on to the landing. By the time I turned, he'd already shut the door. I made a note of the number of the pay phone, an optimist ever, and drove home.

Harry was just finishing vacuuming the living room. Every surface had been dusted and polished, the books tidied, the rubbish hidden away somewhere. It was unrecognizable as my flat.

'I couldn't leave it the way it were, Mike,' Harry explained. 'I could catch all manner of diseases. The dust were half an inch thick in places. Think of the mites.'

'What mites?'

'The dust mites. They live off tiny fragments of human skin.'

'Can you see them?'

'No, of course not.'

'So why worry about them?'

'I 'ave to think of me chest. Especially sleeping on that floor. Me lungs aren't up to 'alf an inch of dust.'

He wound up the flex of the vacuum cleaner and put it away in the hall cupboard. So that's where I kept it. I went into the bedroom. He'd been in there too. I lay down on the bed and dozed off with the stench of Mr Sheen in my nostrils.

# 9

Sometimes in this business, information comes easily. A word in a pub, a phone call, a tip off from a contact. Other times it's harder. The result of hours of painstaking research, checking methodically through the records. I didn't like it, but when it had to be done, I preferred to get it over with early in the morning.

I was back in the library of the *Evening News*. Leafing through cuttings. I'd been there since seven, with one break for coffee, but I still hadn't found anything of interest. The problem was, I didn't really know exactly what I was looking for. I was fishing more than anything. Reading every file, every clipping that might have a connection, however remote, with Mexborough, Jamie Hynes or the CPL Agro-Chemicals plant.

I'd ploughed my way through dozens of envelopes, hundreds of tedious, irrelevant articles on local politics, the council, crime, accidents, shops, bazaars, deaths, marriages, trivia, the whole parochial gamut of local newspaper coverage.

Time was running out. It was now ten-fifteen. The inquest on Rob Fielding was due to start at eleven. I set myself a deadline of ten-forty-five. After that I would abandon the search.

I checked yet another cross-reference from a file. It was a dead end, like all the others. The librarian asked pointedly if I'd finished yet. She was getting fed up of replacing all the envelopes I'd removed. Half an hour, I said. She gave me a look and sighed. I buried my head in a pile of clippings and resisted the temptation to give up now. While I was still relatively sane.

At ten-forty-three I found it. Not a stunning revelation, not even a particularly promising opening, but it was the only new lead I'd discovered all morning. It was tucked away in an article on a horticultural show at Mexborough, dated almost two years earlier. Next to the text was a photograph of a middle-aged man in wellies and an anorak. In one hand he was holding a garden rake, in the other a leek which had to be close on two feet long and about three inches in diameter. The caption read: 'Mr Frank Helliwell displays his prize-winning leek.'

It was an unlikely piece to draw my attention. But it was a single paragraph in the main body of the story which had aroused my curiosity. 'Frank will now have more time to devote to his vegetables since he recently retired from the CPL Agro-Chemicals factory after a works accident.'

It could have meant anything, of course. 'Works accident' was a vague enough term to cover anything from a finger caught in a door to a nuclear explosion, but it was worth following up. Just talking to someone who'd worked at the plant might be useful. I checked the librarian wasn't looking and slipped the cutting into my pocket.

I made it to the inquest with a minute to spare. The press bench was more crowded than I'd seen it for a long time. The ghoulish fascination of a murder. Even the television boys from Leeds were there. There were no cameras inside, naturally, but the two dorks with blow-dried hair and slick suits at the far end had to be TV reporters. No one else could've looked so vacuous.

I squeezed on to the back row and looked around the courtroom. Cathy Fielding was there in the centre, Maria sitting next to her. I nodded at them both and continued my casual examination of the public gallery. Eddie Greaves was the only other face I recognized. He scowled at me then turned his head away.

Bob Davis came in on the dot of eleven, followed by

the coroner. It was a short hearing. The coroner opened the inquest, said police murder inquiries were continuing, released Rob Fielding's body for cremation and adjourned the case. I was back out in the foyer fifteen minutes later.

I waited for Maria and Cathy to come down the stairs from the courtroom and approached them. Cathy was holding up well. Inquests, even just the opening of them, were ordeals for anyone who knew the dead person. She didn't smile, but she shook my hand longer than necessary. Maybe to show it was nothing personal. I didn't know what to say to either of them.

'Let's go outside,' Maria suggested.

I shook my head. 'There're two television crews out there. They'll be on your back the minute you step through the door.'

'I have to pick up Jenny,' Cathy said anxiously. 'Is there another way out?'

'There is,' I said. 'Did you come by car?'

She nodded. 'I borrowed a neighbour's. The police are still examining ours.'

'Where's it parked?'

'At the front.'

'Give me the keys. I'll bring it round to the side for you. What make is it?'

'A dark blue Nova. I don't know the registration.'

'Wait here a moment.'

I went to the receptionist at the desk near the exit. It was a different one from yesterday, a longer-serving part timer called Monica. She knew who I was. But that probably wasn't an advantage.

'Would you do something, please?' I said. 'For Mrs Fielding over there. Show her the side exit.'

Monica looked doubtful. 'I can't do that, Mike. I can't give any help to the press.'

'It's not for me. I'm not whisking her off to some hotel for an exclusive interview, you know. I'm asking for her.'

'Everyone has to use the front entrance.'

'Look outside,' I said. 'See the cameras, the reptiles waiting for her. Would you want to walk out there and be bombarded with questions about your dead husband?'

Monica pursed her lips. She glanced through the window. The creeps from Yorkshire TV and the BBC were preening themselves, adjusting their ties and egos for their moment of glory in front of the cameras. Then she looked at Cathy waiting in the middle of the foyer.

'OK. But for God's sake, don't let Mr Davis know I did it.'

'Thanks, Monica.'

I returned to Cathy and told her what was happening. 'Couple of minutes and I'll be there.'

I found her car quite easily and drove it around the block to the side exit of the Medico-Legal Centre. They were waiting just inside the door. As I pulled in, the press hounds came running round the corner, baying for copy. They must have suspected something was going on. Sometimes, I swear, they can actually smell human pain.

I waved frantically to Maria and Cathy. They hurried out of the building, but it was a close thing. The dogs were nearly on us. I got out of the car, leaving the engine running. Cathy scrambled into the driver's seat and I slammed the door behind her, then moved round to meet the slavering pack head on.

One of the TV greasers tried to push past me and somehow managed to trip over my outstretched foot. He tumbled to the ground, his cameraman toppling over after him. Ten thousand quid's worth of high-tech equipment landed in the gutter and was almost crushed by the nearside car wheel as Cathy took off down the road. In the ensuing confusion I slipped back through the side door with Maria.

'Disgraceful scene,' I said. 'Let me take you away from here immediately. Coffee?'

'I really ought to be getting back to the office.'

'Yes, you're absolutely right.'

'Well, just a quick one.'

We had cappuccino in a café near Cole Brothers department store. I asked Maria if she fancied a cake to go with it. She said no, she was watching her figure. I was watching her figure too, but I kept it to myself.

Maria said: 'You tripped that man up.'

'Is that an accusation?'

'More a compliment. I'd have done the same if my legs were longer.'

'They look fine to me.'

'You don't have to stare at them quite so obviously,' she said.

'Sorry. I'll try to stare at them more discreetly in future.'

Maria spooned the froth and chocolate off her cappuccino and swallowed it, turning the spoon over in her mouth and sucking it for a moment. I'd never seen anyone drink coffee so sensuously.

'Cathy told me to thank you. She appreciated what you did.'

'That's OK. I wouldn't want anyone subjected to an ordeal like that at any time, never mind after an inquest. Sensitivity is not a strong point of the press.'

'You manage to find a bit somewhere.'

I shook my head. 'Me? I'm just a hard-nosed hack, like the rest of them. I hate those TV blokes, that's all.'

'Professional envy?' Maria said.

'Yeah. I wish I could have a manicure and teeth like them. How did Cathy take the inquest?'

'She found it distressing. Who wouldn't? The funeral will be even worse.'

'When is it?'

'Next week sometime. She's got to arrange the exact date.'

'And Jenny?'

Maria made a face. Part anguish, part sympathy. 'She's missing Rob. She still can't understand where he is.'

'Poor kid.'

Maria nodded. We said nothing for a while. I didn't want to talk about grief, but it seemed wrong to change the subject too abruptly. Maria did it for me.

123

'I'm sorry our dinner got cut short the other night,' she said.

'Me too.'

'Your friend has lousy timing.'

'I know. But I couldn't turn him down.'

'He still with you?'

'Yes. And driving me crazy. He's cleaned the flat.'

Maria gave me a dry look. 'Yes, I can see that might have been a traumatic experience for you. For the flat too.'

'Are you implying something by that? It's counterproductive, cleaning.'

'How would you know?'

I let that pass. 'You see, if you allow dust to lie, it settles to a certain finite thickness. After that point the layers become denser, but they don't get deeper. It's a scientific fact. Leave it undisturbed and it does no harm. But the moment you start dusting you just move it about the place. You don't get rid of it, you simply redistribute it.'

'And you prefer to leave it where it is.'

'I call it McLean's First Law of Domestic Happiness.'

She smiled and made no comment. Sipped her coffee thoughtfully. She was sitting sideways at the table, her legs crossed below a very short black skirt. I didn't look down.

'Have you got any further?' she asked.

I knew what she meant. 'A little.'

'I thought something might come out at the inquest.'

'It never does. Not at this stage. But I found out why I didn't cover the inquest on Jamie Hynes. It was held in camera.'

'No press?'

'Or public. Just the parents. But they were excluded at one point too. No doubt something our masters didn't want even his mother and father to know.'

'Our masters?'

'You know who I mean. You can bet it wasn't the

coroner who decided to hold it in camera. Pressure would've been exerted on him from on high.'

'Is this another of your conspiracy theories?'

'Part theory, part informed guesswork. The government's involved somewhere. That's a certainty. Someone pleaded national security interests. State secrets, damaging to the nation, that kind of bullshit.'

'For a child who died of asthma? Why would the government be involved?'

'*If* he died of asthma. I took a look at his death certificate. According to that, he died of asphyxiation due to blockage of the bronchial tubes.'

'So it was his lungs.'

'Yes. But what caused the blockage? That's what I want to know. Jamie died on some wasteland near a fertilizer factory. CPL Agro-Chemicals.'

'And you think the factory played a part in his death?'

'Not necessarily. But I'm looking into it.'

'You have any evidence?'

'Pure conjecture.'

'I assume you're suggesting he was poisoned in some way.'

'It crossed my mind. Jamie had convulsions, he was sick, he foamed at the mouth. It doesn't take much medical knowledge to speculate it might have been poison. He and his mate Dean were mucking about near a stagnant pond. What if it was contaminated in some way.'

'Did he go into the water?'

'I don't know exactly what he did. They were throwing stones into it, that I do know. What if Jamie got splashed, or swallowed something toxic?'

Maria stroked one of her cheeks with her finger, smoothing the skin, the finger coming to rest on her lips. She chewed the tip gently.

Then she said: 'How would the pond have got contaminated?'

I shrugged. 'Accidental leakage, illegal dumping.'

125

'I can't see them being stupid enough to dump stuff on their own doorstep.'

'Me neither. It's a big factory, an established company. On the face of it, it doesn't make sense for them to take a risk like that. I'd rule them out at once if it weren't for one thing. Rob broke into the factory seven months ago.'

Maria stared at me. 'Rob? Why?'

I told her about my conversation with Eddie Greaves.

'But that's completely unconnected,' she said. 'What have animal rights got to do with this?'

'Nothing at all,' I said. 'But that's not why Rob went in that night.'

'But you just told me –'

I held up a hand to stop her. 'The raid was Rob's idea. Up until then he'd shown no interest in animal rights campaigning. It was the first time he'd done anything like that. So why then? And why CPL Agro-Chemicals in particular?'

She finished her coffee and spooned the last few dregs into her mouth, letting me continue.

'I think he had another reason for breaking into the plant. Only he needed help. That's where Eddie and his three pals came in. Rob took them along as unwitting decoys. He knew they'd be caught. But he wasn't with them when they were. Eddie said he just disappeared, but he wasn't sure exactly when.

'My guess is that Rob had no interest in the labs containing the animals. It was a useful front, a way of conning Eddie and the others into coming along. They were a diversion. To keep the security guards busy while Rob slipped away to do whatever it was he *really* went in to do.'

'Which was?'

I grinned. 'That's as far as I've got.'

'You're losing me in all this. There are too many loose ends, too much guesswork.'

'That's how I work. I don't have access to the truth so

126

I have to try and build a plausible framework and see if it stands up to scrutiny.'

'Maybe it was pure coincidence Rob wasn't caught too.'

I shook my head. 'He had it planned. He was nowhere near the others when the security men nabbed them. Why wasn't he, if they all had the same objective in mind? There was no good reason for him to be separated from the group unless he was heading somewhere else at the time.' I drained my cup. 'You want another coffee?'

Maria looked at her watch. 'I really have to go, I've work to do.'

'I'll walk some of the way with you.'

We went down Barker's Pool and stopped on the corner with Leopold Street. Neither of us moved.

'I'll give you a call,' I said.

'I'd like that.'

She waited a second, her eyes on my face. Then her shoulders lifted in a tiny shrug of resignation. She had turned and was walking away across the road before I realized I should have said more.

I had no home address for Frank Helliwell, but the cutting from the *Evening News* I'd filched gave the location of his allotment. It was by a modern housing estate on the outskirts of Mexborough, mostly flats and starter homes, one of a group of allotments clustered together by a small stream.

I left the car in a cul-de-sac and walked down a public footpath which ran alongside the stream. A hundred yards away, partially screened by trees, was the sluggish brown ribbon of the River Dearne. The allotments were to my right, a patchwork of cultivated smallholdings interspersed with dilapidated wooden sheds and a couple of derelict greenhouses, virtually all their panes shattered by stones. A man in a checked flat cap and an NCB donkey jacket was digging a strip of land a few yards in. He leaned on his spade, drawing breath, and saw me watching him. He nodded.

'Afternoon.' His manner was open, friendly.

'That looks hard work,' I said.

'Aye. I'm getting too old for this lark.'

He was probably pushing fifty, but no more. Stocky, his cheeks flushed from the cold air and exertion. From his jacket and age, I guessed he was a redundant miner. There were plenty of them about round here.

'I was looking for Mr Helliwell,' I said.

'Frank? He doesn't come here much these days. Not since he were taken poorly.'

'He's been ill?'

'Aye. These past two year or thereabouts. That's his patch over there.'

He indicated an adjoining strip of land which was untidier than the others, the soil being gradually taken over by weeds and grass.

'We try to keep it under control, but most of us have enough on wi' us own patches,' he said. 'I put some beans and potatoes in for him this year. Very poor crop. Not like Frank would've got. Green fingers he used to have.'

'Is that where he grew his leeks?'

'Them big uns? No, he had them in his back garden. Some bugger'd pinch 'em down here. You a friend of his?'

'Not really. I was hoping to see him, but I don't have his address. I just knew where his allotment was.'

'You'd have found him here like as not a few year ago. He were always here. You should see the prizes he's won. Leeks, potatoes, carrots. He once had a marrow what took two men to lift, it were that big.'

'Does he live far away?'

'Naow.' He gave me an address. 'You in a car? Back up the road, third turning on your left, then second right. You going there now?'

'Yes.'

'Will you do summat for me? Take him these.'

He dug his spade into the earth and left it there while he went into a small shed. When he emerged he was holding a long string of onions tied up in the cut-off leg of a pair of nylon tights.

'I promised Annie a week ago and never got round to it.' He handed me the onions and veered away towards a line of cauliflowers. 'And one of me autumn caulies.' He deposited the vegetable in my arms.

'Who shall I say sent them?' I said.

'Just Jack. She'll know. Tell her I'll pop in at the week-end if I can.'

The Helliwells' house was a small two-up two-down terrace in a street of identical homes. A narrow passage-way took me through to the back where there was a strip of garden, once cultivated but now just bare earth, and an enormous greenhouse which looked as if it hadn't been used for a long time. I went through a waist-high slatted gate and knocked on the door.

The woman who opened it was tiny. She came to some-where near my breast bone but she had a pronounced stoop which made her appear even smaller. She was wear-ing a plain blue housecoat and pink slippers with woolly bobbles on the toes.

'Mrs Helliwell?'

'Yes.'

She tilted her head to look at me. She had features like a sparrow. Fragile bones, a thin beak of a nose and pointed chin. But her eyes were bright and alert.

I held out the onions and cauliflower. 'Jack asked me to bring you these from his allotment.'

Her face broke into a smile, stretching the skin of her cheeks into a lacework of wrinkles.

'How kind of him. And you too. You must come in and have a cup of tea.'

She waved me into the kitchen, lifting the vegetables into the air to show to someone hidden away out of sight behind the door.

'Frank, look what Jack's sent. Look. Onions and a cauli-flower. Aren't they nice?'

From her tone I would have taken her to be addressing

a child. But from the name I knew it was her husband. I stepped over the threshold and closed the door.

Frank Helliwell was sitting in an armchair in the corner of the room. I could see at once I wouldn't be talking to him about the CPL fertilizer plant, nor anything else come to that.

He was a frail shadow of the man in the photograph in the paper. The flesh was gone from his face, the ruddy, outdoors complexion changed to a sickly white. He was gripping the arms of his chair with bony hands, his chin tucked against his chest. A trickle of saliva glistened at the edge of his mouth. I wondered what had happened to bring about such a transformation.

'Sit down,' Mrs Helliwell said. 'I'll just put the kettle on.'

She went to the sink, chatting to me as she made a pot of tea.

'Jack's ever so good to us. Always sending us things. A bag of potatoes, a few carrots, runner beans. He brought us some parsnips only the other week. It makes all the difference. We used to grow nearly all our own vegetables. You don't realize what a saving it is until you have to start buying them in the shops. Do you have an allotment, Mr . . . ?'

'McLean,' I said. 'No, I was just talking to Jack down there. He said he'd call in at the weekend.'

'That'll be nice.' She turned to her husband. 'Frank, Jack's stopping by at the weekend. You'll look forward to that.'

Frank made no response. At least, not verbally. He lifted his head awkwardly and looked at me. I expected his eyes to be vacant, but they flickered with a dim light of understanding. And something else I couldn't place. Maybe it was sadness.

'Jack comes round and plays dominoes when he can. Frank enjoys a game of dominoes. He used to play down the pub but we don't get out much nowadays. Here you are. Help yourself to milk and sugar.'

She put a mug of tea down on the table beside me. I contemplated telling her who I was, but held back. Not for any devious reason. She was an open person; she'd tell me anything I wanted regardless of my job. But I didn't want her to think I'd come with a purpose. I sensed they didn't get many visitors. I didn't want this to be an interview. I was just someone who'd called in for a chat and a bit of company.

'Your husband used to win prizes for his vegetables, didn't he?' I said.

'Oh yes. Dozens. Come and see.'

She beckoned to me, heading through the door to the rest of the house. I followed her. A steep staircase led off to the right from a minute hall. Then, through another door, was the front room. I noticed the change in temperature immediately. Whilst the kitchen had been warm, cosy, this room had a cold, chilling atmosphere seasoned with the musty smell of damp. I guessed it was hardly ever used.

On the mantelpiece over the open hearth was a line of silver trophies of varying sizes and designs. Framed certificates and rosettes covered two of the walls.

Mrs Helliwell took down one of the trophies to show me.

'This is the one he was most proud of. Mexborough and District Horticultural Society Gardener of the Year, 1990.'

It was a silver cup, polished to perfection. She handled it carefully to avoid putting fingermarks over the gleaming surface.

'For all-round achievement. That was a good year for him. He broke the record for the longest carrot. Twenty-eight and a half inches.'

I tried to imagine a two-and-a-half-foot carrot. 'I didn't know you could grow them that long.'

'Oh yes. Of course, you don't do it in the ground. There's not enough depth of soil. Frank grew his in oil drums, in a special mixture. They need a lot of feeding, do carrots.'

She put the trophy back on the mantelpiece and adjusted it until it was positioned to her satisfaction. When she looked back at me her expression was regretful.

'He used to love his gardening so much. It's heartbreaking now. He hardly ever leaves the house. Just sits and mopes in that armchair.'

'Jack said he'd been ill.'

'Ever since the accident. It's got worse these past few months.' She sighed. 'Still, we cope. Come on, your tea'll be getting cold.'

We went back into the kitchen and sat down at the table. Frank was asleep in his armchair, his head lolling sideways over his shoulder.

'Your husband's accident,' I said. 'What exactly happened? If you don't mind my asking.'

'No, I don't mind. It was a couple of years back, at the factory down the valley. The fertilizer place.'

'CPL?'

'That's the one.'

She told me her story. Frank Helliwell had been a fitter at the plant. One afternoon he'd been sent to mend a pipe in a research laboratory. The pipe was supposed to have been sluiced out, but there was some liquid left in one of the joints. When Frank opened it up he inhaled some of the fumes from the liquid. They were so powerful they knocked him backwards and he fell off his ladder, injuring his back. He'd had to give up his job and had been off work ever since.

'He's got worse since then,' Mrs Helliwell said. 'Some days he seems to have lost his senses. Says he can't remember anything. The other day he didn't know who *I* was. That's very upsetting.'

'Do you know what it was he inhaled?'

She shook her head. 'The company said it was just water in the pipe. They said Frank had got careless, overbalanced and toppled off his ladder.'

'Do you accept that?'

'It's nonsense. He'd never do a thing like that. Besides,

if it were true, he'd just have a bad back now. Not all these other things.'

'What other symptoms does he have?'

'Well, you can see.' She nodded her head at her sleeping husband. 'He's a sick man. Not just physically. He gets headaches and cramp in his arms and legs, and some days he gets blurred vision and can't breathe too well. But it's affected him mentally too. He gets these fits of depression. You know, not feeling a bit down like most of us get, but really serious. He was never like that before.'

She looked at Frank. I saw affection, pity, sorrow in her face. And weariness also. The travails of caring for him were slowly grinding her down.

'He's a changed man. Thirty-five years he worked there. He had a spotless record. The one accident he has, they say was his fault.'

'Have they paid you compensation?'

'They gave us fifteen hundred pounds just after it happened. I can't remember what they called it. Said they weren't admitting responsibility.'

'An ex gratia payment.'

'That's it. They made us sign something saying we wouldn't take legal action against them. We didn't realize then how little it was. I suppose we thought Frank would be back at work after a couple of months. But it's been two years now. You don't get much on sick benefit and it'll be another five years before Frank gets his pension.'

So he was only sixty. He looked closer to seventy-five. Mrs Helliwell looked old too. Worn out by stress, worry, financial insecurity and, perhaps worst of all, the prospect of no improvement in the future. I wished there was something I could do to help them.

'Maybe you should see a solicitor,' I said. 'Try to get that agreement overturned. Sometimes you can if they're unreasonable.'

'Solicitor? We can't afford that.'

'You could get legal aid.'

133

Mrs Helliwell screwed up her nose. 'Well, you know, we don't like to make a fuss.'

The English disease. 'Blow the fuss,' I said. 'You've got a sick husband and barely enough to live on. They can't pretend it's nothing to do with them. He was injured at work. They have a duty to pay you compensation. Shame them into giving you more. Companies like that will do anything to avoid bad publicity.'

I was making her uncomfortable, I could tell. She stood up from the table and went to the sink to wash her mug. She wanted a quiet, soothing conversation, not a lecture. A few minutes with a stranger to help her forget her worries. All I was doing was bringing them to the front of her mind.

'I'm sorry,' I said. 'It's none of my business.'

I changed the subject. Asked her how long they'd lived in the house, if they had family nearby, if they had children and what they did. She came back to the table and chatted away amiably. For a time, her husband's health faded into the background.

I'd been there almost an hour when I said I ought to be going.

'Is there anything I can do for you?' I added, standing up. 'Some shopping maybe.'

'No, it's all right. I have to go out later anyway. To pick up a prescription for Frank from the doctor's.'

'Is there much they can do for him?'

'He's on pills. But they don't seem to have much effect. Some days he's better than others. I don't know why. Dr Farrell comes and gives him a check-up every few weeks, but even he doesn't know why he changes from day to day.'

The name registered with a jolt. 'Dr Farrell? Is that Dr Stephen Farrell?'

'Yes, I believe it is Stephen.'

'He's your GP?'

'Oh, no. Our GP comes too, of course. No, Dr Farrell's the company doctor. At the factory.'

134

She turned away from me as Frank suddenly started coughing. Violent spasms that shook his whole body. A glob of thick yellow mucus appeared on his lips. Mrs Helliwell took a damp flannel from the sink and wiped his mouth. He continued coughing, a harsh bark. The very sound jarred.

I stepped forwards, concerned, but before I could speak Mrs Helliwell said: 'He's got medicine for that. I'll just get it.'

She left the room. I heard the light tread of her feet on the stairs. I watched Frank anxiously. His mouth gaped wide, his face contorted as each cough racked his gaunt frame. I could see he was in pain. Then the spasms subsided. He panted for breath, the air wheezing into his lungs. He opened his eyes and looked at me. The sadness I'd seen in them earlier was now a bleak, irredeemable hopelessness. I felt my skin go cold.

Mrs Helliwell came back into the room carrying a bottle of pale pink liquid. She poured some on to a spoon and forced it between her husband's lips. He swallowed it with difficulty, his jaw quivering. It seemed to help for he calmed down within seconds. His arms went limp and his breathing returned to a more normal rhythm.

'Should I call the doctor?' I said.

'It's passed now. He gets these attacks. He'll be all right in a few minutes.'

She put the medicine bottle down on the table and glanced at me apologetically.

'I'm sorry. It's not nice.'

'Don't be silly. Look, are you sure there's nothing I can do to help you?'

'You're very kind, but no, we can manage.' She opened the door to let me out.

'Thank you for the tea,' I said.

'Stop by again.'

I went out into the yard, pausing while the door shut behind me. Through the kitchen window I saw her crossing the room to her husband and wiping his face with the flannel again. I heard her voice in my mind. *We can manage*. Like thousands of others caring for the sick and elderly in quiet anonymity. Not living. Just managing.

I drove around the streets for a time, trying to forget what I'd just seen. Yet remembering every detail of it. Remembering it with an anger that only served to harden my determination to find out what had happened to Frank Helliwell.

I found a call box, looked up the number of CPL Agro-Chemicals and rang it. The switchboard connected me to Dr Farrell's extension. He had a deep, throaty voice with the burr of the West Country in his accent.

'My name's McLean,' I said. 'I'm a freelance journalist.'

'Oh yes.' The wariness was there suddenly.

'I've just been to see Frank Helliwell. I want to talk to you about him. And Jamie Hynes.'

There was a sharp intake of breath at the other end of the line. I prepared myself for a curt refusal, or even the phone going dead. But he said quickly: 'Give me a number I can call you on later.'

I gave him my home number.

'Don't ring me here again, you understand?' he said.

The connection was broken abruptly. I put down the receiver and thought about his reaction. Not uncooperative. Brusque, busy with other things perhaps. Willing to talk, though not on an open line. But underneath it all, a worried man.

On my way home, I returned to the wasteland near the factory. I parked on the verge and walked across to the pool of water Dean Clayton had shown me. I examined it cautiously, keeping my distance. I could see nothing remarkable about it. Dirty, opaque, green algae colonizing the surface but devoid of life below, it was pretty much like any other stagnant pond you'd find on industrial wasteland. I sniffed the air. There was a fetid, sulphurous taint to it, but that too was not unusual given the surroundings.

I walked round the pond until I was standing by the

perimeter fence of the fertilizer factory. On the other side of the mesh was a tarmac roadway with a gulley along the near edge. Set into the surface of the gulley was a drain covered in a heavy metal grid. I looked back at the pond, considering taking a sample of the water. But I had no container to put it in. Maybe I'd come back.

I retraced my steps and drove off along the road which passed the entrance to the factory. As I approached the gates, a lorry pulled out of them in front of me. It was a fixed-wheel truck with solid sides painted plain white. There were no markings on it at all. I held back and followed it for a few miles. It was going the same way as me. Through Swinton, Rawmarsh and Rotherham.

When we reached the M1 it went underneath the viaduct, heading south-west into the centre of Sheffield. I stayed behind it all the way. From the city centre it took the A625 out the other side. This was off my route, but I was curious to know where it was going. It was an innocuous-looking vehicle but that was partly what had aroused my interest. It was too much of a blank. No company name on the outside, no logo or phone number. That was odd.

For another half hour we followed the A625, through Hathersage and along the Hope Valley. Then we turned left towards Bradwell and went up the steep hill past the cement works. At the top we cut sharp right along a single-track road. A quarter of a mile further on, the lorry turned off through some gates on the left. I slowed down and held back, letting it continue up the dirt track. By the time I reached the gates, the lorry had disappeared over the brow of the hill, a cloud of white limestone dust lingering in its wake.

A sign next to the gates read simply: 'Private, no entry.' I didn't go any further. As far as I knew, there was nothing up there. I made a mental note of the location and drove on, descending now past the upper end of Pin Dale and down into the village of Castleton. I turned back on to the A625 and drove east towards the city.

# 10

Harry insisted on cooking an evening meal for me. 'Proper food. None of this takeaway and sandwich rubbish. It's important for your 'ealth, Mike. You've only got one body. You've got to look after it.'

I sat at my desk scribbling a few notes, collating the information I'd gathered on Rob Fielding, Jamie Hynes, the CPL factory. Putting together the pieces. Harry confined himself to the kitchen, making a huge amount of noise with the pots and pans, occasionally shouting out through the closed door: 'Nearly done. You're going to love this.'

When, finally, he emerged, floral pinny strapped around his waist, he was carrying two enormous fry-ups, piled high on the largest plates in the flat. He slapped them down on the table.

'Right, grub's up.'

I sat down and contemplated the mound of steaming grease in front of me. It was like a miniature volcano composed of sausages, bacon, fried potatoes, eggs, black pudding, baked beans and tomatoes.

'Is this your idea of a healthy meal?' I asked.

' 'Course.'

'You never heard of cholesterol, or saturated fat?'

'That's just bollocks, Mike,' Harry said. 'Get it down you. Cholesterol's good for you.'

'One or two doctors might disagree with you on that.'

'What do doctors know? They change their minds every couple of minutes. One day they're telling us summat's good for us, next they find out it's not.' He sprinkled salt over his sausages. 'Just the other month I were reading about margarine in *Grocer's Weekly*.'

'You read *Grocer's Weekly*?' I said.

'My dentist gets it. They've done a big study in America, found out there's summat in all this vegetable fat margarine what's even worse for you than they claim butter is. They don't know what they're doing. It's all a big con by the food companies to make us buy the refined crap they produce when we'd do better sticking to us traditional nosh. Climate like ours, we need fat. Look at the Eskimos.'

'What about them?'

'Lowest rate of 'eart disease in the world, but you wouldn't catch them eating bloody Flora.'

He dug into his fried potatoes and went on, his mouth bulging: 'Or take my late Uncle Ned, God rest 'im. All his life he ate what he liked. A fry-up for breakfast, fish and chips in the evening. Never did 'im any 'arm. Butter, lard, sugar, salt, he loved 'em all whatever anyone else said about 'em.'

'And how old was he when he died?'

'Twenty-seven.'

'*What*?'

'He got run over by a taxi in Scarborough. On 'is summer 'olidays. But he enjoyed life to the full, that's the point. If you're going to kick it tomorrow, and we all could quite likely, why fart around eating tasteless food cos some bugger tells you it'll lengthen your life?'

He shovelled in some baked beans and a slice of sausage and chewed them with relish. 'Bloody good stuff.'

I tackled a corner of my plate, realizing I hadn't eaten anything all day. Harry was right, it did taste good. Afterwards, we staggered to the armchairs and drank strong tea around the gas fire. It seemed odd, having someone else in the flat. I hadn't shared since my divorce, but it made a pleasant change to have some company.

Then Harry announced: 'I've been thinking. About

what I should do. You know, the wife and all that. I can't stay 'ere much longer.'

'You can stay as long as you like, Harry,' I said.

'No, I've got to sort it out.'

'Have you spoken to your wife since you left?'

'No. I can't summon the nerve. I don't really know what the problem is. Women, you know.'

'Didn't she say anything when she threw you out?'

'Plenty. She said I were a complete waste of space.'

'Yes, but you've been a complete waste of space for years. What made her decide to throw you out now?'

He gave me a look. 'That's not funny. I reckon if I wait a couple more days for things to settle down, I could probably move back in wi' 'er.'

'That's not tackling the root cause of the problem.'

'The root cause? The root cause is we've been married twenty year. That's too long for people to live together. Without a budgie,' he added bizarrely.

'A budgie?'

'They say you should always 'ave one if you don't 'ave kids. Gives you summat to talk about. Not that the wife needs much else to talk about.'

'I think you mean a dog.'

'Do I? Even better. It'd give me an excuse to get out of the 'ouse, taking it for walks.'

'This doesn't sound like the right attitude for a successful reconciliation,' I said. 'Are you sure you really want to stay with her? You ever thought of finding someone else?'

Harry stopped his mug in mid-air. 'You mean another woman?' He completed the movement, gulping down a mouthful of tea. 'Nah, couldn't be fagged. All that courtin' again. Meals out, the pictures, 'aving to shave reg'lar. Just thinking about it makes me feel exhausted.'

'What about your wife? Maybe she's got another man.'

Harry gaped at me incredulously. 'You kiddin'? You've seen 'er, 'aven't you?'

'Yeah, silly question.'

'No, I'll take 'er a box of chocolates. Milk Tray, summat

like that. Settle down in me armchair and it'll be like I've never been away. She's let off a bit of steam now. I'll just go 'ome and pretend it never 'appened.'

I didn't argue with him. It never pays to get too involved in other people's marriages. You're apt to find yourself under fire from both sides.

' 'Ow about you?' Harry said. 'You've kept 'er a bit quiet, 'aven't you?'

'Who?'

'You know who. That woman the other night. Nice-looking.'

'She's my accountant,' I said.

'Oh yes?' He didn't sound convinced.

'She is. You want some more tea?'

'You're changing the subject.' He grinned at me. 'You got something going with 'er?'

'She just came round for dinner. That's all.'

'So 'ave you got something going with 'er?'

I was spared the need to answer by the telephone ringing suddenly. I got up to cross the room thinking, have I got something going with her? Do I want to have something going?

I picked up the receiver. It was Stephen Farrell. I hadn't expected him to call. He dispensed with any polite introductory pleasantries.

'Is that McLean?'

'Yes.'

'When can we talk?' he said.

'The sooner the better.'

'Not on the phone.'

'Where do you live?' I said. 'I could come over.'

He didn't like that. 'No, that's not possible.'

'What about a pub?'

He didn't reply. I gave him time to think.

Then he said: 'Do you know Redmires Reservoirs?'

'Yes.'

'I'll meet you there at the end of the road. In half an hour. Alone.'

141

'Half an hour . . .' I was about to say I needed more time but he'd already hung up on me.

'I have to go out,' I said to Harry, flinging on my windcheater and going to the door.

' 'Aven't you got a scarf? It's cold out there. You should wrap up warm a night like this.'

'Harry,' I said. 'Since when did you become my mum?'

I drove hard across the centre of town. The traffic was light, but I was pushing it for time. Redmires Reservoirs were way out on the western side of the city, beyond the built-up area on the edge of Hallam Moor. I would need all of half an hour to get there.

The location worried me. It was a strange rendezvous to choose. Isolated, far from any houses, likely to be deserted at this time of night. Farrell was being ultra-cautious. He clearly didn't want anyone to witness our meeting, but Redmires Reservoirs were taking precautions perhaps a little too far.

I'd have liked time to arrive early, before he got there. To check out the surrounding area. He'd made sure I wouldn't have that opportunity. I didn't enjoy the prospect of going in blind. Maybe it was a touch of paranoia, but I was delving in murky waters. I couldn't rule out the possibility I was being set up.

Lodge Moor Hospital went past on my left, a scattered collection of flickering lights in the darkness. Then the Sportsman Inn and the Three Merry Lads pub. The houses had stopped by now. The ground was open on both sides, falling away steeply into the Rivelin Valley to the north, pasture land to the south. I passed some farm buildings before the road narrowed and dropped down to the head of Wyming Brook, dense forest closing in oppressively along one edge. My headlights picked out a barn, the entrance to the water authority treatment plant and then, around a curve in the road, a glistening expanse of water.

I was completely alone. No lights showing anywhere, no buildings. Just forest to my right and that unnerving

142

lake a few feet to my left. I tried not to look at it. There's something frightening about man-made reservoirs at night. The concrete sides, the inky, bottomless waters, the sense that if you step too close you'll be sucked in and ever downwards.

I reached the last of the three reservoirs and continued round along the western bank. The road started to deteriorate. I slowed down and wound my way past potholes and deep puddles of muddy rainwater. Towards the end, the metalled surface disappeared entirely and I was driving over stones and bare earth.

Ahead of me, parked in the turning area at the end of the road, was a car. I stopped fifty yards away and examined it in the beam of my headlights. It was a dark Rover saloon. Its lights were off. There appeared to be no one in it. I widened my field of study, looking beyond the car and away into the shadows of the plantation on the right behind a dry stone wall. I could still see no one.

My breathing was a little forced. The insistent thud in my chest was more than nerves. I was scared. The temptation to turn around and get the hell out was overpowering. But the urge to know was stronger. Discretion had no place in my make-up, curiosity did.

But I turned the car around nevertheless. Did a U-turn in the track and left the car in the middle, facing back the way I'd come. I took a torch from the glove compartment and got out.

The wind gusted into my face and the front of my open jacket. The thin material billowed out. Harry had been right. I should have brought a scarf. I zipped the wind-cheater up to my neck and turned to look at the Rover.

There was an outside possibility it wasn't Farrell's, that he had yet to arrive. But if it wasn't, what was it doing out here at eleven o'clock at night, unoccupied? The road led nowhere. I'd come to the end of it. I'd been here before and knew how unfrequented it was. The occasional water board employee, adulterous couples looking for somewhere private for a hurried back-seat coupling, hikers leaving their cars to walk up the footpath to Stanedge Pole. None of those was a plausible explanation. It had to be Farrell's. But where was he?

I started to walk towards the car. The torch swung loose in my hand, not switched on. There was enough light to see my way, and I wanted to let my eyes adjust to the darkness. It also made it harder for anyone else to pinpoint my location. I kept well away from the edge of the reservoir so I wasn't silhouetted against the faint orange glow down the valley, the lights of the hidden city. I wanted to blend in as far as possible. Undue caution, maybe, but I knew something wasn't right.

The car was less than twenty yards away now. I approached it obliquely, my eyes scanning the windows, then the road behind, then the forest. My nerves were at snapping point. I tried to ignore the rising sense of panic in my mind, concentrating instead on my senses. Watching, listening for sounds beneath the howl of the wind.

I reached the car and peered in through the driver's window. It was empty. I tried the door. It opened smoothly. I fumbled around the steering wheel. The keys were still in the ignition. Very quietly, I pushed the door closed. The catch only half-engaged. Then I felt the bonnet with the palm of my hand. It was warm.

I twisted round suddenly, sensing I was being watched. I probed the black depths of the plantation. Nothing. For a moment I contemplated calling out Farrell's name. But decided against it. I was so on edge the very sound of my own voice would scare me. I moved away from the car, my eyes registering every shape, every outline, every movement of the trees in the wind.

It was then that I saw it. A shadow, an indistinct mass over by the wall. It seemed out of place, not part of the background. Not a rock, nor a log either. Motionless, shapeless. I studied it intently. The lines became more defined, the textures, the shadings more perceptible. And I saw staring out at me the face of a man.

The shock numbed me. My stomach tightened as if a

fist were crushing it. The man's face didn't move. It took me a long moment to realize it never would. He was dead.

I walked across carefully and looked down at him. He was slumped against the wall, eyes and mouth gaping wide. I didn't switch my torch on even now. I didn't want to see the details. The light from the moon behind the clouds was enough for me to see the bullet hole in the centre of his forehead.

I shivered. It wasn't the cold. I'd never seen the man before in my life but I knew it was Stephen Farrell. Then a chilling thought struck me abruptly: his killer couldn't be far away. Whoever it was must have come by car. There was only one road in and I'd passed no vehicle or person on my way around the reservoir. That meant the car was still here, maybe hidden away up one of the forest tracks.

I backed away from the wall, my mind afflicted with a growing sense of terror, but alert enough still to realize that if Farrell's killer were going to shoot me too, he had already had more than enough opportunity. But in the dark, confronted by a corpse, I trusted my instincts more than my reason. And my guts said: run.

I headed back to the Rover and ducked down behind it, the reservoir immediately below me. I recovered my breath, watching the plantation and praying to God I didn't see anyone move.

Then the moonlight caught the bonnet of the car. On the polished metallic surface I saw the imprint of my palm where I'd tested the temperature. And my fingerprints would be on the door handle on the other side. Leaving either behind on a dead man's car would not be sensible.

I pulled my handkerchief out and slowly leaned across the bonnet to wipe off the palm print. Then I crouched low and scuttled round to the driver's door. I wiped it clean and sprinted for my own car, expecting any second the crack of a gun or a looming figure on the track in front of me. But I made it in one piece. Breathless, quivering, but untouched.

I started the ignition and put my foot down, one eye

on my rear-view mirror, the other on the road ahead. I was in the city centre, five miles away, before my body stopped shaking.

Harry was asleep on the living room floor. I crept in quietly and poured myself a brandy in the kitchen. The glass trembled in my hand. I took a gulp and started coughing.

'Mike, that you?'

I went through the door. 'Sorry. Did I wake you?'

Harry sat up on the cushions and took in the brandy, the expression on my face. 'You all right?'

I nodded. My legs felt wobbly. I stumbled over to an armchair and collapsed into it. I took another gulp of brandy. It seared going down, but the afterglow relaxed me a bit.

'What happened?' Harry said. He crawled out from his blankets and sat in the other chair in his vest and long johns.

I told him. Sipping the brandy more slowly now, soothing my nerves. Harry's eyes were wide open, appalled and fascinated at the same time.

'Blimey, and 'e were just there, against the wall?' I nodded. 'No wonder you're all shook up. You see who did it?'

'No, but they had to be somewhere nearby. They cut it pretty fine. Farrell had only just arrived. I was due any minute. They shot him and then disappeared before I got there. I'd guess into the plantation by the road, but I wasn't going to go looking for them.'

'Who was 'e, the dead bloke?'

'A doctor.'

'Funny place to meet, funny time too.'

'He was scared. I think he had some information for me. And someone else didn't want him passing it on.'

Harry frowned. 'But 'e only called an hour ago. 'Ow did anyone else know 'e was meeting you there?'

'That,' I said, 'is what I've been asking myself all the way home.'

146

I'd asked myself a few other questions too. Running over everything I'd found out since the murder of Rob Fielding, searching my brain for a fact, or a guess, which might possibly be the solution to this whole messy business. And I'd come to a conclusion. It wasn't the answer, but at least it was the next step in the process of discovering more.

'I need your help, Harry,' I said.

'Oh no, you're not getting me involved in this. You've done it to me before and I've learnt my lesson.'

'Just listen.'

I explained to him what I intended to do. And the role he would play. He wasn't having any of it.

'You're out of your mind. We'll get caught for certain.'

'Not if we do it properly. That's why I need you. There's no one else I know with your skills. You're the best, Harry.'

Flattery wasn't going to work either.

'It's too risky. Call the police, Mike. 'And it all over to them.'

'You think I've no pride? No professional integrity? I'm not giving anything to the plods.' I softened my voice. 'You've always been someone I knew I could turn to in times of trouble. Just like you knew you could come to me when you needed somewhere to stay.'

'Oh hell,' Harry said. 'Don't do this to me.'

'We won't have any problems. It's a piece of cake. Someone died tonight. I've got to find out why. I'm appealing to you, Harry. Just this once.'

He sighed resignedly. 'You're a shit, you know that.'

'Thanks, you're a pal.'

'Have I said I'll do it?'

I stood up and patted him on the shoulder. 'Get dressed while I make a phone call.'

Eddie Greaves was well and truly pissed off that I'd woken him up.

'You any idea what time it is?' he said.

'I'm sorry. But this is important.'

'What the hell do you want?'

'I need to know how you got into the CPL factory that night.'

'You're ringing me about that? Look, what I said the –'

I didn't let him finish. 'It'll go no further.'

'Sod off, McLean.'

'Hang up and I'll be round hammering on your door,' I said quickly. 'Don't mess me about, Eddie. I don't work for the police. I'm trying to find out why Rob Fielding was killed. This is part of it. He was a friend of yours. Do it for him.'

'Listen, McLean –'

'No, you listen. I know I'm a capitalist lackey, a tool of the Establishment. But I'm doing something here that matters. To you as well as to me. You might think you can change nothing but don't deny others the chance to try. Two people have been murdered and that factory is connected to both. I want to know why, so just shut your mouth and tell me how you got into the compound.'

There was silence at the other end. I thought maybe I'd overplayed my hand.

'*Two* people?' he said.

'A doctor named Farrell was shot tonight,' I said. 'Ever heard of him? He was the CPL company doctor.'

'No.'

'Tell me, Eddie.'

'You going in?'

'I don't think you want to know. How did you do it?'

I'd convinced him. 'There's a patch of woodland near one end of the site,' he said after a pause.

'I know it.'

'The trees come up almost to the perimeter fence. There's a clearing, maybe four, five yards wide between the two. Inside the wood, hidden by the undergrowth, there's an old culvert. There's a grid over the end of it and it's bricked up inside. Or rather it looks bricked up. Rob had already chipped away the mortar before we went in. Enough to remove a few of the bricks to leave a hole we could crawl through.'

'Where does it come out?'

'Near the huts, the laboratories. You come up through a manhole cover.'

'And you're sure no one knows about it?'

'We didn't tell them. Maybe they went looking and found it, who knows? You'll just have to take that chance.'

I thanked him and put down the receiver. It wasn't the only chance I was taking. There were probably a dozen others. But I didn't like to think about them.

Harry said: 'We going to search the whole bloody wood for this thing?'

'We've only been here five minutes,' I said. 'Look along there. It'll be well hidden.'

'Me feet are freezing,' he grumbled. 'I knew this were a crackpot idea. I should 'ave me 'ead examined, letting you persuade me.'

I let him chunter away to himself while I hunted through the dense undergrowth for the entrance to the culvert. There was a bigger area to search than I'd anticipated, and the forest was pitch black. The moon was obscured by thick cloud, the canopy of branches overhead cutting out what little other light there was.

We were at the bottom of a steep earth bank which flanked one side of the wood. At the top of the slope, and beyond the cleared strip of land, was the high metal fence surrounding the CPL Agro-Chemicals site. We'd kept well away from it.

'Psst!'

I looked up to see Harry waving at me from further along the bank. I pushed my way through the bushes to join him.

'This it?'

He was shining his torch down at a metal grid set vertically across the opening of a wide concrete pipe. It was well concealed by a couple of young rhododendrons

149

which I pushed aside to get a better view. I used my own torch to probe the inside of the pipe. About four feet in it had been bricked up.

'Looks like it,' I said. 'Let's get the grid off.'

The circle of thick wire mesh appeared to be bolted to the concrete rim. But when I examined it more closely I discovered it had been carefully cut along one edge and bent back into place. I stuck my fingers through it and pulled it out far enough for me to crawl into the mouth of the pipe.

' 'Ow are we going to get through that brick wall?' Harry asked.

I studied the lines of mortar in the beam of my torch. Rob Fielding had been very careful. He'd chipped away the cement around the bricks in the centre of the wall so that a whole section could be removed in one piece. Presumably, as he hadn't been caught with Eddie Greaves and the others, he had also come back out this way and replaced the bricks behind him.

I pushed hard on one side of the loose section. The bricks moved backwards an inch or so, pivoting on the central axis so the bricks on the other side edged out towards me. I did it again until it had revolved enough for me to get a grip on both edges. I strained and heaved the whole section out. Beyond the wall the pipe stretched deep into the bank, apparently without end.

'I don't like the look of that,' Harry said with feeling. 'You expect me to crawl along it?'

'It can't be far to the manhole,' I said.

'There could be 'owt in there. It's an old drain, innit? What if there's rats? I could catch myxomatosis.'

'That's rabbits, not rats.'

'Well, there might be rabbits 'n' all.'

'I'll go first and flush them out,' I said.

I pulled my balaclava down over my face. Harry had one too. We'd picked it up along with various tools when we'd called in at his locksmith's shop on the way over. He adjusted it so only his eyes and cheeks were showing.

'We look like the bleedin' SAS,' he said.

He ducked down into the pipe behind me and we started to crawl along it on all fours. It was hard going. The concrete hurt the knees and the roof was so low we had to keep our heads bowed, our eyes fixed on the floor. As we progressed, the sides seemed to close in on us, making the tunnel even narrower.

'I don't like this,' Harry said.

'You get claustrophobia?'

'Not until now.'

Something scuttled along the pipe in front of us. In the confined space the noise was amplified. I shuddered at the thought of what creatures might be lurking down there.

'I told you there'd be rats,' Harry muttered.

'They'll keep well away from us.'

'You 'ope.'

We crawled a few more yards. I tried to forget we were in a pipe barely three feet in diameter. My eyes stayed locked on the tiny patch of concrete immediately below me. I knew if I looked up and down the tunnel there was a risk of a sudden panic attack.

We'd covered something like fifty yards when the pipe opened out suddenly into a small brick chamber. I looked up, directing the beam of my torch at the roof. There was another pipe leading upwards. A broader pipe with rusty iron rungs set in the concrete walls. At the top, perhaps twenty feet above us, was the underside of a manhole cover.

'This is it,' I said.

'Thank God for that. Me knees are killing me.'

We stood up and stretched our backs.

'You stay down here,' I said. 'I'll just check it out.'

I started to climb towards the surface, hoping the manhole cover still opened. The culvert obviously hadn't been discovered or it would have been sealed up again. There was no reason to believe the manhole would have been tampered with either.

I reached the top and pushed upwards on the steel

cover. It moved fractionally. I opened up a narrow crack along one rim and peered through it. My eyes took a moment to adjust to the outside light. There was a wide expanse of tarmac around the cover and, beyond that, a low one-storey hut with a corrugated iron roof and windows all along the side. It looked like a leftover from the war.

I checked the other direction. There were no buildings there, just what appeared to be an access road and then the perimeter fence. From the way I could make out the details so clearly, I knew there must be floodlights some-where out of sight above me.

I flashed my torch down at Harry. 'Come on up.'

He joined me at the top of the ladder, clinging to the rungs just below my feet.

'I'll go out first,' I said. 'Then you. No hanging about.'

'You don't need to tell me that,' Harry said. 'The sooner we're out of 'ere the better.'

I lifted the manhole cover and pushed it to one side. It scraped along the surface but the noise would hardly have been discernible more than a few feet away. I poked my head out and did a quick three-hundred-and-sixty-degree check. There was no one around. I pulled myself out swiftly and leaned back in to give Harry a hand. He clam-bered out and together we slid the manhole cover back into place. Then we ran to the hut and took cover in the shadows. We waited, listening.

'What now?' Harry whispered.

I looked in through the nearest window of the hut, pressing my face to the glass. I could see benches, labora-tory equipment and, in the dark at one end, what looked like cages.

'Let's take a look inside here.'

We moved to the door and Harry examined it cau-tiously. 'No alarm.' He took out a small tool kit, selected a thin metal probe and went to work on the lock. Half a minute or so later we were inside.

'Lock it behind us,' I said, already moving down the

laboratory. I didn't use my torch. There were various pieces of chemical apparatus on the benches: glass jars, retorts, complicated arrangements of tubes and flasks, like a school chemistry lab only more sophisticated. I examined the bottles of chemicals on a shelf. I recognized ammonia and sulphuric acid but the other labels were just meaningless compounds and formulae to me.

Harry came up beside me. 'What we looking for?'

'Anything that seems suspicious.'

'And 'ow will we know what's suspicious?'

'Trust me, Harry. We'll know it when we see it.'

'What *is* this place anyway?'

'Some kind of research lab.'

'It stinks, you noticed?'

'Yes.'

There was a peculiar odour of chemicals, none of them readily identifiable, but mixed with other smells that were distinctly animal. We walked to the far end of the hut and what I saw there turned my stomach.

In rows of metal cages, stacked four high against the wall, was a collection of animals. Rats, mice, guinea pigs and rabbits. At least, that's what they had been originally. Now they were all so deformed it was only just possible to identify their species. Rats with no hind legs, dragging themselves painfully around their cages; rabbits with huge growths on their backs and skulls. Open wounds, tumours, stumps of limbs, horrific mutations, patches of shaved skin where chemicals had been applied, burning and blistering the tissues.

'Jesus Christ,' Harry said.

'Let's get out of here,' I said. 'Before I puke up.'

There was another door at this end of the lab. Harry unlocked it and we stepped outside, gulping in the fresh air. My skin felt clammy, the sensation of nausea diminishing only gradually.

'Who'd do that to an animal?' Harry said angrily. 'What kind of bastards would do that? You see them rabbits?

153

Poor little buggers. Let's go, Mike. I've 'ad enough of this place. Gives me the creeps.'

I nodded. I wasn't sure I wanted to see any more. I started to say something, but stopped. I could hear the sound of an engine approaching. Harry had heard it too.

'Back inside,' I said.

We slipped back into the lab and closed the door. 'Lock it,' I said to Harry.

I went to the window and took a peek out. A small white van was coming down the road which ran through the centre of the group of huts. It was moving slowly. I could see two men in the front. The one in the passenger seat had a torch which he was holding out of his window, playing it across the sides of the buildings. I prayed this was just a routine patrol. I ducked back and leaned on the wall with Harry, holding my breath, listening to the sound of the van engine. It went right past the lab and faded away into the distance.

Harry moved towards the other end of the room. I caught his arm.

'Where're you going?'

'Back to the other door, then down into the drain double-quick.'

'Not yet. I want a look round outside.'

'*What*? Don't be stupid, Mike. That were the security guards, weren't it? Let's get out while we can.'

'It won't take long. Unlock this door again.' He opened his mouth to speak, but I beat him to it. 'The longer we spend arguing, the longer we have to stay here.'

Harry shook his head. 'If we get caught . . .' But he bent down and unlocked the door.

'Stick close to me,' I said when we were outside.

'Like shit on a sheep's arse,' Harry replied.

I checked in all directions and ran across to the next hut. There were floodlights on high gantries at intervals around the whole site, but by hugging the walls of the buildings they could be avoided. I looked in through the windows. It looked like another laboratory. We got to

154

the other end where, adjoining the lab, there was an open-sided storage shed. Inside, stacked on wooden pallets, were drums of chemicals with serial numbers and the words, 'Danger, hazardous materials,' printed on their sides. There was no indication as to what exactly they contained.

We went on past the shed and stopped. To our left, across another access road, was a high fence. Not the perimeter fence for we were barely in the middle of the site and there were more buildings beyond it, one or two of them lit up. I was intrigued. There appeared to be a compound within the compound.

We crossed the road and I knelt down, pulling the ruck-sack off my back to get out the bolt cutters.

Harry said in alarm: 'What're you doing? You're not planning on going through, are you?'

'Why not?'

'Because it's wired, you cretin. Can't you see?' He indicated a thin filament running horizontally through the wire mesh about eighteen inches off the ground. 'Touch it and we're done for.' His voice changed. 'We might even be done for already.'

He tugged at my sleeve. I looked at him. His eyes were staring over my shoulder at something beyond the fence. I turned to look but he was dragging me away.

'Now,' he whispered urgently. 'Just do as I say. Back off.'

He ran in a crouch to the cover of the nearest hut and pulled me behind the wall.

'Harry, what's . . . ?'

'Shut it,' he hissed.

He had one eye cocked around the corner. He withdrew it. 'Take a look. Along the fence. You see a light moving?'

I swapped places with him and scanned the line of the fence. There was a light all right, getting gradually nearer. A torch. I could make out the dark shape of a man behind it. He drew level with us and I saw he was wearing the uniform of a security guard. But there was something odd about him.

I watched him pass and I knew what it was. His walk, his posture, even his short back and sides. He didn't look like a security guard, he looked like a soldier. The light from his torch glanced off his belt and what I saw only confirmed that impression: in a canvas holder on the right side he was carrying a handgun.

Harry had seen it too. 'I think it's time to go,' he said.

'My thoughts exactly.'

We retreated along the side of the hut and paused at the end. I checked to make sure the coast was clear and froze. On the wall of the hut opposite, pointing straight at us, was an infrared camera.

'Oh, shit,' I said. 'What do we do now?'

'We get the fuck out,' Harry said, taking off at a run before he'd even finished the sentence.

I sprinted after him. I could hear a bell ringing faintly somewhere far off. Someone had acted quickly. We crossed a gap between huts and, looking to my right, I saw two pairs of headlights coming down the perimeter road from the main manufacturing part of the site.

'The last hut, Harry,' I said breathlessly. 'We have to get inside it. It's our only chance.'

He nodded, pulling out his tool kit as he ran. We'd come in further than I thought. It was probably eighty yards to the laboratory where we'd started. Eighty yards on foot with two vanloads of security men less than two hundred yards away. And closing. The engine noise was now all around us, bouncing off the walls of the buildings so it was impossible to tell exactly which direction it was coming from.

We kept close to the wall, the hut between us and the approaching vehicles. If the vans had split up we were doomed. Our only hope was that they were both still on the perimeter road. The end of the laboratory appeared suddenly before us. We raced recklessly across the intervening space, not bothering to check if it was clear.

156

There was no time for precautions now. It was all or nothing.

Harry fell to his knees and picked at the lock. The engine noise pounded in my ears. The vans were nearly on us.

'Move it, Harry,' I said desperately.

His mouth was clenched, his eyes concentrating on the lock. I risked a look around the corner and down the side of the hut. One of the vans skidded to a halt at the far end while the second came on towards me. I pulled back and in two strides I was next to Harry again. The last tumbler clicked and he whipped the door open. We dived through and swung the door shut. Without prompting, Harry locked it behind us.

We waited in the darkness, trying to muffle the sound of our breathing. The second van had stopped outside. There were voices, then footsteps. Someone rattled the door handle. I looked at Harry and pointed to the floor. Very quietly, we dropped to our bellies and slithered underneath one of the benches under the window.

A torch probed the interior of the lab through the glass, flashing over the apparatus, the cages of animals. We lay very still, watching the beam moving around the room. Only when it had gone and we'd listened to the footsteps receding outside did we dare move.

Staying on our knees under the benches, we moved down the length of the laboratory. At the other end I peeped out over the windowsill. The first van was still parked nearby, but I could see no sign of the occupants. We had to move immediately.

'Get the door open,' I said softly.

'You sure?'

'They don't know exactly where we are. They're searching the whole area. That gives us a minute or two's reprieve. No more. We have to go now.'

Harry didn't argue. He worked on the lock and I heard a dull click as it popped back. I pulled the door open an inch and looked out. The two security guards were further down the perimeter road, checking the doors to the other huts. They weren't looking my way. I readied myself for the sprint to the drain. And stiffened.

The manhole cover was nowhere to be seen.

I closed the door gently and leaned back on the wall of the lab, my pulse drumming inside my head.

'What's up?' Harry said.

'The manhole cover. The van's parked right over it.'

'Shit! Can we get to it?'

'I'm going to try.'

'Let's 'ang on. Until they go.'

I shook my head. 'If they don't find us outside, they'll search every hut on the site until they do. I'll flash my torch when I'm down the drain.'

I opened the door again and surveyed the area. The two guards had disappeared, I had no idea where. I hesitated. It could be seconds before they reappeared, or minutes. There was no point in wondering which. I went for it. Dashed the fifteen yards to the side of the van and slithered underneath it.

I lay on my stomach, the van's exhaust pipe almost touching the back of my head, and peered out. I hadn't been spotted. The manhole cover was, quite literally, in front of my nose. There were two ring handles set flush with the surface. I hooked my fingers around them and tugged upwards. The cover moved, but only slightly. It was heavy and, in my prone position, it was very hard to get enough leverage to lift it out. I tried again, the muscles across my shoulders and back knotting under the strain. The cover lifted clear of the ground and I managed to slide it a few inches to one side.

I took a momentary break to recover before I pushed it out of the way to expose the drainpipe below. I made another quick survey. The guards were still out of sight.

Getting into the hole was tricky. I didn't fancy going in head first so I spun round and manoeuvred my legs in. I let them drop until my feet found the iron ladder inside, then I lowered the rest of me through. There was just enough headroom, though my hair got smeared with oil.

I looked back at the hut, only my head visible above the ground. Harry was watching me. I flashed my torch at him. He didn't hang about. A quick look in all directions and he was off. He rolled under the van and we both held our breath, waiting for a response. None came.

''Ow do I get down?' Harry whispered.

'Legs first. Turn around.'

He twisted his body in a half-circle. I caught his ankles and guided his feet into the pipe.

Halfway through, while Harry's torso and head were still above ground, the security guards came back to the van. I heard their boots first, voices next. I looked over my shoulder and saw two pairs of legs approaching. Harry was rigid with fear, his face pressed to the tarmac, his legs dangling down into the drain beside me.

The two guards walked to either side of the van and opened the doors. I tugged at Harry's jacket. He resisted at first, then suddenly relaxed as I tugged harder. I pulled him down into the pipe and we both clung to the top rung of the ladder. We could hear the guards above us talking on the radio to their control. Harry pointed frantically at the manhole cover. I shook my head and put a finger to my lips. They'd hear the noise for certain.

I waited for the right moment, resisting the urge to simply drop down into the culvert and back along it to the woods. If they found the open manhole, they could cut us off by road in minutes. We had to time it just right. I knew Harry was staring at me, imploring me silently to get out of there. I held up a finger. Then it came.

The van's engine started, practically deafening us. I nodded at Harry. We reached out with a hand each, the other hanging on to the ladder, and dragged the manhole cover back towards us. The van pulled away above. I prayed the guards weren't looking in their wing mirrors. The cover scraped noisily across the edge of the hole. We ducked down and it clanged into place over our heads.

Harry wasted no time in clambering down the ladder and scuttling back along the culvert. I didn't bother to replace the brick wall or grid over the end. It didn't matter if anyone found them. We weren't going back in there again. No way.

We were in the car, heading home through Mexborough, when Harry finally turned his head from its slumped position on the back of his seat and looked at me.

'Told you it'd be a piece of cake,' I said.

# 11

We slept in late and had breakfast around noon. Then Harry went out to open his shop and I made a fresh pot of coffee and rang Gordon Crieff.

The murder of Stephen Farrell was the first thing he mentioned. He gave me the few details they were releasing to the press. The circumstances of the death, the victim's age, occupation and address – a cul-de-sac off Redmires Road, which explained why he'd chosen to meet me at the reservoirs. No leads so far, Crieff said. I wasn't surprised. And Rob Fielding's murder? I asked. Same answer. Someone wasn't trying very hard. I hung up and called Chris Strange.

'The doctor who was shot last night at Redmires,' I said. 'You got the ballistics report yet?'

Strange was his usual cooperative self. 'If we had, you'd be the last person I'd tell. Now piss off.'

'Well, when you do get it,' I continued, undeterred, 'check the details against the Fielding case. Maybe it was the same gun.'

'What? Now, just a minute –'

I put down the phone before he could finish. Feed them the bait a bit at a time. It was the only way to make them bite.

Martin Furness was next in line for a call. We'd trained together on the *Evening News* years ago and kept in touch, though our career paths had long since diverged. He'd gone to London and made a name for himself on the City desk of one of the upmarket Sundays. While I . . . well, I didn't like to think about that too much. He was an assistant editor on one of the national dailies now. But I never let titles intimidate me.

'Would you do something for me, Martin?' I said.

'Sure, anything.'

'You still got good contacts in the City?'

'I assume that's a rhetorical question.'

'I want a check on a company. CPL Agro-Chemicals. Ever heard of them?'

'No. What do you want to know?'

'Anything you can get. Who owns it, what they manufacture, whether they do any defence work.'

'Defence work? An agro-chemicals company?'

'Just a long shot.'

'I'll see what I can do. It might take me a while, I'm pretty busy at the moment.'

'Really? What exactly does an assistant editor do?' I asked.

'Oh, you know. Oversees the smooth and efficient running of the editorial operation, liaises with management and the general public, that kind of thing.'

'In other words, bugger all.'

'Got it in one. I'll call you back later.'

There was a thread here. Thin and fragile, it was true, but clear enough to see. It was broken in places, its beginning and end obscured, yet I was starting to feel it was almost tangible enough to grasp.

A couple of Special Branch officers snooping around, an inquest held in camera for national security reasons and now a fertilizer plant with a compound inside guarded by what appeared to be armed soldiers. They were all linked, that much was obvious to me. But it was the missing links that counted. And they were not going to be easy to find.

I took a shower to consider my next move. Then the phone rang and the decision was made for me. It was Cathy Fielding.

162

'I think I know where Rob went that weekend just before he died.'

'I'm on my way,' I said.

She looked terrible when she answered the door. There were purple shadows around her eyes, an unhealthy, and for her unusual, pallor to the skin and her shoulders were sagging underneath her hand-knitted pullover as if she lacked the energy to stand up straight.

'Are you all right?' I said.

'Yes. I'm not sleeping too well, that's all. It's Jenny, not me. She's up half the night, then all day too.'

She led me down the hall to the kitchen. On the way, I glanced into the sitting room. Jenny was on the floor playing listlessly with a doll's house. She didn't look up as we passed.

'I don't think it's grief,' Cathy said. 'She's too young. But she's aware I'm upset and that's disturbing for her.'

She picked an envelope up off the table and handed it to me.

'Rob's Visa statement. It arrived this morning.'

I pulled out the sheet of paper and ran my eyes down it. Even after death our debts come back to haunt us.

Cathy put her finger on one of the entries. 'That one there. The dates match.'

'September 6th, the Clarendon Hotel, Idmiston. Ninety-six pounds,' I read.

'That was the weekend he went away without saying where he was going.'

'Idmiston,' I said. 'Do you know where that is?'

Cathy shook her head. 'I've never heard of it.'

I went back down the hall and telephoned Directory Inquiries. I asked for the number for the Clarendon Hotel, Idmiston, and wrote it down on a notepad. I asked where it was.

'Wiltshire,' I said, putting the phone down. 'Why would Rob go to Wiltshire and not want to tell you?'

'I don't know.'

'Do you have relatives or friends down there?'

'No one.'

'Did he ever mention Wiltshire? Did he go there at any other time?'

'Not to my knowledge.'

I handed her back the credit card statement. 'Do any other entries strike you as odd?'

'I've already looked. No. Only that one. That's why I called you.'

I tore off the note with the hotel number on it and put it in my wallet. 'I'll give them a call later. See if they remember him.'

'Why not now? Go ahead. Don't worry about the cost.'

'No, I'll do it later.' It wasn't the cost that concerned me but something else. Something I didn't want to do in front of Cathy.

I opened the front door and turned to go. Cathy touched me on the arm. She seemed about to speak, but the ring of the telephone interrupted her.

'I'll let you know how I get on,' I said.

She nodded and picked up the phone, listening, then frowning.

'A sample? My husband? I'm sorry, I don't know what you're talking about. What sample?'

I stepped in quickly, taking the receiver out of her hand.

'Perhaps I could help,' I said.

'Is that Mr Fielding?' a man's voice said. 'This is Sygma Laboratories. The sample you sent us, we've finished the analysis. The report's ready for collection, or would you rather we posted it out?'

'I'll come and pick it up. Where are you again?'

He gave me the address. 'Ask for Dr Murray Johnson at reception. I'm the senior chemist.'

'I'll be there in about ten minutes,' I said. I replaced the phone.

Cathy gave me a funny look. 'What's going on? Is there something you're keeping from me?'

164

I shook my head.

'So what's this sample he was talking about?'

'I'm just going to find out.'

Sygma Laboratories occupied the top two floors of a modern three-storey building near the university. The ground floor, according to the sign just inside the main entrance, was taken up by a medical supplies company.

I went up the stairs into a brightly lit reception area and asked the young girl typing at a word processor behind the desk for Dr Murray Johnson. She picked up a phone and pressed a button. 'Your name, sir?' 'I've come for Mr Fielding's report,' I said. She spoke to someone briefly then smiled at me. 'He's just coming.'

Murray Johnson appeared through a set of double doors to my left. I'd expected someone who looked like a scientist, a boffin in a white coat with unruly hair, thick glasses and a selection of nervous twitches perhaps. But Johnson looked more like a merchant banker. Dark suit, pearl tie, a smooth, self-assured manner.

'Mr Fielding, how do you do?' He shook my hand firmly, moving aside almost immediately to usher me through the doors. I didn't put him right about the name.

We went down a corridor flanked on one side by offices and on the other by a series of high-tech laboratories which had internal windows opening out on to the corridor. Inside the labs I could see technicians working at consoles, computer screens flickering with data and lights glowing on complex-looking machines whose purpose I could only guess.

Murray Johnson opened a door and I followed him into an office overlooking the car park at the front of the building. He offered me a seat then sat down behind a gleaming oak desk.

'I'm sorry it's taken us longer than I said it would originally on the phone, but we've had a bit of a rush on this week. And when your sample arrived on Tuesday it sort of got lost in the pipeline.'

165

He took a Manila envelope from the top drawer of the desk and removed a sheet of paper from it.

'It wasn't too complicated. We carried out all the tests on it as you arranged.'

He turned the paper around so I could read the report.

'As you can see, the substance is dichlorethyl sulphide.' He paused and smiled apologetically. 'Our service is, of course, completely confidential, but given the nature of the sample, I wonder if you could tell me where you got it? It is rather unusual.'

'Dichlorethyl sulphide?' I said. 'I'm no chemist, I'm afraid. What is it?'

'Well, in layman's terms it's generally known as mustard gas. Although it was in liquid form in your sample. It has no connection with mustard, but that's how it's come to be known. From the smell.'

I stared at him. 'Mustard gas? You mean the stuff they used in the First World War?'

He nodded. 'A very unpleasant compound. That's why I'm curious to know how you came by it.'

I looked down and pretended to study the sheet of paper, wondering where Rob had found his sample. I didn't answer Johnson's question. Instead, I picked up the paper and folded it carefully before slipping it into my pocket. Johnson was watching me. Then his eyes flickered towards the window. I'd heard it too. Car engines, the screech of brakes.

I stood up and went to the window. Two police cars had pulled in across the entrance to the car park, blocking the way out. I counted three, four uniformed officers running towards the building. I had no doubts why they were there.

'Thank you for your help,' I said as calmly as I could. 'I'll show myself out.'

I left the office and automatically headed down the corridor away from the reception area. A sign at the far end said, 'Emergency Exit'. I pushed through the door and found myself on the back stairs. I ran down them two at

166

a time. I'd reached the ground floor when through a window in the stairwell I saw more police officers coming round to the back of the building.

I hesitated. My escape route was cut off. Yet going back was impossible. The police were nearly at the rear entrance now. There'd be more upstairs. I spun round, looking for another way out. There was a door at one side of the stairwell. I had no choice. I pulled it open and ran through.

I was in another long corridor lined with doors. I opened the first and stepped into a storeroom of some kind. There were shelves on every wall, stacked with boxes and jars and plastic containers. I examined the labels. They had to be medical supplies. On a peg on the back of the door was a soiled white coat, like a hospital doctor's. I put it on then scanned the shelves. I saw a box marked 'goggles' and pulled it down. I ripped off the lid and took out a pair of large Perspex goggles. I put them on hurriedly and went back out into the corridor. I had to move fast. Murray Johnson would tell the police where I'd gone and it wouldn't be long before they were down here checking all the rooms.

I opened the door to the rear stairwell and walked out. The back exit was open. I ran for it. And almost collided with Inspector Jack Carson who was on his way in with a uniformed constable. I lifted my hands to my face, pretending to adjust my goggles, shielding my features, but Carson wasn't interested in me. His eyes were fixed on the stairs.

'Get out of the way,' he snapped, hitting the bottom flight at a run, not looking back for even a second.

I ducked out through the exit and glanced around. No coppers visible. But there'd be plenty round at the front. That narrowed my options pretty much. I walked across the yard and climbed over the brick wall at the end. On the other side was an alley. I ran down it a short way, then vaulted over another wall into the delivery area at the back of the Children's Hospital. I dumped the white coat and goggles in a large dustbin and went through the rear entrance of the hospital.

I followed the signs to the main entrance, emerging on to Western Bank, then turned left back into the top end of Northumberland Road where I'd left my car. I sat in the driver's seat for a while and let my heartbeat get back to somewhere near normal. There are times when exercise is definitely bad for the health.

Maria's secretary, Muriel, looked me over with unconcealed distaste, her nose wrinkling as if she'd just detected a particularly unpleasant odour in the room. Odour, not smell. Muriel was far too genteel to use a word like smell.

I gave her a wave. 'Hi, Muriel, how're you doing?'

She declined to answer that so I sat down in the chair opposite her desk and made polite conversation.

'I'm not disturbing you, am I? You're looking well. Very trim. You still go to the tea dances at the City Hall?'

She continued to ignore me.

'What do you say I come with you one Saturday? Then we could go back to my place afterwards for some hot, sweaty group sex? Get the neighbours in, you know. Maybe a couple of sheep.'

She didn't rise. Just glared at me icily, her features set rigid underneath about three inches of foundation. Her dress was a profusion of orchids on a cream background, à la mode circa 1953, and her cologne reminded me of industrial-strength fly repellent. Not that any fly would have dared go near Muriel.

'Any chance of seeing Maria?' I asked.

'No.'

'Give me a straight answer, I can take it.'

'She's busy.'

'It won't take me a minute. I'll just go through, shall I?'

I made a move towards the inner office, but Muriel beat me to it. She stood there in front of the door, blocking my path. I checked out the set of her jaw, the biceps rippling beneath the ruched organza and decided to retreat.

'OK, when isn't she busy?' I said.

'Her diary is full for most of the day.'

'What, on a Saturday? I'll wait then.'

I sat back down in the chair and beamed at Muriel. 'Don't worry about me. Just pretend I'm not here.'

'I will.'

She lowered her head and started tapping away on an electronic typewriter. I looked around the room idly, calculating how long it would be before she cracked. We both knew I'd get in to see Maria eventually. It was just a point of honour with Muriel to delay me for as long as possible.

I'd been there ten minutes or so when the door to the inner office opened and Maria came out anyway. She was carrying a slim leather briefcase in one hand.

'I'll be back in about an hour,' she said to Muriel. Then she saw me. 'Michael! Have you been waiting long?'

'No, it just feels like it.'

Her lips moved at the corners. She glanced at Muriel, then back at me.

'I've got a meeting. Come with me to the car.'

We walked outside together.

I said: 'You should get a Rottweiler for a secretary. It'd be more welcoming.'

'You know you ask for it. Muriel gets overprotective the minute you walk through the door.'

'I do my best to be nice to her.'

'You do your best to annoy her. You should have called first. To let me know you were coming.'

'It wasn't planned. I wanted to ask a favour. Would you keep something for me in your safe?'

'What?'

I took out the Sygma Laboratories report and gave it to her. She unzipped her briefcase and slid the piece of paper inside without looking at it.

'You going to tell me what it is?'

169

'Tomorrow. We'll have more time then.'

She stopped by her car and opened the door.

'Will we?'

'I'll pick you up at ten.'

'Morning or evening?'

'Morning. You've got some walking boots, haven't you?'

'Where exactly are we going?'

'Hiking. Wrap up warm. Cagoule, gloves, hat. I'll bring the Kendal Mint Cake.'

Maria lowered herself into the driving seat of her Mazda MX5 and swung her legs round under the steering wheel. It really was a very short skirt she was wearing.

'I do have work to do tomorrow, you know.'

'It's Sunday,' I said. 'Which sounds more appealing, a long day in the office toiling over columns of figures, or a date with me?'

'That's a tough one. I'll give it some thought,' she said.

Accountants, you have to wonder about them.


The door to my flat was slightly ajar. I approached it cautiously, the back of my neck starting to tingle with trepidation. The lock had been smashed in. I could see the indentation in the surrounding woodwork where the sledgehammer or something similar had struck home. There were voices inside, the sounds of people moving around.

I pushed the door open and saw Chris Strange standing by my desk in the living room, leafing through papers. That was all I had time to register before a pair of hands grabbed me by the lapels of my jacket and hurled me up against the wall just inside the hall. A jolt of pain shot up my spine, blurring my vision. I blinked and saw Jack Carson's ugly face a few inches below mine.

'Welcome home, sunshine,' he said. He pulled me away from the wall, then slammed me back into it.

I grunted, my eyes closing involuntarily. I became aware of another voice, of other hands coming between Carson and me, dragging him off. I opened my eyes. Chris Strange was holding Carson at bay with a hand on his chest.

'That's enough . . . Sir,' he added with heavy irony.

'I'll break his bloody neck,' Carson spat out. 'Fucking journalists.'

'Back off.' Strange pushed him away hard.

'Don't fucking tell me what to do, Sergeant,' Carson said. 'Or I'll have you busted so fast you –'

'Back off, Jack,' said a third voice.

Detective Superintendent Ray Coltrane was watching from the door into the living room.

'Bring him in here.'

Strange took me by the arm and led me through.

'Sit down, McLean.'

I flopped down into an armchair and looked at the three of them in turn.

'This official?' I said. 'Or are we making up a foursome for bridge?'

Carson came for me again.

'Jack!' Coltrane said sharply.

Carson stopped a foot away from me, his fists and teeth clenched.

'Just a couple of minutes, Ray. Just give me a couple of minutes with him.'

'Leave it.'

Carson glared at me, getting his aggression under control, then he moved away and sat down on the edge of the desk. Coltrane eased himself into the other armchair. I took in the mess on the floor, the scattered papers, drawers removed, possessions tipped out on to the carpet.

'I assume you've got a search warrant,' I said.

Coltrane held it up. 'Watertight. We've got a few questions too. Like where were you an hour ago?'

'What business is that of yours?'

'You know it's an offence to impersonate someone else?'

'No, it's not. I can impersonate whoever I like. You,

Sergeant Strange. I could even impersonate an arsehole named Carson, but that role's already spoken for.'

Carson got up from the desk. 'Right, you shithead. I don't have to take that from you.'

'Sit down, Jack,' Coltrane said quietly. He turned back to me. 'To impersonate someone with a view to obtaining their property by deception. That's an offence.'

'You accusing me of it?'

'We have a description of someone remarkably like you who took away a report from Sygma Laboratories this afternoon by pretending to be one Rob Fielding, deceased. I'm sure Murray Johnson would be able to pick you out in an identity parade.'

'He'd also be able to tell you that I never said I *was* Rob Fielding. He just assumed I was because he'd spoken to me on the phone. Check your tap. You hear me say at any point that I was Rob Fielding?'

'Our tap?'

I rolled my eyes. '*Please*. Do you think I don't know?'

'You admit you took that report?'

'I was acting for Mrs Fielding. It was her husband's. It's hers now. But it's still none of your business.'

'Where is it?'

I looked around the room. 'You mean you didn't find it?'

Coltrane came forwards out of his chair. 'Don't piss us about, McLean. You're way out of your league here.'

'Well, you'd know all about that,' I said.

'Let's take him in,' Carson snarled. 'I'm sick of pansying around with this dick.'

'You got a charge,' I said, 'or do you not bother with things like that in the Branch?'

Coltrane ran his fingers over his chin. The flesh rippled along his jowls like pockmarked jelly. I almost expected to see an imprint when he took away his hand.

'How about section one of the Official Secrets Act, 1911?' he said.

'One of my favourites. Which bit? I'm paraphrasing

172

now: obtaining, collecting, communicating any secret, sketch, plan, note calculated or intended to be useful to an enemy? That bit?'

'It's a start.'

'Do me a favour, Coltrane. Finish your search, then get out. But don't make me laugh with these pathetic threats. You got any evidence for this? A one-sheet report on a chemical analysis of a toxic substance. No mention of where it came from. You think that's of use to an enemy? Take me in, ask me a few questions, but I guarantee that even the worst solicitor in this city will have me out in a couple of hours and you and your pal there will look even bigger jerks than you do now.'

Carson finally snapped. He lunged towards me, lashing out with a fist, his face contorted with anger. Coltrane made no move to stop him. Chris Strange did. He stepped between us in one smooth motion, catching Carson's arm in mid-air and twisting it up behind his back.

'I don't think that's wise, sir,' he said mildly.

'What the fuck . . . You get your . . . Jesus, he's got it coming, you know that.'

'Touch him again and it's in my report. Sir.'

'What do you care? He's got no witnesses.'

'He's got me.'

Carson twisted round and broke free. 'What?'

'I said he's got me,' Strange repeated. 'Now, are you taking him in, or are we going to spend the rest of the day tossing off here?'

Carson stuck his face to within an inch of Strange's nose. The veins were standing out on his forehead. His breathing was laboured, hissing through his teeth. Strange looked him in the eye, inviting him on. Coltrane took Carson's arm and dragged him away. He shot Strange a look of fierce animosity.

'We'll remember that, Sergeant,' he said. 'It's not what I call cooperation. Let's go, Jack.'

'Hey, you think I'm going to let this bastard . . .'

'*Let's go.*'

Coltrane paused at the door and pointed a finger at me. 'You're a marked man, McLean. Remember that.'

He pulled open the door and the two of them walked out.

I took a deep breath. 'Charming pair, aren't they?'

Strange settled himself in the armchair and crossed his hands over the swelling mound of his beer belly.

'Thanks, Chris.'

'I didn't do it for you. I did it for me,' he said, echoing his words in the pub a few nights earlier. 'Call me sentimental, but I still think this job deserves something better than that. I don't really care one way or the other if you get the shit beaten out of you, McLean. Might do you some good. But I'm not going to stand and watch it.'

'Thanks all the same. You not going with them?'

'They only brought me because I knew where you lived. They can find their own way back to Snig Hill.'

'You found out what they're doing up here yet?'

'I was hoping you were going to help me on that one.'

I shrugged. 'I'm pretty much in the dark too.'

Strange snorted. 'Don't bullshit me, McLean. Why do you think those two are out to get you? You know exactly what's going on. I think maybe it's time you shared it with someone else.'

'I want to know who killed Rob Fielding, that's all. You and your mates don't seem to be getting too far with it.'

'That's Ripley's case, not ours. What's this report Coltrane wants?'

'Rob Fielding sent a sample for chemical analysis before he died.'

'Sample of what?'

'Mustard gas.'

Strange's mouth dropped open a fraction. 'Where did he get that?'

'I don't know. But I think Coltrane and Carson do. And they want it kept quiet.'

174

'You got the report on you?'

'You know better than that, Chris. Did you check with ballistics?'

He pulled a face. 'You have a habit of changing subjects when anyone asks you questions. You know that?'

'So what did they say?'

'They weren't the same guns for a start. Different calibre, different markings on the slugs. No reason to connect the two. But you obviously did.'

I started to get up. 'I'd better tidy this place up. You blokes leave a hell of a mess.'

'Sit down, McLean. This time I want an answer.'

I sank back down into the chair. 'Just a guess, I suppose. Two murders in the space of a couple of days. Both shootings. That's out of the ordinary. I wondered if there might be a link. I was obviously wrong.'

'Bollocks.'

'That's the truth.'

'You don't know the meaning of the word.'

'You making much progress on the Farrell case?'

'Jesus, you're doing it again.' He eyed me narrowly, gnawing at the tip of his thumbnail. 'What's his connection with Fielding?'

'Does he have one?'

'I'm wasting my time, aren't I?'

'Yes,' I said.

Strange pulled himself to his feet. He was irritated, maybe angry.

'This will sound familiar, McLean, but I'll say it all the same. This time you'd better listen. You think Coltrane and Carson won't be back? You think they won't want another friendly chat somewhere private, when I'm not around to pull your balls out of the fire? Wise up. You've got my number. Give me a call when you feel like telling me what's going on. And make it soon.'

I nodded noncommittally. But he hadn't finished.

'You remember in the pub the other night,' he said.

175

'When I told you to watch your back? Well from now on I'd watch your front too.'

I was in the middle of cleaning up the flat when Martin Furness called me back.

'I haven't got much,' he said.

'Every little helps.'

'It's a pretty obscure company. No stock market listing. Small operation. One factory. Mexborough in South Yorkshire. I take it that's why you're interested in it.'

'Yes. You find out what they make?'

'Agricultural fertilizers, nitrates, sprays, pesticides. Nothing for the Ministry of Defence as far as anyone knows.'

'Ownership?'

'Tricky. It's a private company. I spoke to a couple of analysts, specialists in the chemical business. They didn't know offhand. You'd have to go to Companies House and check the records for that.'

'Any bad vibes about it?'

'No. It makes modest profits, seems to have a good reputation. Nothing spectacular. But no dirt either.'

'Thanks, Martin. I appreciate it.'

'Give me a call next time you're in London.'

'I will.'

I went into the kitchen to put the kettle on. The police had been in here too. The contents of all the cupboards were piled on the worktop. They'd been through every jar, every tin and packet. No one could say they weren't thorough. I started to put it all back where it belonged.

Harry's voice wafted through from the living room. 'Mike?'

'In here,' I shouted.

He came to the kitchen door and looked around.

'Blimey. What's 'appened? You 'ad burglars?'

'Police,' I said.

'Bloody vandals. The front door lock's all smashed in.'

'They didn't have a key.'

'Look at it. They can't get away with this, surely.'

'They just have. Give me a hand, will you?'

'I'll start in 'ere. Bastards! After I'd just cleaned the place 'n' all.'

I finished off in the kitchen, then made us mugs of tea and took them out into the living room. Harry had picked everything up off the floor and was holding a piece of paper in one hand. It was the drawing of a cow that Jenny had given me.

'Where does this go?'

'It was on the wall. Above the desk. It must've fallen off.'

He swivelled round to stick it back up, and as he did so the light from the window shone directly through the paper. I saw something on it I'd never noticed before.

'Harry, just a moment. Give it here.'

He handed me the drawing. I turned it over. On the back was some writing. A small, cramped hand, but easily legible. A row of numbers which looked like a telephone number and a name, Sarin. Something about the number was familiar. I took out the note I'd made at Cathy Fielding's house and checked the number of the Clarendon Hotel, Idmiston. They didn't match, but the area code was the same.

I dialled the number on the back of the drawing. I let it ring for some time. There was no reply.

I tried the Clarendon Hotel instead and got through. I told the manager I was Detective Sergeant Strange of the South Yorkshire police, investigating the death of Rob Fielding.

'I believe he stayed in your hotel the weekend of September 5th and 6th,' I said. 'Could you confirm that?'

He went to check the records and came back on the line.

'That's correct. Two nights.'

'Was he alone?'

'I'm afraid I don't remember. But he booked a single room so I have to assume he was on his own.'

That seemed to rule out the dirty weekend theory I'd had at the back of my mind. Obvious explanations first, then look for the alternatives.

'I don't suppose you know why he was in your area, do you? He didn't talk to you or any other member of the staff?'

'I'm sorry, I don't recall anything about his stay. He was just another guest. I could check with my colleagues and ring you back, if you would give me your number.'

'That's all right,' I said hastily. 'We'll be sending someone down in due course. Thank you for your cooperation.'

I put down the phone. Harry was watching me disapprovingly. He shook his head.

'Impersonating a police officer. You could land yourself in deep shit, Mike.'

'I'm up to my neck in it already,' I said.

# 12

Somehow, at the back of my mind, I'd known that Maria would turn out to be revoltingly fit. She was that kind of person.

We were halfway up Cave Dale and my body was urging me to lie down on the ground and die. Maria, on the other hand, was five yards in front of me, striding casually up the almost sheer incline as if she were out for a stroll on the prom at Blackpool. She paused to let me catch up. She was barely out of breath, not a trace of sweat on her serene features.

I stumbled to a halt just below her on the hill and wheezed a bit more air into my tortured lungs. I knew I looked a complete wreck, a walking – or rather staggering – metaphor for the terminal decline of modern man. I felt even worse. Maria smiled at me. She didn't even have the decency to gloat so that I wouldn't feel so bad about hating her.

'I'm enjoying this,' she said ambiguously, not making it clear whether she meant the walking, or watching me gasp along behind her.

'Me too,' I said. She wasn't going to see me crack.

'I don't get out here very often.'

'Once is more than enough for me.'

'Shall we go on?'

'Whenever you're ready.'

We continued on up the valley. The ground was rocky beneath our feet and running with so much water we were virtually picking our way through a stream. Around us the sides rose steeply, the lower slopes grass-covered, the higher surfaces bare outcrops of limestone. Behind us, on the top of the hill, was Peveril Castle, its ruined keep and the vestiges of the walls just visible beyond the interlocking spurs of the dale. I struggled to keep up with Maria, thinking: and people do this for *fun*?

A mile further on we passed through a gate and the ground began to level out. I found I could take in enough oxygen to talk and walk at the same time.

'Do you have to get back for anything later?'

'I've nothing planned,' Maria said. 'Are you intending to tell me where we're going, or is that a big surprise?'

'To the top here, then I want to go round and over to the back end of Dirtlow Rake.'

'What's that?'

'Some old lead mines. All disused now. It's a long time since I was there, but most of them are filled in or covered in iron grids, if I remember correctly.'

'They mined lead round here?'

I nodded. 'Dates back to the Romans. It was very valuable to them.'

'What for, plumbing?'

'Currency. Derbyshire lead ore contains silver. The Romans refined it to extract the silver for their mint.'

'And what's your interest in these mines?'

'I'm not sure. You know the factory I mentioned, CPL Agro-Chemicals at Mexborough?'

'The one Rob broke into?'

'Yes. Well, I followed a lorry from there two days ago. It came all the way across here and ended up turning off along a track at the bottom of Dirtlow Rake. I thought we could come over the back way and maybe figure out where it was going.'

'Just a lorry? Sounds pretty innocuous to me.'

'Does it? I don't know. There's something very peculiar about that factory. It's got a fenced-off compound in the middle of the site which is guarded by armed men.'

Maria stopped and turned her head to me. 'Armed?'

180

'Now what kind of fertilizer factory needs armed guards?'

'You sure?'

'Saw them with my own eyes the night before last.'

It took her only a moment to work out the implications of that.

'You broke in, didn't you?'

'I didn't break anything. Harry came with me. He used to be a burglar. He's pretty good with locks.'

'Harry?'

'You met him a few nights ago.'

'Ah, that one.'

'I've got no proof, but I'm certain Rob went into that inner compound the night he broke in with Eddie Greaves and the others. That's why he wasn't with them when they were caught.'

'Did you get into it?'

'Unfortunately no. We had a bit of a setback, had to run for it.'

She gave me a look. 'You have an exciting life, don't you?'

'That's only half of it.'

I told her about finding Stephen Farrell's body at Redmires Reservoirs and the incident at Sygma Laboratories.

'Wait a minute,' she said. 'This is too much to take in. What is going on, Michael? Someone else has been killed?'

'Farrell was the CPL company doctor who tried to save Jamie Hynes's life on the wasteland by the factory. He signed the death certificate. He knew what really killed Jamie and I think he was going to tell me, only he was dead when I got to the reservoirs. A bullet through the head, just like Rob.'

Maria winced. 'The same killer?'

'It was a different gun. It could have been the same person using another pistol, or someone else entirely.'

'I suppose they might not be connected.'

181

I shook my head. 'That's stretching credibility too far. They're connected all right.'

We'd reached the end of the footpath. In front of us was a five-barred gate with a high stile across the wall next to it. I went over first and jumped down on the other side. I held up a hand to help Maria down behind me. She took it in her own and held on after she'd reached the ground.

'Where now?' she asked.

'Left.'

We turned and followed a muddy track between two dry stone walls. I kept hold of Maria's hand. She didn't seem to mind.

'So what's dichlorethyl sulphide?' she said.

I grinned at her. 'You read that piece of paper I gave you.'

'You knew I would.'

'Is it in your safe?'

'I put it in as soon as I got back to the office.'

'It's mustard gas.'

'Mustard gas!' She pursed her lips, her brow furrowing. 'Really? And it was Rob's sample? From where?'

I didn't answer.

'That factory?' Maria ventured.

'I don't know. He went into the factory seven months ago. If he took it from there, why did he wait until now to have it analysed?'

'Maybe he went back in more recently.'

'That's always possible. I've been trying to piece together the facts. Rob was killed sometime in the early hours of Monday morning. Sygma Laboratories received the sample from him in the post on Tuesday. So when did Rob get hold of it, and when did he post it?'

'Presumably he posted it at the weekend,' Maria said. 'For it to have got there on Tuesday.'

'What if he posted it Monday?'

She stared at me. 'He was dead.'

'Before he died. It was all planned in advance, you see.

The chemist at the lab said he'd talked to Rob about the analysis on the telephone. The lab was expecting the sample. What if Rob got hold of it Sunday night, when he went out without telling Cathy what he was doing? And he had with him a small container and an envelope, already stamped? He put the sample in the container, popped it in the envelope and posted it just before he was killed.'

'That's hardly the most obvious explanation.'

'But it is. Sunday night is important. Why else did Rob go out at that time if it wasn't to find, or to collect, that sample? And if he did, he could only have posted it during Sunday night or early on Monday.'

'Unless someone else posted it for him.'

The muddy track we were on had now turned into an even muddier road. Unmetalled and churned up by tyres, but wide enough for a couple of lorries to pass. On one side was a huge mound of earth and rock with an excavation next to it. A bulldozer was pushing piles of soil up the sides of the mound. A truck came towards us along the road. We moved aside and watched it turn into the excavations.

'What're they doing here?' Maria asked.

'Looks like a quarry of some sort. Cement, minerals, I don't know.'

'The lorry you followed, maybe it was coming here. To be loaded up with raw materials.'

'It was the wrong sort of lorry. It wasn't an open-backed quarry truck. It was enclosed, high sides, like a delivery lorry.'

We walked on in silence for a quarter of a mile, then came to a sharp bend in the road. A narrower track led off it at this point, going uphill past another enormous spoil heap. A dilapidated sign by the junction read: 'Keep Out, Mine Workings.'

'Let's try this,' I said.

'You sure we should? What if it's dangerous?'

'Look at the track. Fresh tyre marks in the mud. It's well used.'

The track took us round the side of the spoil heap and down a gentle incline towards another quarry. It was only when we reached the edge of the excavations that we saw how massive they were. A hole some two hundred feet deep had been carved out of the hillside. The track branched into two here, one part continuing along the edge, the other winding down steeply into the bottom of the quarry where I could see a JCB and a couple of lorries waiting to be loaded with rock.

I bent down and examined one of the boulders scattered along the rim of the workings. It was rust-coloured, laced with veins of white and small clusters of glassy crystals.

'Fluorspar,' I said.

'What's that?'

'They use it as a flux for making steel. The old lead miners used to throw it away. It's probably worth more than the lead now, if you can get it out in big enough quantities.'

'They haven't exactly stinted themselves here. What an eyesore.'

I nodded. 'Another twenty years and half the mountain will have disappeared. What with this and the limestone quarry down the road. You see it?'

I pointed into the distance. Maria followed my finger. 'I can see a chimney.'

'That's the Hope cement works. There's a quarry behind it the size of a small town. And growing. Not exactly one of the natural beauties of the Peak District.'

We skirted round the hole in the ground, splashing through puddles of murky water the colour of tomato soup. At the far side the track seemed to peter out as it reached a high wire fence.

'We'll have to go back,' Maria said.

'Fences are there to be climbed,' I said. 'I'll give you a leg up.'

184

'Michael, I don't think we should. What if we're caught?'

'By whom? And so what if we are? What are they going to do to us? Just ask us to leave, that's all. Come on.'

I cupped my hands in front of me. Maria hesitated, then lifted her right foot. I gripped it and launched her upwards. Her hands found the top of the fence. She pulled herself up and swung one leg over athletically. Her body followed and she hung from the full length of her arms before dropping down on the other side. I scrambled over after her.

'Dead easy, see.'

The terrain was more undulating now. Small hillocks broken up by clefts in the earth and stark outcrops of rock. We passed a tiny fenced enclosure, about a quarter of the size of a boxing ring. On the ground inside, set in concrete, was what looked like a heavy steel cattle grid. I leaned over the fence and peered down through the grid into a narrow shaft.

'One of the old lead mines,' I said.

Maria took a look. 'It's so narrow. They used to climb down there?'

'On wooden ladders. With only candlelight to work by. Then they'd haul the ore up behind them in wicker baskets.'

She pulled a face. 'A grim existence.'

'Daniel Defoe came here in the eighteenth century. He said the miners looked like corpses. Skeleton-thin, their skin the same hue as the lead they dug.'

'Are these holes all over this area?'

'Pretty much. Though a lot of them have been sealed off completely. There're horizontal shafts deep underground too.'

We descended a little way down the hillside. There was no footpath so we stuck to the easier ground, avoiding the treacherous slopes of the old spoil tips where we could have snapped an ankle in one of the numerous fissures between boulders. A hare popped up from a tuft of grass in front of us and bounded away out of sight behind a patch of thick gorse.

We passed another fenced-off mine shaft, then dipped down and around the side of a low hummock. I stopped and caught hold of Maria's arm quickly. I pulled her back a couple of feet. She turned towards me, her mouth opening to speak. I touched a finger to her lips. She heard it too. Voices.

'Stay here,' I whispered in her ear.

I dropped to a crouch and clambered carefully up the side of the hummock. Nearing the top, I lowered myself on to my belly and slithered the last few feet. There was a slight rustle behind me. Maria came up and lay down next to me. I frowned at her.

'I'm not going to be left out,' she said softly.

I didn't argue. I pulled myself to the brow of the hummock and looked over. I sensed her following.

Below us, maybe fifty yards away, was a shallow ravine enclosed on three sides by walls of smooth, unbroken rock. At the deepest point was a wooden building with a shiny metal roof and no windows. A wide sloping track led down to it from the fourth side of the ravine. Through an open doorway on the front of the building I could see a lift cage.

Three men were walking up the track towards a Land Rover parked at the top. They were talking to each other, but the words didn't carry well enough to be comprehensible. By then, in any case, I wasn't listening to their voices. My whole attention was fixed on their faces. The third man I didn't recognize, but the other two were Russell Stamford and his sidekick, Vince.

They stopped by the Land Rover. Stamford and Vince got into it and drove away down the hill. The third man returned to the building in the bottom of the ravine. I slid back down the hummock and brushed the dirt off my clothes. Maria joined me.

'Was that a lift I saw inside the hut?' she said.

'Looked like it to me.'

186

'I thought you said the mines were all disused now.'

'That's what I thought. Maybe one's still operational. Although there can't be much lead left down there of any real value.'

'They could be mining something else. What about fluorspar?'

'No way. You saw the quarry back there. They just blast holes in the ground to get fluorspar out.' I took her hand again. 'I think we should leave.'

The high perimeter fence we'd climbed over encircled the whole of the area. A short distance down the hill we encountered it again. We didn't scale it immediately, but tracked along beside it until we reached a couple of metal gates across the access road. The Land Rover must have passed through them. They were fastened shut with a heavy chain and padlock.

'They certainly don't want anyone straying in here by accident,' I said.

I helped Maria over again before climbing up myself. The track on the other side ran all the way down to the main road near the top of Pin Dale.

'This is the track the lorry came up,' I said. 'No question about it.'

'I still don't find that odd,' Maria said. 'It was simply delivering something from the factory.'

'I don't think it's that simple. I didn't think so before. I think it even less now I've seen those men.'

'What's so special about them?'

'One of them was Russell Stamford.'

Maria came to an abrupt halt, pulling me up next to her.

'Stamford?'

'Makes a difference, doesn't it? Rob was checking him out. He was checking out the CPL factory as well. Now there's a definite link between the two. Still think the lorry isn't relevant?'

She didn't reply. We walked down Pin Dale and were

on the main road into Castleton before she said: 'Mustard gas. Is that what killed the little boy?'

'No. He died too quickly for it to have been mustard. It burns severely, blinds, destroys the membranes of the lungs, but it doesn't always kill. Certainly not in the space of the ten or fifteen minutes it took Jamie Hynes to die.'

'Even in large quantities?'

'I doubt it. Think of those pictures of the First World War. The gassed soldiers. Lines of them holding the shoulder of the man in front, unable to see. Coughing up mucus, burns on their skin. They were crippled for life but many of them lived for years afterwards.'

'But Rob's sample. What if he went into the factory Sunday night and got it there?'

'If he did, why was his body found at the bottom of Winnats Pass, thirty-odd miles away?'

We entered the outskirts of Castleton, the tiny cottages lining the edge of the road, curtains drawn to keep out prying eyes. Then through the village square and past the youth hostel to the pub.

'Lunch is on me,' I said.

We had a ploughman's each, and a couple of halves of bitter. I pulled off my walking boots and stretched my legs in front of the log fire. My feet felt as if they'd been massaged by a navvy with a piledriver.

Maria had removed her cagoule and the thick jumper underneath. The sleeves of her tartan shirt were rolled up beyond her wrists and her cheeks were flushed pink. It was pretty hard keeping my eyes off her.

'Feels good, doesn't it?' she said, smiling at me. 'Fresh air and exercise followed by food and a warm fire.'

'Personally, I think we should have missed out the first two and got straight down to the second,' I replied.

'You wouldn't appreciate it so much.'

'Oh, I think I would.'

'I enjoyed this morning. I haven't had a proper walk for ages. It seems such a waste, having all this beautiful

188

countryside on the doorstep and not taking advantage of it.'

'You should ease off on the work. You'd have more time.'

'Mmmm.' She sipped her bitter thoughtfully. 'I suppose that's a habit I ought to get out of. Working Saturdays, evenings, sometimes Sundays. I never used to. I started after my divorce. It took my mind off things.'

I nodded. 'Dulls the pain, doesn't it? But it was a long time ago.'

'It's still clear in my memory.'

'Regrets?'

'None. You?'

'No.'

I smiled at her. It felt comfortable. We could have said more, but I sensed we both felt there was time ahead of us for talking. Right now, it didn't matter.

Maria stared at the fire in the hearth. There were horse brasses all round it, glowing dully in the flames. I watched her, thinking back to my own marriage. Remembering not the bad times, but the moments of companionship. Missing those Sundays with someone else, those mornings in bed with coffee and the papers, the warmth of another body nearby. Feeling no regrets for the end, but plenty for the emptiness of the years since.

We stayed in the pub until closing time, then walked out to the car which was parked up against the wall by the church.

'Do you mind if we just take a short stroll around the village?' I asked.

'I thought you'd had enough exercise for the day.'

'This is more my style. Window-shopping, gentle pace, no hills, pub on every corner. That's how the countryside should be.'

We turned on to the main road and wandered past the cluster of gift shops. The illuminated displays of souvenirs, trinkets, twee bits of pottery, tea towels, silver spoons and rows of jewellery set with Blue John, the fragile-veined fluorspar extracted from the hill behind the village. Maria slipped her hand into mine.

Just round the next bend I found what I was looking for. A red pillar box outside the post office. The newsagent's over the road was open. I went in and asked if there was another pillar box in the village. I was told there wasn't.

'I suppose this has a purpose?' Maria said.

'If Rob posted that sample Sunday night, that's probably the box he put it in. So why then did he drive up to Winnats Pass? I think we should go and see.'

We took the road towards Mam Tor and turned off left for Winnats, pulling into the car park at the bottom of the pass. No matter how many times I went there, it never failed to impress me. The towering outcrops of limestone, the precipitous sides, the sheer, awesome size of the gorge. It had a stark, inspiring beauty that was easy to admire, harder to comprehend.

Maria said: 'This is the car park, isn't it?'

She didn't have to explain what she meant. It was impossible to think of the place without remembering the details of Rob's murder. I took a walk around, wondering exactly what had happened that night. It was an exposed spot, scoured by the wind blowing down the pass. In daylight, with people around, cars parked, the entrance to Speedwell Cavern across the road, its atmosphere was hospitable enough. But in darkness it would be sinister, threatening, the open mouth of the gorge a constant lowering presence.

'What are you thinking?' Maria said.

'Nothing.' I didn't want her to know what grim passageways my mind was exploring.

She stood directly in front of me. 'Do you think I'm not doing the same? It's better out in the open than festering inside us.'

'I'm wondering whether he was killed here, or just dumped here afterwards.'

'Why?'

'Because I can't work out what good reasons he had for being in Winnats Pass in the middle of the night. Why here?'

'Why dump him here if he wasn't killed here?' Maria said.

'It's out of the way, no houses nearby.'

'Maybe he met his killers here,' she suggested. 'Or what if he picked up the sample from someone here?'

I shook my head. 'Then went into Castleton to post it before coming all the way back up here again? Why would he do that?'

'He doesn't have to have posted it in Castleton.'

I looked her in the eye, a possibility occurring to me.

'Let's check something out. It's a wild idea, but it might just be right.'

I crossed the road and went into the Speedwell Cavern souvenir shop. There was a woman behind the till, sorting through a pile of Derbyshire guidebooks. She looked up when I approached her.

'The next tour's in fifteen minutes,' she said. 'If you don't mind waiting.'

'We haven't come for the cavern,' I said. 'I wanted to ask you something. Were you working last Monday?'

'Monday? Yes, why?'

'You didn't find a small packet on your doorstep by any chance, did you? First thing.'

She screwed up her forehead. 'What kind of packet?'

'Like a small parcel. Or maybe a thick envelope.'

She shook her head. 'Not me. Did you lose it?'

'A friend might have. Thanks anyway.'

We turned to leave.

'Hang on a sec. I'm not first here in the mornings.' She called out a name and a man appeared in the doorway at the back of the shop. She explained to him what I'd been asking. He nodded.

'Well, yes, I did. I thought it was a bit funny. It was leaning against the door down to the cavern. About so

191

big.' He held his fingers approximately five inches apart. 'Bulging in the middle.'

'What did you do with it?'

'I thought it was for us to start with. I brought it in here. Then I noticed the address was completely different. And there was no postmark on it.'

'But it had a stamp?'

'Oh yes. I thought, nerve of some people. Dumping it there as though this was the post office. Was it you?'

'No. What happened to it?'

'I stuck it in the box when I went into the village. Not much else I could do with it.'

'Do you remember the address on it?'

'Can't say I do. Somewhere in Sheffield, I think. Is there a problem?'

'Not at all. Thanks for your help.'

We were back in the car heading down the hill towards Castleton when Maria said: 'How did you know?'

'I didn't,' I said. 'It was partly what you said earlier, remember? That maybe someone else posted it for him. That immediately made me think of an accomplice of some sort, but of course it could have been anyone. Then you questioned whether it had actually been posted in Castleton and it started me thinking.'

'So he got hold of the mustard gas sample,' Maria reiterated. 'Put it in a pre-prepared envelope and left it outside the cavern. Why?'

'There's only one explanation that makes sense. He knew his killers were closing in on him, and he wanted to get rid of the sample before they got to him.'

'And having the envelope with him? That presupposes he knew in advance what was going to happen.'

'He was a careful man. A planner. He knew what he was doing was dangerous. Regardless of who was after him, he'd have wanted the sample off his person as quickly as possible. Only instead of posting it himself, he was forced to dump it in the nearest convenient place and hope someone else would dispatch it for him.'

192

I thought of Rob in that car park. In the pitch black. Probably scared. Fumbling with an envelope. Hurriedly popping the container inside it. Running across the road and leaving it by the cavern entrance. Aware that someone was close behind him, maybe closer than he imagined. Returning to his car, his killer arriving. Then one shot. And darkness. I shuddered.

'You all right?' Maria said.

'Yes. Do you mind if we stop in at Cathy's on the way home?'

'No, it'll be nice to see her.'

'You busy tomorrow?'

'During the day, you mean?'

'I'm taking a trip to Wiltshire. I wondered if you'd like to come with me.'

She thought about it. 'This have something to do with Rob?'

I told her about his weekend at the Clarendon Hotel, Idmiston, and the phone number on the back of the drawing Jenny had given me.

'I want to know what he was doing down there.'

'I've got something on in the morning I can't cancel,' Maria said. 'What about going after lunch? We could go in my car, it'll be faster.'

'I'll fix up somewhere for us to stay overnight,' I said casually. 'Then we can come back Tuesday.'

She didn't raise any objection. I glanced at her. She was looking at me, half smiling. I hoped it was in anticipation, not amusement.

Cathy gave us tea and home-made fruitcake at the pine table in her kitchen. She seemed pleased to see us, but distracted nevertheless. Something weighing on her mind.

I took out Jenny's folded drawing and turned it over for Cathy to see.

'Is that Rob's handwriting?'

'Yes.'

'Do the number or name mean anything to you?'

'Sarin? No, I don't know anyone of that name. I don't recognize the number either. What is it?'

'Jenny gave it to me earlier in the week. Is she around?'

'She's upstairs. I'll go and get her.'

Cathy went out. Maria took the drawing from me and studied the phone number.

'I suppose you tried it?'

I nodded. 'There was no answer. We'll check it out when we go down there.'

'You think Rob went to see this Sarin?'

'Seems pretty likely. He had a reason for going to Wiltshire. So far this is the only indication we've had of what that reason might have been.'

Jenny came in holding her mother's hand. She looked up at us shyly. I wanted to pick her up and hug her, but instead I just smiled and said: 'Hello, Jenny.'

She gave me a guarded glance, then a more open one at Maria.

'Hello, Aunty Mia.'

'Hello.' Maria smiled at her and held out her arms. Jenny came to her, letting Maria pick her up and hold her on her knee.

'What've you been up to then?' Maria said.

'Nothing much.'

'Have you been out today?'

'No, I did some painting.'

She pointed at a sheet of paper pinned to the noticeboard. There was a patch of blue powder paint in the centre with a daubed green object superimposed on it.

'It's a frog. On a pond.'

'It's very good,' Maria said. 'Now you remember Michael, don't you?'

Jenny stole another glance at me and nodded.

'You did this for me,' I said, showing her the drawing. 'I keep it on my wall. Can I ask you where you got the paper?'

She didn't understand me. A blank look was all I got.

Cathy said gently: 'Did you get it off Daddy's desk? It doesn't matter if you did. We just want to know.'

Jenny studied her mother's face, gauging whether she was going to get into trouble. Finally, she nodded.

'It was all right, wasn't it?'

'Of course it was.'

'I ran out of paper. There was some on the desk. I only took a few bits.'

'Have you got any left?' I asked.

She shook her head.

'Did you draw on them all? Can you remember which drawings?'

'No.'

'We can check,' Cathy said. 'Most of them are in here or in her bedroom.'

'Would you mind?'

'I'll go upstairs. You looking for anything in particular?'

'Just any notes that might be on the back.'

Maria and I took a wall each in the kitchen, removing Jenny's drawings and paintings one by one and examining the reverse sides. Every one was blank.

When Cathy returned she shook her head. 'Sorry, nothing.'

'It was worth a try.'

'I phoned you earlier,' she said. 'I wanted to show you something.'

'Did you leave a message on the machine?' I asked quickly.

'No.'

'Use a call box if you've anything confidential to say. There's a tap on your phone.'

Her jaw dropped. 'A *what*?'

'The police are listening in. So be careful who you phone from here.'

'But why would they . . . ?' She held out her hands in bewilderment.

'Because you're Rob's wife. He was deep into something very controversial and, no doubt, they believe you're a part of it. Now what did you want to show me?'

She waited a moment, recovering from her astonishment – 'Oh, yes, of course' – before going out and returning with a large heavy-duty transparent plastic bag. There were various objects in the bottom of it.

'The police brought the car back this morning. They've finished their tests on it. These are the things that were in it when they found Rob.'

She poured the contents of the plastic bag out on to the table. I saw maps, an umbrella, a windscreen ice-scraper, a Vauxhall manual, nothing much of interest.

Then Cathy picked through the pile and lifted out a curious polystyrene object. She handed it to me. It was a long cylinder, about the length and diameter of a wine bottle with a join around the middle where it could be split into two sections. Attached to one end was a short piece of nylon cord. I pulled the tube apart. It was hollow inside. And empty.

'What is it?'

'The container Rob kept his spare torch batteries, sandwiches, valuables in when he went potholing.'

'Potholing?'

'It's waterproof and it floats. He used to tow it along behind him through the underground streams.'

'Did he keep it in the car all the time?'

'Only when he went caving. The rest of the time it was stored upstairs with all his other gear, his ropes, ladders, wet suit, helmet.'

'And are they . . . ?'

'I've already checked,' Cathy said. 'They're all missing.'

I nodded slowly. 'So now we know what he was doing out at Winnats.'

Maria held up a hand. 'You're losing me here. You mean Rob went potholing last Sunday night?'

I nodded again. It made sense. The hillsides around Castleton were riddled with caves and passages. And it also explained why he'd been stripped after death. That left the pressing question of which cave he'd gone down and why. But I already knew the answer to that.

196

# 13

It was a long, tedious drive to Wiltshire. Motorway to start with – M1, M69, M40 – then the A34 heading down around Oxford and on into the heart of southern England. I would have dozed off in the passenger seat only Maria kept saying: 'Talk to me, or I'll fall asleep too. Keep me awake.'

'How about some music?' I said.

'You choose.'

I browsed through her collection of CDs. It was nearly all classical. Brahms, Schumann, Mozart, Chopin. I held up some Mahler.

'What's this?'

Maria glanced at it. '*Des Knaben Wunderhorn*. You know it?'

'Know it?' I said. 'I can't even pronounce it. You got any James Last, or Bobby Crush?'

She gave me a look. 'You work hard at pretending to be a philistine, don't you?'

'It's not hard work,' I said.

'Oh, just shut up and put something on.'

We arrived at the Clarendon Hotel in Idmiston as dusk was falling. Set back from the road up a short drive, the hotel was an old stone house with various more recent extensions added on at the sides. It looked welcoming enough. Not too grand, well maintained and, at first sight at least, blessed with a little more character than most hotels. But then that wasn't difficult.

We checked in and I carried our bags upstairs to the

197

room. It was on the first floor in the old part of the building, with a bathroom en suite and a bay window overlooking the terrace and formal gardens at the rear of the
house. Maria looked at the double bed, then at me. She
didn't say anything.

'I tried to book us a couple of singles, but this was all
they had left,' I said, not entirely convincingly.

Maria rolled her eyes. 'Michael, how old do you think
I am? I don't mind you trying to bed me, but for God's
sake do it in style. Don't be so bloody apologetic about it.'

She went into the bathroom and closed the door with
a bang behind her.

Did I say something?

I pulled the curtains and switched on the bedside lamps.
Style? That wasn't one of my strong points. But I had to
try. I rang room service and asked them to send up two
glasses and a bottle of champagne. It wasn't stylish, but I
couldn't help asking how much it would cost. Twenty-
eight pounds, I was told. I almost asked if I could pay in
instalments.

The champagne had been delivered by the time Maria
emerged from the bathroom. I popped the cork and filled
her glass. She sighed.

'This isn't what I meant.'

'Then what did you mean?' I said.

She moved away from me, running her fingers through
her hair in exasperation.

'I'm thirty-nine years old. You don't have to pussyfoot
around me as if I was some teenage virgin.'

'I'm trying, Maria. What am I supposed to do?'

'How about this?'

She came close and kissed me hard on the mouth. More
aggression than passion. Then she sat down on the end
of the bed as if nothing had happened.

'There, that wasn't difficult, was it?' she said.

I recovered my breath. But before I could say anything, Maria changed the subject. Suddenly businesslike,
detached.

'So how are we going to find this man Rob came down here to see? Sarin, or whatever his name is.'

I blinked, trying to get my thoughts together. 'Well, we could always try him.'

I pulled out the paper with the phone number on it, picked up the receiver on the bedside table and dialled out. It rang for a long time before a man finally answered. He had a frail, slightly plummy voice, quavering a little at the back of his throat. He sounded elderly.

'Hello?'

'Is that Mr Sarin?' I said.

He didn't reply. I could hear his heavy breathing in my ear.

'Hello?' I said.

'I'm afraid there's no one here of that name.'

The line went dead. I replaced the phone. Maria raised an eyebrow at me.

'Wrong number?'

'I don't think so. It's just a feeling I get.'

I hunted around in the drawers of the desk that occupied one corner of the room and found a local telephone directory. There was no listing for anyone called Sarin.

'Maybe he's ex-directory,' Maria suggested.

I called Directory Inquiries. There was no Sarin, listed or unlisted, anywhere in the county.

'There's only one thing for it,' I said. 'The number must be in someone else's name.' I opened the phone book on the desk and pulled up two chairs in front. 'You take the left-hand pages, I'll take the right.'

'You're kidding?'

'It's not very thick.'

Maria pulled a face. 'You certainly know how to give a girl a good time, don't you?'

We started to work our way through the directory, checking every column for a number that matched the one on the paper.

'What if we don't find it?' Maria asked as we reached letter G.

'Then we revert to Plan B,' I said.

'And what's Plan B?'

'I've no idea. If you think of something, let me know.'

It was nearing half past seven, and the champagne was long finished, when we found it. It had to be under the letter S, of course. Edward Salter was the name by the number. Yew Tree Cottage, Vicarage Lane, Newton Langford.

'Picturesque sort of address. You planning on visiting him?' Maria said.

'Let's have something to eat first.'

The dining room was practically empty when we went down. We found a table for two near the window and picked at a couple of starters. Neither of us seemed to have much appetite. There was a knot in my stomach, a vague feeling of nausea. I was nervous.

Maria said: 'I'm sorry I got ratty earlier. I think it was the drive. It wore me out.'

'That's all right.'

'Maybe I'm a little on edge too.' She looked me in the eyes. 'You feel as tense as I do?'

'Probably worse.'

She put her hand over mine on the table. 'I don't want us to spend all evening circling around each other. We both know what's going to happen. Let's just relax and enjoy it. The next move is yours, OK?'

I nodded. She grinned at me. 'And if that's not a proposition, I don't know what is.'

I took her hand and held it, entwining her fingers in mine.

'We should have done this a long time ago.'

'You're telling me.'

We didn't linger over dinner. Some of the tension went, but not all. We were entering uncharted waters. It was impossible not to be just a little apprehensive. Somehow, each first time, age and experience make no difference at all.

The village of Newton Langford was a couple of miles

from the hotel. I got rough directions from reception but they couldn't tell me exactly where Vicarage Lane was. It seemed a pretty obvious address to find. Simply look for a church and the vicarage couldn't be far away. Maria drove again while I navigated.

We entered the fringes of the village as a clock somewhere nearby was striking nine o'clock. I saw the tower of a church over some houses to our right.

'Next turning,' I said.

We left the main road and went along a narrow street lined with tiny houses and one or two shops. Lights glowed behind curtains but the pavements outside were deserted. A village that went to bed early.

Maria slowed to a crawl, studying the buildings. The church came up on my side. There was a crenellated stone wall all around it, a graveyard scattered with headstones beyond.

'Try first left,' I said.

Maria turned and I saw a sign at the junction. Vicarage Lane. On the opposite corner was a large detached house with steps leading up through a wrought-iron gate to a lawned front garden. There was no garage or drive. I guessed it was the vicarage.

Further along the lane was a row of four terraced cottages, almost hidden behind bushes and a hedge of flowering currant. The last cottage had a yew tree in the front garden.

Maria said: 'That must be it. At the end.'

She moved over to park on the pavement at the side of the lane but I said quickly: 'Keep going.'

'But I thought . . .'

'Straight on. Don't stop.'

Across the lane from the cottage I'd seen a small car park at the back of the church. There was a car waiting in it, two men in the front seats.

I looked over my shoulder at them as we passed. It was too dark to make out their faces.

'Which way?' Maria said as we reached a T-junction at the end of the lane.

'Doesn't matter. Right.'

We were outside the village now, hedgerows and fields on both sides of the road.

'You see them?' I said.

Maria nodded. 'Watching the cottage?'

'Well, they didn't look much like a courting couple to me.'

'What now? Back to the hotel?'

'How long have you known me?' I said.

She turned her head. 'You won't get near that cottage without those men seeing you.'

'From the front, no. But there must be a back door. Turn right here.'

We circled around the outskirts of the village and came back in from the opposite direction, pulling into the car park of the Bell and Candle pub which lay immediately behind the vicarage.

We got out and explored the edges of the car park. The backs of the four cottages were visible above a chest-high wooden fence.

'I thought there might be a back lane,' I said. 'Nothing's simple, is it? You want to stay with the car?'

'No fear, I'm coming with you.'

'OK.' I cupped my hands in front of me. 'You know what you have to do.'

Maria groaned. 'Do you ever go anywhere where there's a gate?'

She stepped into my hands and I hoisted her up and over the fence. I checked no one was observing us before I went over after her. The ground on the far side sloped away steeply into a muddy ditch. I took a step down the bank and stretched out my hand to Maria.

'Here, it's slippery.'

She gripped my fingers and came down gingerly behind me. Halfway down she lost her footing and started to fall. I grabbed her arm, but overbalanced myself and the two

202

of us tumbled over and landed in a heap in the bottom of the ditch. Maria's face was only inches from mine. Somehow my right hand had come to rest on one of her breasts. She took a breath to get over the shock of the fall.

Then she said: 'I know we're sharing a bed, but I hope this isn't your idea of foreplay?'

I kissed her lightly. 'Well, you did say the next move was mine.'

'This is not exactly what I had in mind.'

I pulled her to her feet and she brushed the mud off her jeans.

'You all right?' I asked.

'Nothing broken, I think. This had better be worth it, Michael.'

'Only one way to find out.' I pushed aside the under-growth. 'After you.'

We crept through the gardens of the first three cottages, sticking to the cover of shrubs and bushes wherever we could. There were no more fences to scale, just a couple of low brick walls. When we reached the garden of Yew Tree Cottage, we stopped and crouched behind a wooden bench on a crazy paving patio near the rear boundary. The house was about twenty yards away. A light was on behind the curtains of the back room on the ground floor.

We flitted across the lawn to the house and I pressed an eye to the window, peering through a narrow gap in the curtains. I saw a wall of books, a table lamp next to an armchair and, sitting in the chair reading, a grey-haired man in a woolly cardigan. He looked about seventy.

I nodded to Maria and went to the back door. I knocked. No one came. I wondered if the old man had heard. I rapped harder. I did it three times before an internal door clicked open and a light came on inside. Slippers shuffled across the floor towards us.

Then a shaky voice said: 'Who's that?'

'Mr Salter? My name's McLean. I know it's late but I need to talk to you.'

'Talk to me?'

'About Rob Fielding.'

He didn't reply immediately. When he did, his voice was little more than a whisper.

'Go away. Please, go away.'

Maria leaned nearer the door and said: 'We've come a long way, Mr Salter. It's important.'

'Is that a woman?'

'I'm a friend of Rob's. Please let us in.'

Something in her voice, or maybe just her presence, must have reassured him for he unlocked the door and opened it on the chain. He looked out at us. Behind the pebble lenses of his glasses, his eyes were frightened.

'I don't know anything. There's nothing to talk about,' he said.

'Rob came to see you, didn't he?' I said. 'What about? We won't stay long. We just want to know why Rob came here.'

'What for?'

'You know he's dead, don't you?'

The eyes moved nervously. He lifted a wrinkled hand to his face and rubbed the fingers across his mouth. He nodded fractionally.

'I read it in the paper.'

I took out my press card and held it up so he could read it.

'Anything you say will be treated with the strictest confidence. No one knows we're here.'

Salter studied both our faces. His lower lip quivered. He lifted a finger to his mouth again and sucked the edge of a knuckle joint. The finger was trembling.

'Did anyone see you arrive?' he asked.

I shook my head. 'We were careful. That's why we came through the gardens.'

He closed the door and unhooked the chain. 'Quickly.'

He let us in and locked the door behind us. We followed him through into the back room. He closed that door too and pushed a stuffed, snake-like draught excluder up against the gap at the bottom. It seemed to make him feel safer. Two doors between us and the outside world. He relaxed a little and sat back down in his armchair.

I looked around for somewhere to sit. There was a settee against one wall but it was occupied by a couple of fat sleeping cats. Salter gestured with a hand.

'Just throw them off. They won't mind.'

Maria and I took a cat each, picking them up and depositing them on a rug in front of the fireplace. They opened their eyes momentarily, yawned and went back to sleep again. We sat down in their place on the settee. Salter watched us anxiously. I tried to put him more at ease.

'No one saw us, Mr Salter, I assure you. We'll go the same way we came.'

'There are two men in a car at the front. I think they're watching me.'

'Do you know who they are?'

He shook his head. 'But you understand, after what happened to Fielding, that I have to be cautious. No one must know you were here.'

'You think your life is in danger?'

'There are powerful vested interests at stake. People who will go a long way to protect themselves.'

'Protect themselves from what?'

He didn't answer.

'Protect themselves from what?' I repeated.

'Exposure,' Salter said. 'As Fielding found out.'

'You know who killed him?'

'No.'

'But you know why, don't you? What did Rob come here to talk to you about that weekend?'

Salter bit his lip, his gaze moving from me to Maria, then back to me. He was old, his body was starting to crumble, but there was nothing wrong with his mind. I could see it in his face.

'He wanted to know about my work,' he said.

'Your work?'

205

'Before I retired. At Porton Down.' He saw my expression change. 'Ah, I see you understand.'

Maria gave me a blank look. 'What's Porton Down?'

'The government chemical and biological warfare research establishment,' I said. 'It's just a few miles from here.' I turned back to Salter. 'Why you?'

'We met last year at an environmental conference. We exchanged phone numbers, then a couple of months ago he rang me and asked if we could meet. If I'd known it would lead to all this, I'd have said no.'

'An environmental conference?'

'In Birmingham. Since my retirement I've taken an interest in Green issues. Doing something worthwhile to make up for all the years I . . .' He stopped. 'Well, let's just say it was a change from everything I'd done before.'

'What was your work at Porton?'

He looked away, staring at the rows of books on the shelves that covered most of the wall space in the room. In profile, I noticed he had fine silvery hairs protruding from his ear. A tiny, irrelevant detail which seemed, unaccountably, to add to his fragility.

I said gently: 'You told Rob, I assume. What difference will it make if you tell us?'

'I'm still bound by the Official Secrets Act. You realize what will happen to me if anyone finds out I've spoken to you. Arrest, a trial in camera, probably twenty years in jail. Do you think I want to die in a cell?'

Maria said, 'You make it sound like Stalin's Russia.'

'That's what it *is* like here when it comes to revealing state secrets.'

'Your work. What was it?' I asked again.

Salter said nothing for a time. Struggling with something inside him. I didn't push. Pressure would only make it worse for him.

Finally he said: 'I was a research chemist. In the chemical warfare section.'

He told us briefly how he'd gone there as a young man shortly after the war. How at first he'd been so sure of the value, the importance of the work they were doing there. Then how the disillusionment set in.

'You're both too young to understand, but I lived through the war. We were genuinely terrified that the Germans would use gas against us. They'd used it in the First World War with horrifying consequences. Chlorine, phosgene, mustard. Do you know how mustard gas works? It burns, it blinds, it strips the bronchial tubes of their mucous membrane so the victim chokes on fluid and pus from the lungs.'

I sensed, rather than saw, Maria shudder. Salter looked at her.

'I'm sorry to be so blunt, but chemical warfare is an unpleasant business. That's why Porton Down was set up in 1916. To undertake research into defences against gas. But of course that's impossible without studying gas as an offensive weapon too. They go hand in hand.

'Then, after the Second World War, it was the Russians who became the threat. We knew they had chemical weapons and were engaged in further research to find newer, even more effective weapons. We had no choice but to continue our own research and development. It seemed vital work at the time.'

'And later?' I said.

Salter closed his eyes for a second and inhaled deeply. He seemed troubled, anguish just below the surface.

'Later,' he said, 'I began to wonder. When you're working on defence it's easy enough to convince yourself it has a morally justifiable purpose. Protecting your own people, your own families from attack. But when your work becomes offensive, when you actually start to make weapons, then it becomes more questionable. Your conscience becomes harder to live with.'

'You made weapons at Porton?'

He shook his head. 'It's not a factory, it's a research centre. But what is a weapon? Is gas a weapon on its own, or only after it's been put in a shell to be fired at the enemy? We're into semantics here. The realm of the politician, not the scientist.'

'I thought we didn't have any chemical weapons in this country.'

'Officially, we don't. That's what the government tells us, but do you really believe them? Do you think they would admit to having them? There's something abhorrent about chemical weapons, the way they kill, the agony in which people die. But we have a chemical warfare capability all right. Why do you think Porton Down is still there?'

'You told Rob Fielding all this?'

'Yes.'

'Even though you knew you could go to jail for it.'

'I suppose it was all on my conscience.' His mouth tightened, his forehead creased in a fleeting moment of what looked like pain.

'You know, my last few years at Porton, I used to come home from work in the evenings and have to go for walks in the countryside for a couple of hours until I felt human again. I'm ashamed of what I did there. I've spent my entire working life devising ever more horrific ways of killing people.'

I didn't say anything. I could think of nothing appropriate. Salter was hunched in his chair, head bowed, hands clasped tightly in his lap. The posture of a penitent.

One of the cats stretched itself on the rug, then strolled across to the armchair and climbed up on to Salter's knees. The old man started as if he'd been asleep. He smiled at the cat and stroked its neck affectionately.

'Do you know someone called Sarin?' Maria said.

Salter lifted his head. 'Sarin?' Only then did he seem to realize what she'd said. 'Sarin. It's not a person, it's a substance. It was discovered by a German scientist called Gerhard Schrader just before the war.'

'What kind of substance?' I asked.

'An organophosphorous compound, isopropyl methyl

208

phosphonofluoridate. Schrader called it sarin. It's a nerve agent.'

'Deadly?'

'A tiny drop on the skin or inhaled into the lungs is more than enough to kill a man.'

'Rob asked you about sarin too, didn't he?' I said, one more mystery becoming clear to me. 'And he asked you about a little boy who died near a fertilizer plant in South Yorkshire.'

Salter nodded. 'Vomiting, frothing at the mouth, convulsions, death within ten minutes. The classic symptoms of nerve agent poisoning.'

I described what I'd seen at Frank Helliwell's house, the circumstances of his accident at work.

'That too?' I said.

'Not sarin,' Salter replied. 'Or he'd be dead. But maybe a milder nerve gas in a very low concentration.'

'Do they do chemical weapons research up there?'

'I don't know. I'd never heard of the factory until Fielding came to see me.'

'What about manufacturing nerve agents? Has Britain ever had that capacity?'

'Oh yes. There was a time when we made sarin at a place called Nancekuke, in Cornwall. Officially, the stockpiles were dumped at sea when we renounced chemical warfare in the fifties.'

'But the research continued?'

'Of course. What governments say and what they do are two entirely different things. It's the first rule of democracy. Never let the people out there know what you're doing.'

'What about mustard gas stocks?'

'Also destroyed.'

'But you have your doubts?'

'I don't know what really happened to them. I was a chemist. I wasn't privy to that kind of classified information.'

He coughed harshly, covering his mouth with his fist.

The cat on his lap craned its neck to look up at him. Salter waited, swallowing hard. When he spoke again he was slightly hoarse.

'I've been talking too much. I'm tired. Go now, please.'

Maria stood up and went to him. 'Can I get you a drink? Water, some tea?'

Salter shook his head. 'Just go. The longer you stay the more dangerous it is for me.'

He came with us to the back door, opening it cautiously and peering into the garden.

'Don't come back. And don't telephone me,' he said.

We slipped out into the night, leaving him there in the doorway. An old man with his cats, his books and memories he'd rather forget.


We were a couple of miles from Newton Langford, driving through open countryside, when it happened.

I didn't notice anything until I saw Maria glance at the rear-view mirror and screw up her eyes. I twisted round in my seat. There was a car directly behind us, headlights on full beam. It moved closer, almost touching our back bumper. I knew at once it wasn't some ordinary idiot playing games on the road. Maria knew too.

'It's the car from behind the church,' she said. 'What shall I do?'

She sounded calmer than I felt. I looked over my shoulder again. Behind the glare of the headlights I could make out two figures in the front seats. Then the lights surged forward suddenly. The car smashed into the back of us.

'Jesus Christ!' Maria said.

She put her foot down automatically and the Mazda accelerated away. The car behind stayed with us, matching our speed. It smashed into our rear again. Maria hung on to the steering wheel, struggling to keep the wheels on the road.

'Ease off!' I shouted above the noise of the engine.

She touched the brakes but that only made things worse. We were hit from behind a third time. I jolted forwards in the seat. I looked across at Maria. Her face was pale, taut, frightened. Eyes fixed on the road, just concentrating on staying alive. This was no warning shot, no attempt simply to scare us. They were out to kill us.

The road started to curve to the right, then back the other way in a tighter bend. A patch of woodland came up on our left. They'd been waiting for it. Their car sharked out and drew level with us on the outside. It was a Mercedes, black and anonymous. I tried to see who was inside it, but the low roof of the Mazda blocked my view.

We were on the left-hand bend now, trees right alongside the road. Maria was hanging on. She braked abruptly, but the Mercedes was expecting it. The nearside wing of the black car swung hard into the side of us and kept coming, forcing us closer to the edge of the road. Maria accelerated, trying to outrun them. Trying to slip away at the front. Then the road took a turn to the right again and we found ourselves on the outside of the bend, the speedometer touching eighty.

Maria started to lose control. The Mercedes rammed into us. Our front wheels skidded on gravel on the narrow shoulder of the bend. There was no room to correct the motion. Maria hit the brakes but it was too late. We shot off the side and into the fringes of the wood. Maria wrenched the wheel over violently, the brakes locking. We missed a couple of bigger trees, ploughing through thick undergrowth, then the ground plunged away suddenly beneath us. The Mazda went over the edge. I hung on to my seat as we rolled upside down and slithered sideways down the slope. Then there was a jarring bang and we came to a halt.

I took a few deep breaths, still clutching the edges of my seat, then I looked across at Maria. She was hanging upside down, suspended by her seatbelt, blood trickling from a gash on her head.

'Maria? Maria? Oh, God.'

I snapped off my seatbelt, then hers, and pulled her gently away from the steering wheel. She was unconscious. I felt the pulse on her neck. She was alive. I could smell burning. A flame licked over the side of the car. The acrid smoke caught at my nostrils. I kicked open my door and pulled Maria out with me. I felt sick with shock, but getting away from the car was the only thing on my mind.

We slid out on to the earth. I stumbled to my feet and picked Maria's limp body up in my arms. I headed down the slope, no idea where I was going, but it was easier than heading up the hill. We were thirty yards away, partially sheltered by trees, when the car blew up.

The explosion threw me to my knees. I hung on to Maria, protecting her from the blast. Lying next to her on the ground, panting for breath, listening to the crackle of the flames as the car behind us burned.

The details of how I got her to hospital were just a blur of disjointed images. Snatches of information that my brain refused to put together in any rational sequence. Getting back up to the road, a car stopping, hands helping me lift Maria into the back, headlights, nurses' uniforms, corridors, voices echoing. And throughout it all, Maria's face. Unconscious, motionless, closed to me.

She was awake now though. Lying back on pillows in the bed. The wound on her forehead had been dressed but she was pale and drawn. Drained by her experience.

'They're keeping you in overnight for observation,' I said. 'You had a nasty knock.'

'I feel all right.'

'You don't look it.'

She took in her surroundings. We were in a side ward, a single room with bright curtains, its own washbasin and armchair by the bed. But it still felt like an institution: cold, sterile.

'I hate hospitals,' Maria said. 'Can't I come out?'

'Maybe tomorrow.'

A look of panic passed suddenly across her face. She clutched at my hand.

'You'll stay, won't you?'

'Of course.'

'I don't want to be alone here. I'm frightened, Michael. They intended to kill us.'

'You're safe. I've given a statement to the police.'

'What if they come back? What if they come here?'

'They won't. You should get some sleep.'

'Mr Salter . . .'

I put a finger to her lips. 'He's OK. I called him from a payphone in the foyer. He's going to stay with friends for a few days.'

I leaned over and adjusted the pillows for her. She smiled up at me. Trying hard, but the energy just wasn't there.

'Seems a shame to waste that double bed, doesn't it?' she said.

I kissed her. 'I can think of a couple more we can use back home. Now go to sleep.'

I stayed with her, sitting in the armchair by the bed. Holding her hand until she fell asleep.

# 14

They let Maria out of hospital at one o'clock the next day. I'd hired a car and picked up our luggage from the hotel during the morning, keeping my eyes open for the black Mercedes or any other suspicious-looking vehicle on my tail. I didn't think they'd try again so soon, but I wasn't taking any chances.

Maria seemed to have recovered well from the crash. A night's sleep had refreshed her, put colour back into her face, but I knew the surface was deceptive. Underneath, though she wasn't admitting it, her nerves would still be raw, acutely sensitive to the slightest shock. Her physical injuries were not great, but psychologically she would need a long time to get over the experience of last night.

I drove home steadily. Maria slept for most of the journey. We didn't talk much, and when we did, it was of inconsequential matters. Neither of us seemed ready yet to talk about what had happened.

We reached Sheffield in the early evening. When I pulled in outside Maria's house, she said: 'Stay with me.'

I nodded. 'I'll come back in a couple of hours. I've got something to attend to first.'

'What?'

'Nothing much. Here, I'll help you in with your overnight bag.'

She put a hand on my arm. Her fingers dug into my flesh.

'Michael, don't hold out on me. I'm in this too, remember.'

'It's better if you don't know.'

'*Tell me.*'

I sighed. 'You're not up to this. You should rest.'

'Don't pamper me,' she said fiercely. 'Those bastards totalled my car, nearly killed us. I'm staying with this to the bitter end. Got me?'

'OK.' I didn't argue any further. I told her where I was going and why. 'You still want to come?'

She didn't hesitate. 'Yes.'

'I have to pick up a few items from the flat, but I'll be straight back.'

'Do I need anything?'

'Warm clothes. A torch if you've got one.'

She nodded, and pulled her bag over on to her knee from the back seat. She looked worn out, the plaster on her forehead emphasizing her vulnerability.

'You sure?' I said.

She leant across and kissed me. 'I'm sure,' she said.

I found a note from Harry on the living room table when I got home. 'Gone back to the wife. Giving it another go. Thanks for everything,' it read. In a postscript he'd added: 'Keeping your spare set of keys, just in case.'

I suppressed a smile and threw the piece of paper in the bin. In a strange way I'd miss him. You can live alone too long.

It took me ten minutes to pack a small rucksack, then I left the hire car parked outside my flat and drove back to Maria's house in my own. She was waiting for me, changed now into hiking boots, a thick polo-necked jumper and a quilted anorak. A torch protruded from one of the side pockets of the anorak.

'I still think you should be in bed,' I said.

'I'm OK. I took a couple of aspirin.' She held up a plastic carrier bag. 'I made us some sandwiches and coffee.'

We ate on the move, passing the cup from the Thermos between us as I drove out into the Peak District. We left the car in a lay-by near the top of Pin Dale and walked

215

up the track to Dirtlow Rake. A quarter of a mile on, we took a right fork, ignoring the 'Private, no entry' sign, and came to the wire fence and the padlocked gates we'd climbed over on Sunday.

Maria sighed wearily. 'Not again. I'd forgotten about these.'

'This time,' I said. 'We do it the easy way.'

I took the bolt cutters out of my rucksack and snapped off the chain. We passed through the gates and walked up the track to the ravine where we'd seen Russell Stamford. I looked down the slope to the wooden hut at the bottom of the ravine. There was no sign of life: no lights on, no vehicles parked outside.

We went down to it and I examined the door. It was fastened shut with another padlock. I chopped it off with the bolt cutters and we slipped inside. I flashed my torch around warily. The beam caught the metal cage and the sliding doors of the lift, then a bank of switches on one of the walls. I stepped across and threw all the switches. A light clicked on above our heads. I heard the hum of an electric generator under a casing at one end of the hut. It seemed unnervingly loud.

'Was that wise?' Maria said.

'There's only one way down,' I said. 'And for that we need power.'

I pulled open the lift doors and stopped on the threshold. The top of the shaft was visible around the sides of the cage, but there was no telling how far down into the earth it went. I tried to ignore the queasiness in my stomach. This was no time for second thoughts.

I stepped into the lift and waited for Maria to join me. There were two buttons on a panel to the side of the doors. One red, one green. I looked at Maria. She licked dry lips and nodded. I pressed the green button. A motor started to whir and the lift descended slowly down the shaft. The walls passed by outside the cage. The rock was smooth, cut by a machine. This might well have been an old lead mine, but it had been enlarged fairly recently.

Maria gripped my hand in hers. I could feel the tension in her body. I didn't look at her. I counted the seconds, trying to appear calm.

Ten, fifteen, twenty . . . On the twenty-eighth second the lift jolted to a halt. We were at the bottom. The temperature difference was marked. We must have been close on two hundred feet down. I opened the sliding doors and walked out into a rock chamber. I could tell from the regular shape, the absence of natural features, that it was man-made. There were lights at intervals on the walls, burning brightly behind thick opaque glass covers. And at one side of the chamber, a tunnel leading off, also illuminated. It was about eight feet high, perhaps a little wider, and so straight and smooth it had to be man-made too.

'It's cold,' Maria said, zipping up her anorak. Her breath was billowing out in clouds and drifting up into the roof of the chamber.

I went to the entrance to the tunnel and looked along it. 'Let's see where it goes.'

We didn't have to walk far before finding out. After thirty or forty yards the tunnel opened out suddenly into another chamber. Only this was natural. A vast limestone cavern whose furthermost reaches were hidden in the darkness. I looked around. There were lights on the nearest wall but even they couldn't illuminate the huge vault of the ceiling, the crevices, holes and recesses. Stalactites draped the sides in curtains of dripping rock, the stalagmites below protruding like the stumps of sawn-off fingers. Massive boulders littered the edges and mounds of fallen stone sloped upwards and out of sight behind buttresses and pillars.

But I noticed the natural features only in passing. For in the middle of the chamber, stacked on wooden pallets, were rows and rows of metal oil drums. I stared at them. There were dozens, maybe hundreds, it was hard to tell. All of them painted bright yellow and stencilled with black serial numbers.

I moved closer to examine them. There were no markings to identify their contents, just the numbers and the painted warning: 'Danger, handle with care.'

'Wow,' Maria breathed. 'What are they?'

'Your guess is as good as mine. But some of them, at least, contain mustard gas.'

'So this is where Rob came?'

I nodded. 'This is where he took his sample. From one of these drums. Then he made his way back through the underground passages to Winnats where he'd left his car. But someone knew he'd been in. They came after him. Shot him and stripped off his potholing gear so no one would start asking awkward questions about what he'd been doing that night.'

Maria said: 'They *stripped* him?'

'He was naked when he was found. They took his clothes, his ropes, his helmet, lamp, but they somehow missed the polystyrene container Cathy showed us.'

Maria moved along the first line of drums. 'That lorry you saw was bringing more to add to the stockpile, wasn't it?'

'Yes.'

'Do they make this stuff there? At the factory.'

'In the inner compound. The fertilizer plant is just a convenient front.'

'What about the nerve agents Salter mentioned? Do some of these drums contain sarin?'

'I don't know,' I said. 'And I don't particularly want to find out.'

I removed my camera from my rucksack and took some photographs of the cavern and the rows of containers. Then I got Maria to take a few close-ups of me standing by the drums to prove I'd been there.

'And Jamie Hynes?' she asked. 'Was that pool of water near the factory contaminated with nerve agent?'

I shook my head. 'I don't think so. There's no plausible way it could have got in the water. They wouldn't have dumped it there deliberately and I think an accident outside the manufacturing area is unlikely. But not inside it.'

'What do you mean?'

'This is guesswork. I went back to check on that pond. Jamie was by the fence of the factory when he died. Just inside the fence, right next to where Jamie was standing, there's a grating over a drain of some sort. What if there was an accident in one of the labs? A spillage. Chemicals accidentally washed down a drain, something like that. Then the fumes drift along a pipe and come out through a grid where Jamie inhales them.'

Maria pursed her lips. 'Maybe, maybe not. You'll never prove it either way, will you?'

Before I could answer, there was a distant click, then the whir of a motor. I spun round.

'The lift!'

We sprinted back along the tunnel to the bottom of the shaft. I peered upwards through the metal cage. I could just make out the underside of the lift as it ascended and disappeared into the darkness above.

'We're trapped,' Maria said. 'They could leave us down here to rot.'

'Sssh.' I was listening. After a few seconds, the whirring stopped as the lift reached the top. The doors clattered open, the noise echoing down the shaft. I glanced at Maria. She was listening too. Then came the sound I'd feared. The doors closing again, followed by the whir of the motor.

'They're coming down after us,' I said.

Maria was frozen to the spot. 'You mean . . .'

I didn't let her finish. I took her hand and pulled her along the tunnel into the cavern.

'Where are we going?' she said. 'There's no way out here.'

'Rob got in and got out somehow, and he didn't use the lift,' I said. 'Take your torch and look around. There has to be a tunnel, a passage somewhere.'

'But he had potholing equipment with him. We have nothing.'

I didn't wait around to reply. I was already heading for

219

the far end of the cavern, skirting round the stacks of chemical drums. I shone the beam of my torch over the walls, probing the cavities and hollows in the rock. Some clearly went nowhere. Others offered possible hiding places, but a hiding place was not what we needed. We needed a way of escape.

Maria came up behind me, her torch flashing over a different section of the walls. We covered the area quickly, but thoroughly. There was nothing that looked like a way out. Yet I knew there had to be one. Rob had come in from somewhere, and even without that knowledge, I knew there would be passages and smaller caves connecting with the cavern. We were in the middle of a limestone hill, chewed and eaten away by rainwater and underground streams over a period of millions of years.

I stopped. Water. That was it. 'Look for water,' I said urgently. 'A trickle, a stream, anything.'

We moved along the back wall. The rock glistened with moisture virtually everywhere but I was searching for a greater, more localized flow. Maria put her hand on my arm suddenly.

'Listen.'

I tilted my head, expecting to hear the sound of a stream or waterfall. Then I realized that was not what Maria meant. I heard voices instead, the heavy tread of footsteps on rock. Our pursuers were coming along the tunnel.

We both clicked off our torches. Maria whispered, 'What now?'

I didn't know. We were cornered, protected for a time by the size of the cavern, the dark and the wall of drums between us and the tunnel. But if we simply waited we'd be discovered for certain. Doing nothing was not an option. We had to make a move.

I scanned the sides of the cavern. Without a torch it was difficult to make out any features, but by gauging the depth and intensity of the shadows it was possible to identify the larger cavities in the limestone. If nothing else, we had to hide.

There was a dark hole above us and to the right, an opening at the top of an ancient rock fall which sloped upwards from the cavern floor to the point on the sides where the curve of the roof began. I nudged Maria and crouched down behind the chemical drums, creeping along to the bottom of the rock fall. I pointed up at the hole. Maria nodded. Slowly, we started to climb.

A few yards up, I looked round and across the cavern. Three, maybe four figures were just emerging from the tunnel, flashlights in their hands. I scrambled higher, moving quickly but watching my feet to ensure I didn't dislodge any of the stones. Hardly any of the light from the wall lamps on the other side of the cavern penetrated this far in. I knew I probably couldn't be seen, but I still felt dangerously exposed. All it would take was for a torch to shine this way and I'd be picked out like a fly on a white wall.

I reached the top and pulled myself into the hollow, Maria scrambling in behind me. The entrance was partially screened by a rock pillar so it wasn't visible from directly below. I felt my way around the inside of the cave. It was small and unbroken by clefts or passageways. We would have to find some other means of escape.

I squatted down next to Maria and whispered in her ear: 'You OK?'

She nodded. She was breathing hard but trying to deaden the sound.

'They'll find us in here,' she said.

'It's only temporary,' I replied. 'We're not staying.'

Although where else we could go was not immediately obvious. One thing at a time, I told myself. We were out of sight for the moment. That brief respite would allow us pause for thought, to consider our next move.

I put an arm around Maria's shoulders and squeezed. She shivered.

'We'll find a way out,' I said, more optimistically than I felt.

'And if we don't?'

221

That wasn't something to dwell on. Nor was remaining in this cave until they found us. I crawled to the entrance and looked out. There were torches flickering around the cavern, a couple along the edges, another in between the rows of drums. It wouldn't be long before they reached this end. I pulled my head back in and thought hard for a time, reviewing the alternative courses of action we could take, none of them appealing.

It was then that I became aware of the noise. A low, continuous splashing, like a dripping tap. I turned my head, trying to locate the source of the sound. It was outside the cave, but not far away. I took another look out, and saw it. Across the top of the rock fall, about twelve feet away was a tiny stream. It trickled over the lip of a rock basin and down into the cracks between the fallen stones. But it was where it was coming from that interested me more. Behind the rock basin was a small waterfall and, above that, a narrow horizontal opening in the wall.

I ducked back to join Maria. 'There's a tunnel on the other side of the rock fall. I can't see into it but there's a stream running through it.'

'That doesn't mean it leads anywhere,' Maria said despondently.

'You want to stay here until our friends arrive? Come on, I'll go first.'

We crawled to the mouth of the cave. I located the torches again, still some distance away, and climbed back out on to the rock fall.

I clambered across cautiously and peered into the opening above the waterfall. I leant in with my torch and flicked it on and off once, hoping that no reflected light leaked out into the cavern. The opening was a couple of feet across but the passage beyond was wider, sloping gently upwards and out of sight. I turned my head and signalled to Maria. She came over and caught my outstretched hand to steady herself on the mound of boulders.

'There's no room to turn round inside. Once we're in we have to keep going,' I whispered.

She nodded. I could tell from her expression she didn't like it, but she knew what the alternatives were and liked those even less.

I lifted off my rucksack and pushed it into the opening. Then I slithered in behind it, my belly dipping into the stream. I pulled myself further in and started to crawl along the passage on my hands and knees, pausing once to crane my neck round. Maria was still outside, hesitating.

'Come on,' I hissed.

She screwed up her courage and pushed her shoulders through the opening. There was nothing I could do to help her. Her torso was into the passage and she was pulling her legs up behind her when I heard a shout from out in the cavern. They'd seen her. Maria looked at me in despair. I gave her a weak smile of encouragement.

'Stay with me,' I said.

I turned back to face the front and scrambled along the tunnel, my torch lighting the way. Maria was right behind me. I could hear her breathing, the brush of her clothes on the rock. The passage started to turn upwards in a gentle incline. It became steeper, and narrower. I forced my shoulders through a tight gap, twisting round to pull myself up on a protruding knob of limestone. Water poured down from above, soaking my face and hair. I climbed upwards and dragged myself out into a tiny chamber, then helped Maria out. She was wet too, her hair dripping over her forehead in gleaming strands.

We looked around the cave. The stream trickled across the middle in a shallow channel, but there was no question of following it further. Its source was a slit in one of the walls, only a few inches high.

'They'll be on us any minute,' Maria said breathlessly.

I explored the walls of the chamber. There were several holes in the rock but only one big enough to squeeze through. Maria shone her torch into it.

'Let's go.'

223

I hesitated. 'It's too obvious. They'll know we took it.'

'It's the only way out.'

I looked higher up the walls. There were a few more openings above us but there was no way of telling which, if any, of them led anywhere.

'Come on, we're wasting time,' Maria whispered urgently.

I pointed upwards. We just had to pick one and take a chance.

'That hole there.'

'It's too high,' Maria said. 'We'll never get into it.'

'Give me your leg.'

I lifted her into the air so she could reach one of the handholds in the rock. She pulled herself higher and peered into the hole.

'Any good?'

'Maybe. I'm not sure.'

'Go for it.'

Maria wriggled in through the opening. I took my camera out of the rucksack and hurriedly removed the exposed film. I put the cartridge in my inside jacket pocket in a plastic bag and left everything else. They were burdens I could do without.

Our pursuers were not far behind. I could hear them back down the passage we'd crawled through. Muffled sounds, the scrape of boots, then a metallic clank I couldn't identify.

I found some purchase on a rock with my right foot and stretched upwards for a handhold, dragging myself slowly up the wall and into the opening after Maria. She was waiting ahead of me, lying flat in the cramped tunnel. I crawled up behind her and we wormed our way through into the next chamber, a tiny cavity barely big enough to sit up in.

'How close are they?' Maria asked.

'Close. But with any luck they won't know which way we went.'

We crawled on further until we reached a point where

the tunnel suddenly divided into three. Maria turned to look at me.

'Which one shall we –?'

I broke in quickly. 'Turn off your torch.'

'What?'

'Turn it off!'

We switched off our torches almost simultaneously, plunging the passage into darkness. I knew Maria could hear the noise too now. More footsteps, more sounds of movement. This time not behind us, but in front.

I slithered up beside her, listening. The blackness was absolute. Not a trace of light coming in from anywhere. Maria was less than a foot away from me but I could see nothing of her. I could sense her presence but my eyes were blind.

I pressed my lips to her ear. 'There are more of them up ahead.'

'Jesus,' Maria breathed. 'How?'

'There must be other ways in. They've come round to cut us off.'

She didn't reply. I felt a chilling sickness in my belly. An ague spreading out into my limbs, permeating my body with fear and despair. We couldn't go back, couldn't stay put, yet to continue might prove even more hazardous.

The noises ahead seemed to fluctuate. Sometimes clear, sometimes muted, occasionally disappearing altogether. It was impossible to tell from which direction they were coming. Or how far away they were.

'We have to keep going,' I whispered.

'We'll walk straight into them.'

'That's a risk we have to take. Stay here and they'll have us for certain. Which tunnel is the sound coming down?'

'I can't tell. It could be all of them. Left, I think.'

'So we go right.'

'I could be wrong, Michael. I just don't know.'

'No torches. We feel our way along the passage.'

It was important now to do something, it didn't matter

225

what. I pulled myself past Maria and let my hand follow the wall of the tunnel, keeping to the right all the time. It was slow work, inching along the floor feeling every bump, every crack, every change in the surface of the rock. Maria followed me, touching my ankle periodically, keeping in physical contact though she couldn't see me.

Perhaps five minutes had elapsed when I gradually became aware I could see the walls around me again, if only faintly. Maria tugged on my trouser leg. She'd noticed it too. Up ahead, light glimmered dimly from some hidden source. Torchlight.

'They're coming down towards us,' Maria said quietly, defeat in her voice.

I peered up the passage. The light was intensifying, the sounds of people growing louder. I focused on the walls, the roof, looking for an opening in the rock that might provide a way of escape. There was nothing.

Then Maria said suddenly: 'Back here. Quickly.'

I looked over my shoulder.

'Here.'

Maria was pointing to the left. At something level with her shoulder. A crack in the wall I'd crawled right past in the dark.

'Where does it go?' I said.

'I can't see. I think it's wide enough to squeeze through.'

I looked back up the tunnel. The torchlight was getting nearer. Only the corkscrew twists in the passage were protecting us from discovery.

'We don't have a choice,' I said.

Maria pushed herself through the crack. I retreated down the tunnel and went in after her. Just inside there was a small cave and enough room to turn around before the cleft dropped away down a steep slope. Maria was sitting on the edge, her legs tucked up against her chest. I switched on my torch for an instant, directing the beam down the slope. I couldn't see the bottom. I paused. The noises outside were clearer than ever now. Maria looked at me. 'We have to,' she said. 'You go first.'

I twisted round and lowered my legs over the side. 'Keep close to me,' I said.

Then I half climbed, half slid down the cleft. I must have dropped ten or twelve feet when the slope became suddenly vertical. I plunged down into space and a few seconds later my feet hit rock with a jarring thud. I rolled over on to my side and took a moment to recover my breath. I pulled myself to my feet. I was bruised but uninjured. I shone my torch around. I was in a chamber some fifty feet across with a pool of cloudy water along one edge.

'It's OK,' I called up softly. 'I'm waiting.'

Maria's legs came into view above me, her feet dangling out through the hole in the wall of the chamber.

'I'm here,' I said. 'Let yourself go.'

'You sure?' she whispered.

'I'll catch you.'

She edged out further then dropped the last few yards into my arms. For a moment she clung to me, trembling.

'They're going to find us,' she said. 'I know it.'

'They're not,' I said forcefully. 'You understand? We can still get out. We have to get out.'

I lowered her to her feet and flashed my torch around the chamber, shielding it in my hands so only a narrow beam was emitted. Maria followed the light, studying the walls.

'There's no way out.'

'There has to be,' I said.

I scrambled round the sides, searching desperately for another opening. But there was only one exit, the shaft above us we'd dropped through and that was now beyond our reach.

Maria slumped down dejectedly against a rock. 'That's it then. We're trapped.'

I clicked off my torch. 'Sssh.' I listened. 'They're up above us.'

We waited in the darkness. Breathing in quietly the cold dampness of the cave. Listening. Then I heard a distant hissing sound. It took me a moment to work out what it was, and when I did my blood turned suddenly to ice.

'Gas.'

I stood up quickly.

'Poisonous?' Maria said.

I didn't answer. I was scanning the walls again with my torch. I could still see no escape route. I swung round and the beam glanced across the pool of water. I noticed the surface was broken and bent down to examine it more closely. I put a hand in.

'There's a current. It's moving.'

'So?'

'So it must be going somewhere. Find the exit.'

We probed the edges of the pool, feeling under the water for a break in the rock.

'Here,' Maria said.

She had her whole arm submerged. I squatted down by her and felt the opening in the rock wall just a few inches below the surface of the pool. It was wide enough to accommodate a man's body, but only just.

'It's impossible,' Maria said. 'We don't know where it goes and it's all underwater. We'll drown for sure.'

I shone my torch back towards the opening high in the far wall. A cloud of whitish vapour was drifting down into the cave.

'Get in,' I said.

'Michael, this is . . .'

I plunged into the pool and pulled Maria in after me. She gasped as the freezing water washed over her chest. I held her under her arms.

'A deep breath, then we go. The gas will hit us in seconds. We have to, Maria.'

She swallowed and nodded. We took a couple of shallow breaths, then filled our lungs, ducking down below the surface and into the submerged passage. I dragged myself along it, feeling my way in the blackness, my hands scraping over rock, my knees banging on every outcrop. My lungs were ready to explode, my head bursting.

228

I pulled myself a few feet further, feeling above me for any break in the tunnel roof. My fingers touched rock, more rock. The pain in my chest was unbearable. I waved my hand in front of my face desperately. It touched rock, the edge of something sharp, then nothing. Not rock, not water. Air.

I burst to the surface and reached down behind me. My hands caught Maria's arms. I tugged hard and she shot out of the water next to me. She gulped in the air, moaning in pain while I supported her shaking body.

After a while she relaxed. I clambered out of the water on to a rock ledge and lifted Maria out. She was shivering violently.

We were in another cave, smaller than the last. The pool we'd surfaced into occupied one side of the chamber, the water overflowing down a slope to join a fast-flowing underground river which entered the cave through a hole in the roof and exited down a wide tunnel some ten yards further on.

We gave ourselves time to recover, then I started to look around for a way out. There was a long, vertical crack in the wall away to our left. From a distance it looked big enough to walk through. I scrutinized it in the beam from my torch which, fortunately, seemed to have survived its immersion.

'Over there,' I said, taking Maria's hand.

We headed for the crack. We were halfway there when a figure suddenly emerged from it clad from head to toe in a grey protective suit. His face was covered by a helmet with a miner's lamp on the front and a transparent panel just below it. On his back was a cylinder of air connected to the helmet. Maria stifled a scream and grabbed hold of my arm. I kept my torch on the man and saw that in his gloved right hand he was carrying a pistol.

He raised his left hand and ripped open a seal around his face. He pulled the transparent panel open and smiled at us coldly. It was Detective Superintendent Ray Coltrane.

We looked at each other. 'Nice outfit,' I said eventually.

'Just a precaution.' He watched us closely. 'You don't seem very surprised to see me.'

'It wasn't hard to work out you were involved. Where's Carson?'

He jerked his head sideways. 'Somewhere back there. There're a lot of passages and caves to check out. I got lucky.'

'You going to shoot us, or gas us?'

'Shoot. The gas doesn't seem to have worked.'

'Like you did Rob Fielding.'

'That was Jack.'

'But Stephen Farrell was you, wasn't he?'

'I can't let my subordinates have all the fun.'

'Official or unofficial?'

He smiled again. A facial twitch devoid of any humour. 'You'll never know.'

'You think it was worth it?' I said. 'To protect a shameful state secret and the hypocrisy of your political masters.'

'Ours is not to reason.'

'Just do as you're told, is that it? Whatever it takes.'

'You know the system, McLean. Expediency, not morality.'

'You can live with that?'

Coltrane's lip curled. 'I'm in the Special Branch, what do you think? You work for the political police, you work for the interests of politicians, not justice. That's the way it goes.'

He lifted his pistol and pointed it at us, unsure who to kill first. I knew I was wasting my breath, but I had to ask him. It was a point of honour.

'Let Maria go. I've told her nothing. She just came along for the ride.'

Coltrane shook his head. 'One ride too many. You took her to see Salter, she's seen the drums out there in the cavern. She knows as much as you.'

'I suppose it was a couple of your boys who forced us off the road near Porton.'

'Does it matter?'

'I like to tie up the loose ends. What about Jamie Hynes?'

'That was an accident.'

'A spillage down a drain?'

He raised an eyebrow. 'So you knew. Jack said we should've taken you out earlier. At the reservoir, he wanted to kill you. I should've let him.'

'You made a mistake with Jamie,' I said. 'Lying about exactly where he died to prevent any suspicion falling on the factory. Then paying off Dean Clayton's father to make sure his son didn't talk to any reporters or let slip what really happened. That was clumsy.'

'It worked until Fielding started poking his nose in.'

'And Russell Stamford? Did he hire the yobs to disrupt the demo outside his landfill site? Or did you?'

'That was all his idea. A crude, diversionary tactic to discredit his opponents.'

'Yet you give him protection. Why? What does he do for you?'

'That's classified.'

I gave a snort. It was almost a laugh.

'Does that make any difference now?'

Coltrane considered. He shrugged. 'He disposes of the waste from the labs. Also various drums and chemicals left over from the war. Unstable, leaking containers.'

'Which he seals in concrete in illegal dumps around the country.'

'What he does with them is his business.'

'I don't think so. Not chemicals as toxic as these. You know exactly what he does with them. You must know about his past too.'

'You think we care?'

I hazarded a shrewd guess. 'That was part of his appeal, wasn't it? You didn't want anyone too legit, anyone who might question what he was being asked to dispose of. It helped that he was a dodgy operator.'

231

Coltrane smiled cynically. His eyes seemed to sink even deeper into his pudgy face.

'Stamford's amoral, unscrupulous, takes his money and asks no questions. Politicians love people like that. Reminds them of themselves.'

'And the stockpile back there in the cavern? What's his role in that?'

'It's his operation. He enlarged the shafts, installed the lift. We just use the space. We deliver the drums, he takes care of them. It's a perfect set up. Low key, unlikely to arouse any attention, all at arm's length from the government.'

'And so all the easier to deny if anyone wants to know whether we manufacture and stockpile chemical weapons. Does Stamford know what's in those drums?'

'Of course not. Only a handful of people with security clearance know.'

'But Rob Fielding found out.'

'He was close to going public. He knew about the factory at Mexborough, the stockpile, Jamie Hynes. He was dangerous.'

I shifted my position. I was uncomfortable. Water was dripping from my clothes, forming a puddle under my feet. The cold was starting to bite.

'What were the stolen documents you searched his home for?' I said.

'There weren't any. That was just an excuse to get in and take away his files. To find out how much he knew, who else he might have told.'

'And Farrell?'

'He had a conscience, like Salter. We'd been keeping an eye on him for months, tapping his phone. Then he arranged to meet you. It was a risk we couldn't afford to take.'

Coltrane raised the pistol again. He was getting impatient. The talking was over. I drew Maria to me. Her hair was wet on my cheek. I looked back at Coltrane. The lamp on his forehead dazzled me. I screwed up my eyes and saw a cloud of white vapour entering the cave through the crack behind him. It drifted in and enveloped his face. His nostrils twitched and he stiffened. A hand went to his nose and he spun round in a panic, looking into the gas. Then he coughed violently and clutched at his throat. He couldn't breathe. His legs gave way and he fell to the floor, his body convulsing.

I didn't wait to see any more. The gas was dispersing throughout the chamber. I hung on to Maria and backed away automatically. It didn't matter where we went. We just had to get out. The river was below us down a steep rock wall. I lowered Maria down on the end of my arm until her feet were on a boulder at the water's edge. I glanced back at Coltrane.

'Michael, come on,' Maria urged.

I took a last look. Coltrane was frothing at the mouth, his eyes bulging, his limbs twitching spasmodically. Dying. I averted my eyes and dropped down the wall to the river.

We eased ourselves into the foaming water, holding hands. Then the current took us suddenly away, swirling us around in the torrent before plunging downwards and into the darkness of the tunnel.

There was nothing we could do to control our descent. I kept my torch on to give us a chance of avoiding any jutting boulders or low ceilings, but we had to go wherever the flow took us. It dropped steeply through a series of caves and waterfalls, interlinked by tunnels, some of them completely underwater. Twice, three times we had to hold our breath and duck beneath the surface as the river poured into a passage with no headroom. But we were through them quickly the current was so powerful, snatching a few hurried gasps on the other side before we plummeted into the next tunnel.

Then suddenly we were in calmer water. The channel had levelled out and we were swirled to the side and deposited on a bank of stones. We crawled out and collapsed on our stomachs, gasping. My body was bruised and pummelled all over. I rolled on to my back, staring up sightlessly. My torch had stopped working and we were in pitch darkness again. Yet there was something different about the darkness. Or about our surroundings. I could see nothing, but I had a sense of space above me. A feeling of emptiness, as if we were in some huge void.

I reached out and touched Maria. 'You all right?'

'Yes,' she mumbled faintly.

I helped her up on to the rocks at the side of the river and gave my torch a couple of bangs on the ground. The bulb came back to life, flickering weakly. I held it up to Maria's face. She was white, drained. The plaster on her forehead had come off and the cut underneath was seeping blood. I examined it gently.

'We have to get you out of here.'

I pulled her to her feet and gazed around. We were in a narrow, high-sided cave, its roof hidden in the impenetrable blackness above us.

'Michael, look,' Maria said.

She was pointing at something on the wall nearby. I directed the feeble torchlight at it. Bolted to the limestone was a Perspex lamp casing with a bulb inside. An insulated cable connected it to another lamp further along.

'And there.' Maria indicated a metal handrail and a set of concrete steps leading upwards. 'Where are we?'

'There's only one place we can be. Peak Cavern.'

She turned to me, a spark returning to her weary eyes. 'You sure?'

'It has to be.'

We practically ran up the steps. A few tunnels and more flights of steps later we were in the mouth of the cavern. For the first time in hours we saw the sky. Royal blue, moonlit, peppered with stars. Maria slipped her arms around me and hugged me tight.

'Thank God.'

We climbed over the fence past the ticket office and walked away down the path into Castleton. Fresh air had never tasted so good.

# 15

We found shelter by the church in the centre of the village, huddled together in the doorway to keep warm. We'd wrung the water from our outer clothes but our bodies were still wet and frozen to the bone. If we didn't dry out soon we'd die of exposure.

Maria's teeth were chattering like castanets. 'What about the car?' she said.

I shook my head. 'We have to assume they've found it.'

'We can't stay here.'

'I know.'

I looked at my watch. It was nearly three o'clock in the morning. Too late to find a hotel or a B & B in Castleton. And anyway, they'd come looking for us in the village. They couldn't know for certain we'd got out of the caves, but they'd cover all the options, particularly after they found Coltrane's body.

'Wait here,' I said. 'I'm going to make a phone call.'

'I'm coming too,' Maria said. 'I'm not staying on my own in a churchyard.'

We went round to a call box near the post office, half jogging to try and keep warm. Neither of us had any coins so I reversed the charges through the operator. Harry sounded half asleep when he came on the line.

'Mike? What the 'ell's going on?'

'I need a favour,' I said. 'I'm in Castleton with Maria. Can you come and pick us up?'

'What?'

'It's urgent, Harry. We need some towels and dry

clothes, too. Anything you've got. Drive round past the church. We'll be looking out for you.'

He was smart enough not to waste time on questions. 'OK, I'll leave straight away,' he said and hung up.

We waited for him back at the church, crouched out of the wind in the doorway, shivering so violently it hurt. Occasionally I stood up and attempted a few exercises to generate more heat, but my body temperature was so low it made no difference. Maria didn't even have the strength to try. I held her in my arms, trying futilely to warm her up.

After half an hour I heard a car engine coming round the side of the churchyard. I looked out and saw a white Astra van moving slowly towards us.

'That's the one.'

We scrambled over the wall, waving to Harry. He stopped beside us and we climbed into the back of the van. He pulled away and said over his shoulder: 'The towels and clothes are in them bags. I brought a couple of blankets 'n' all.'

'Thanks, Harry.'

Maria was already removing her clothes and towelling herself dry. I dug into one of the bags and pulled out an assortment of shirts, jumpers, trousers.

'I didn't know what you wanted,' Harry said. 'So I brought a whole load. Some are mine, some are the wife's, but don't tell 'er.'

I stripped to my underwear, rubbed myself down with a towel and slipped on a shirt, two jumpers and a pair of baggy trousers. Maria was pulling a man's long-sleeved shirt on over one of Harry's woollen vests.

'As many layers as you can,' I said.

She wriggled into some ancient flannel trousers and then topped it all with an enormous jumper and a thick woolly cardigan. I wrapped a blanket around her and she leaned back on the side of the van with her eyes closed.

I touched her cheek gently with my fingertips. She opened her eyes briefly and forced a smile. Then closed them again, breathing peacefully now. I watched her for

236

a time before kneeling up and leaning over the passenger seat to see out of the windscreen. We were on the Hope Valley road, approaching Hathersage.

'Sorry to get you out of bed, Harry,' I said.

'I weren't in bed,' he replied morosely. 'The wife wouldn't let me near it. I 'ad to sleep on the sofa.' He glanced back at me. 'Am I going to get an explanation or what?'

I told him what had happened. Then I said: 'We need somewhere to hole up for a time. Can we stay at your place?'

'My 'ouse?' He sounded doubtful. 'The wife'd 'ave a fit. It's only small, you know. What about the back of my shop? There's a fire, a kettle, a toilet, a sink, a couple of armchairs. No one'll find you there.'

'That'll be fine.'

He came in with us when we got there and turned off the alarm.

'I'll be back at 'alf-nine to open up,' he said, then left us to it.

I made coffee. Maria sipped hers slumped in one of the armchairs, too exhausted to speak. She fell asleep as soon as she'd finished it. I tucked the blanket around her, hung our wet clothes on a couple of chairs in front of the gas fire and dozed off myself.

It was half past eight when I awoke. I went out to a bakery and bought rolls and croissants for breakfast. Maria was stirring by the time I got back.

'Coffee?' I said.

She nodded weakly.

'Sleep all right?'

She stretched and sat up in the chair, pulling the blanket around her shoulders.

'I had a nightmare about that cave. That man dying. I kept seeing him choking, his limbs twitching.' She covered her eyes with her hands and shuddered.

'Shut it out,' I said. 'He was a killer.'

'I know. But it doesn't make any difference. It was a terrible way to die.'

237

I gave her a mug of coffee and a croissant. She took a sip, holding the mug in both hands.

'Were they acting under orders?' she asked. 'Or were they just a couple of rogue coppers?'

'Coltrane was right. We'll never know. Not for certain anyway.'

'If Special Branch were involved, that means the government was involved too, doesn't it?'

'It's an MoD factory at Mexborough. It's their stockpile at Dirtlow Rake.'

'They'll just deny it.'

'They'll try. But those chemical drums will still be there in the cavern. There's no way they can move that number in a hurry, and I've got photographs. I've also got you to back me up.'

'You going to write a story?'

'Yes.'

'Will anyone print it?'

'I've got to call a friend in London to find out.' I checked my watch. 'Now's as good a time as any.'

'I think I'll have a wash,' Maria said. She fingered her hair. 'I feel so dirty.'

She went to the sink at the far end of the room while I phoned Martin Furness. I told him the story from beginning to end.

'Shit,' he said softly when I'd finished. 'You sure about this?'

'No question. You interested?'

'I'll talk to the editor and call you back. What number are you on?'

I gave him Harry's number. 'Martin,' I said, 'keep this tight. Any leaks and the MoD will slap an injunction on you.'

'You think I don't know? Give me an hour.'

I was making notes on a pad I'd found in the desk when Harry arrived to open up his shop.

'You got everything you need?' he said.

'Do you have a typewriter?'

'There's an old Adler in the cupboard. I use it for me invoices. Help yourself.'

I spent the rest of the day writing and rewriting my story. Martin Furness rang back in the middle of the morning to confirm they'd print it. I said I'd fax it through late. 'Give me a time. I'll be waiting by the machine,' he said.

Harry took the roll of film I'd shot in the cavern to a quick process lab to be developed. The cartridge had stayed dry inside the plastic bag in my pocket and the prints were better than I'd hoped. Then I typed up the final neat copy of the story and Maria checked it over for errors.

'This is going to upset a lot of people in high places,' she said.

'That really cuts me up,' I said.

'You thought about the consequences?'

'I'm trying not to. I might lose my nerve.'

In the evening we went to Maria's office. She turned on the fax machine and on the dot of seven I started to transmit my story, pictures and the Sygma Lab report Maria had kept in her safe for me. I gave Martin fifteen minutes to return to his office after the transmission had finished, then telephoned him.

'You read it?' I asked.

'Give me a chance. I'll call you back.'

He took down Maria's office number. We waited impatiently, hardly talking, until he rang.

'I'm with the editor,' he said.

'What's the verdict?'

'You've got yourself a splash. We're running it on one, and on the inside too.'

'You know the risks, don't you?' I said. 'You could end up in jail for this.'

'What the hell. Why else are we journalists?'

For the next hour he quizzed me, going over every fact in the copy, verifying, as far as he could, every detail of the story. He spoke to Maria too, asking for corroboration on some of the points. When, at last, he hung up I felt utterly drained. The trip to Wiltshire, the night underground, the mental stress of getting it all down on paper had caught up with me.

Maria let out a sigh of relief. 'Let's go home,' she said. 'We can't spend the rest of our lives in the back room of a shop.'

We drove back to her house in Ranmoor, picking up a bottle of Beaujolais at an off licence on the way. She pulled the curtains, switched on the gas fire and curled up next to me on the settee. We didn't say much. There wasn't any need. We drank the wine, then kissed, then drank some more, holding each other, drifting off into sleep together.

'Why don't we go to bed?' Maria said.

'You mind if I take a shower first?'

She shook her head. 'I'll keep you company.' Then she turned to me, suddenly serious. 'How long have we got?'

'I don't know,' I said.

'Let's make the most of it.'

She took my hand and we went out into the hall. We were almost at the top of the stairs when the front door was smashed open suddenly. Three uniformed police officers ran into the house. Inspector Jack Carson followed.

I walked down the stairs to meet him. I felt very tired. I looked him in the eye. He didn't get any prettier.

'Michael McLean,' he said. 'I'm arresting you on suspicion of obtaining and communicating information which might be directly or indirectly useful to an enemy contrary to the Official Secrets Act. You do not have to say anything unless you wish to do so, but what you say may be given in evidence.'

I turned to look at Maria. She came down the stairs to me.

'We never do get this quite right, do we?' she said.

I kissed her on the lips. 'I can wait.'

They led me out to the police car. Before I got in I looked back at Maria. She was standing on the doorstep, framed in the light from the hall. She was smiling at me. I didn't care about anything else. I smiled back and glanced at my watch. It was almost midnight. Somewhere in Docklands, the presses were running.